the bad dog's diary

a year in the life of Blake: lover... fighter... DOG

Martin Howard

Illustrations by Tracy Hecht

PORTICO

For Mum and Dad,
with love and thanks from both of us.

First published in hardback in the United Kingdom in 2007 by
Portico
10 Southcombe Street
London
W14 0RA

An imprint of Anova Books Company Ltd

This paperback edition published 2008

ISBN 9781906032340

A CIP catalogue record for this book is available from the
British Library.

10 9 8 7 6 5 4 3 2 1

reproduction by SX Composing DTP
Printed by WS Bookwell, Finland

This book can be ordered direct from the publisher.
Contact the marketing department, but try your bookshop first.

www.anovabooks.com

JANUARY

Tuesday, January 1

New Year's Day. Bow, but definitely not wow. My bladder was at breaking point by 8 a.m. while the Owner* was comatose and smelled like an explosion in a brewery toilet, very tantalising to my ultrasensitive nose. Interestingly, the human muzzle has about five million scent receptors, right? Mine has 220 million, at least. I can pick up scents better than the most sensitive scientific equipment. Not that I need to around here. Not with his bowels being in such terrible shape.

Anyway, the usual barking and licking routine just made him curse, roll over and cover his head with a pillow, so what else could a poor crossbreed do but pee on his duvet? Even the zingy scent of fresh urine failed to wake him though, so I just barked for an hour or so until he finally crawled out of bed clutching his head, looking pale, ill and with his fur all over the place. They say that dogs start to look like their humans, but I damn well hope not. It's no wonder he can't get a bitch; looking like that I wouldn't touch him if he were covered in steak. But what a stroke of luck, he was muttering about something called tequila and wetting the bed at his age. A good start to the year at last! Although it wasn't strictly a 'welcome home' moment, I treated him to the full works: some fine bass barking balanced with excited yapping in my upper register (I've got an excellent range), just the right amount of tugging on his pyjamas and some boisterous jumping up; it was hard to see how it could be improved. One particularly graceful twisting leap from a stationary position allowed me to get my tongue right into his ear. Now that's a welcome!

After a frankly mediocre walk to the wasteland and back I decided that in the interests of canine–human relations, and with a nod toward the quaint tradition of 'man's best friend,' I would introduce a few concessions in my New Year's Resolutions that might even pave the way toward some kind of *entente cordiale* if his own behaviour is good enough. So I settled down in front of the fire to think of some while he watched some terrible old movie on the TV. I farted a bit. So did he. Domestic bliss.

* I call him 'Owner' only because it's more succinct than 'that guy who walks and feeds me'. In this context it does not imply actual ownership or dominance. I am definitely the alpha male in this den.

Wednesday, January 2

Blake's New Year's Resolutions

1. Be a ~~good~~ better dog. If I lead by example there may be thaw in relations and maybe even a return on the investment in terms of longer walks, more and better food, fewer threats about *that* trip to the vet. This breaks down into sub-resolutions as set out here.

> (i) ~~Fetch paper, slippers, pipe, whatever.~~ Not a chance.
> (ii) My 'welcome home' routine is pretty honed, but could become spectacular with a little more work, perfecting the jumping, licking, barking etc.
> (iii) Quit chewing so much of his stuff (delicious hand-stitched, Italian leather shoes excepted of course).
> (iv) Bring things back when thrown. It goes against my instincts to indulge him, and Marx would have said that the game of 'fetch' is a physical reinforcement of the values of the ruling class. By constantly doing the bidding of the holder of the can opener the dog fixes himself within a hostile socio-political ideology. But, bless him, he does love it when I drop that little ball in his hand, and I am one thirty-second retriever. I think.

2. Expand my territory in the Western Park. This will provide a beachhead into the East as far as the pond. The empire will grow.

3. ~~Develop a mature and enlightened attitude to cats.~~ Make cats suffer. Nasty little cats with their smug faces and washing.
4. Stop kicking up an enormous fuss any time a bath is threatened.
5. Stop jumping in every cold, muddy puddle, ditch or pond that I come across.

6. Quit scooting. Though the sensation of rubbing one's posterior at speed along the ground is pure ecstasy, even Denny the Flea has the social grace to do it in private.
7. Prevent Owner from becoming romantically attached. The last thing we need is another human female cleaning the place up and complaining about the 'doggy smell'.

Thursday, January 3

A small misunderstanding about a missing sausage I thought he'd left on the kitchen counter for me, plus I broke his laptop a little bit, but he did leave it on my part of the sofa and I'm sure that 'e' key will fit right back on with a bit of glue. Other than that not a bad day, but then no day is completely wasted when you can lick your own genitals.

Friday, January 4

Disaster! The Owner made his own set of resolutions while I was busy lapping at my crutch last night and left them in plain sight for anyone to read.

Numbers 1, 2 and 4 were respectively: 'Take Blake to obedience school'; 'Join a dating service'; and, worst of all, 'If obedience school does not improve behaviour, have Blake neutered.' There was also some rubbish about not drinking, getting fit, redecorating and keeping the place tidy.

Saturday, January 5

Usually, his resolutions last as long as it takes to open a can of beer, but today the Owner was awake at dawn (with the aid of a snuffling wet nose to the face). For once he didn't push me away with a 'Fuuuurgghhofff Blake,' but gave me a cheery good morning, jumped out of bed and into the ludicrous training outfit he bought in the sales yesterday. I'm not well versed in human fashion, but I know my Prada from Versace and this is neither. He thinks it makes him look like Sylvester Stallone in *Rocky*.

After cleaning the den, he took me for a long walk in the park, during which he *ran* and did *press-ups*. Purely out of fear for my testicles I returned the tennis ball properly for half an hour, though it's much more fun to almost give it to him then run away laughing. Playing fetch may make him forget his evil plans even if it is just another example of him expecting me to fill an outmoded stereotype. The whole fetch thing was started by wolves bringing food back to the den over 10,000 years ago, do I ask him to sit in a tree scratching his armpits and eating bananas? Not that human evolution's changed much. Substitute the tree for a sofa and the banana for pizza, and your basic monkey remains completely unchanged, though in all fairness he never throws actual poo at me. Just the metaphorical stuff.

Sunday, January 6

Getting a little bit bored with the Good Boy routine already, though it seems to be doing the trick: no calls to the vets or obedience classes yet. Even came back when he called today. Am I going too far? Much more of this and he'll get delusions of alpha. When I think that my virility and the happiness of the neighbourhood bitches are subject to the whims of such an idiot human my tail runs out of wag. I mean, who is the superior species here? A dog can understand human commands, plus we can read their body language and scent so well we know what they're going to do before they do it and respond appropriately.*
The stupid human, on the other hand, makes no effort to learn to communicate. Ha, he can't even comprehend the most

obvious raised eyebrow, let alone discern the wealth of personal information packed into my glands and pheromones. I tell you, life in this den would be a lot more harmonious if he got down on his knees and sniffed my backside once in a while.

* Or not, in my case.

Monday, January 7

On the way back from my morning constitutional in the park today I put Stage One of my military campaign into action by marking one of Scottie's lampposts. I really should have done more reconnaissance first – Scottie might be geriatric and a bit forgetful, but he's still feisty. 'Know your enemy, and in one hundred battles you will never be defeated,' as Sun Tsu says, but all this fetch business is putting a strain on my naturally ebullient spirits and I was feeling a bit pettish.

Talking about Sun Tsu, it was leftover Chinese food tonight. I adore Kung-po Chicken and breathed it down before the dish hit the floor, though to be honest I do that with all my food and would scoff a bowl of scorpions just as quickly. Again, it's a wolf thing; feast and famine and all that. Credit where credit's due though, the Chinese know what to do with a dead hen and sometimes the Owner is smart enough to make a dog happy. I always like to give a little something back, so I spent the evening pushing my nose up his bum. Just my way of being friendly, but you'd think from his reaction that I'd wired him up to the mains. A few scraps went in the bin. This must have been a mistake when he could see my bowl was empty so I'm sure he won't mind if I have a quick dig around in there when I get hungry later.

Tuesday, January 8

Started the day with the Rolled-up Newspaper. I really don't understand why he's got such a shocking position on my very sensible attitude to wasting food, but I tried to be conciliatory by putting my head down, whining, juggling my eyebrows and retreating to the corner while he cleaned up. I can't say it did me much good; *en route* to the park he was yanking my chain like he wanted to flush me.

There was a bitch there today so I sauntered over. Like me, she was a cute mixed-breed (it's worth noting that we find the term 'mongrel' highly offensive). Keeping it casual I had a sniff at her nose then went round the back end to get to know her a bit better. What a set of anal glands! I was in dog heaven, even though she's not even in season. I checked her tag, which said her name was Ella, and the little cutie barked, 'Is that your tail or are you just pleased to see me?' After that we had a great romp around the lake, a bit of play-fighting and more sniffing. I love being a dog, we're so direct about romance.

The usual processed chunks of hooves, lips and eyelids for dinner and not a lot in the bin, though I emptied it again and had a thorough investigation. The vet threat seems to have receded, so I'm reducing the state of alert to orange, which means getting that extra lick or two out of a not-quite-empty tin more than compensates for a Slap on the Nose.

Wednesday, January 9

Saw Ella again today, but not for long as the idiot with the lead was soon rushing around, red-faced and shouting, 'Blake! Blake!' as usual. Nevertheless, I managed to lick her in all the right places, but figured that after another garbage incident I ought to keep him sweet and strolled over to see what the fuss was about. Oblivious to having interrupted my date, he was all happy encouragement when I 'came,' so I licked his face. He kept patting me and calling me 'Good Boy.' Ha, he wouldn't have said that if his nose was good enough to tell him where my tongue had just been. Out of pique I peed on two more of Scottie's lampposts and scooted on the Owner's bedroom carpet when he wasn't looking, which was bliss, but very bad behaviour. On the bright side, still no calls to the obedience school.

Thursday, January 10

Under this polished, sophisticated exterior I am basically a pack animal and like to be sociable, so when he was asleep last night I let myself into the bedroom and made myself comfortable. There was nothing submissive or affectionate going on. Nevertheless, I thought it would be sensible to make sure he knew I had the protection of the den well in hand and growled at the slightest noise all night. The old 'ever alert and faithful watchdog' ploy. For all the gratitude he showed, I needn't have bothered. There were a couple of minor nocturnal altercations, but I stand by my judgement call; that leaf brushing against the window might well have been a predator and I was right to throw myself at it barking. In consequence, he was a bit sluggish getting out of bed and spent much of the day being downright surly. I was, of course, a model of support and when not catching up on my sleep could be found sympathetically drooling and moaning into his lap while he worked. Not that he understands that a dog's gentle moans are a sign of pleasure. They certainly do not mean, 'Push me away and tell me I'm an annoying mongrel.'

Friday, January 11

Not a good day. The Owner has turned jailer and spent half the day patching holes in the fence in the tiny yard at the back of the den. Then he went out and bought a kennel. A bloody kennel! A proper little wooden house without even basic modern conveniences such as a toilet to drink out of. How very clichéd. From now on I'm supposed to spend the night out in the cold where I can't get at the bin or disturb his precious sleep. Surely he understands that he's putting his own life in danger if I'm not there to protect him? And surely there's a law against such blatant cruelty? It's just another example of keeping dogs down, as if shouting it at us all the time isn't enough. Well, I'll pit my ferocious jaws and canine persistence against his hopeless D.I.Y. any time. Let's see how long this gaol can hold me.

Saturday, January 12

Less than one night! A blow to his pretensions of alphadom. If he'd bothered to learn anything about dogs he'd know that the way to summon a member of the pack is to howl, and like it or not he is a member of my pack. By three in the morning he had a queue of neighbours knocking at the door and was forced to let me back in. (Between howling I made a good-sized hole in his fence. Next time he tries to take away my freedom, I'm off.) It seemed a good time to practise my 'welcome home' routine. I got some good licking in and the jumping up was so beautifully choreographed that he crashed into the shelves and broke some glass stuff. Admittedly, I then got a bit carried away and lost control of my bladder for a second or two, but the way he carried on you'd have thought I'd sprinkled his pyjamas and the lounge carpet with napalm.

For the rest of the day I was very good, mainly on account of being asleep in front of the fire. Woke up to a tummy rub and some very good leftover pizza.

Sunday, January 13

Halfway down the road to the shops a black cat crossed my path. Talk about lucky, the Owner was apologising to a neighbour and didn't see me start pointing like a professional: front paw raised, tail straight out, nose and ears alert – I should have been a hunting dog. When I launched my attack he wasn't expecting it and I easily got the lead out of his hand. Ah, the joy of the hunt. Tearing down the high street was like running down prey across the freezing tundra. Well, sort of. Less elk, more pizza-delivery mopeds. It was a mighty chase, and one I would have won if the craven pussy hadn't found a tree. I gave it the fright of its life though. I don't know what was more fun, chasing the cat or seeing the Owner trying to negotiate a path through all the other humans at a flat-out run over my shoulder. When he eventually caught up with me I got the old 'Bad Boy' routine and a sharp Slap on the Nose, but for goodness' sake what does he expect – I am a dog after all.

Monday, January 14

Gulp. He made the call today; I am booked into a course of obedience classes, starting tomorrow. Bastard. Obedience school! Do I look like the kind of geek that goes to obedience school? Sit, stay, down, roll over. He'll be lucky. But if I don't, what then? The white coat and the knife.

Tuesday, January 15

Passing over the tussle to get me into the car, during which I racked up a bit of damage, obedience classes are outstanding fun! The trainer, Molly, had amazing insight for a human. As soon as we got there I met a cheeky minx called Bonny and we got a bit carried away. Molly took one look at the Owner dragging at my collar while yelling at me and saw straight away that he's the problem, not me! She gave him a thorough dressing-down about his needing to be an alpha that I could rely on and was it any wonder I wouldn't obey commands if his responses to me were inconsistent and violent. He looked so dejected I couldn't help rubbing it in a bit. When Molly offered me a treat and asked very nicely for me to do a couple of things, like sit and stay, I did it all perfectly. When he tried to do the same I just cocked my leg up and peed up the leg of the dog owner next to us, then ran off with him tearing after me trying to be gentle and cajoling. Molly told him sternly that he had obviously lost my trust and that this would need some very hard work and restraint on *his* part to correct. I haven't laughed so much since I pulled him into the pond.

Wednesday, January 16

Oh, Good Dog. He's all fired up by Molly and her psychological approach to training and this morning he wouldn't give me my breakfast until I 'sat.' The ignominy. I ignored him, of course, and dived in regardless. We reached some sort of compromise when I forced the bowl out of his hand and its contents onto the kitchen floor from where I wolfed them up before he could stop me. He wasn't impressed though, and rather than a decent run around in the park, checking out who's been on my territory and what they're up to, I had to endure more pathetic attempts to 'train' me. Molly told him to start again with the basics, be firm but kind with me and not let me get the upper hand, so I got dragged around on a short lead while he constantly bellowed 'Heel.' It would have been more impressive if I hadn't been towing him around like a deranged water-skier.

Thursday, January 17

Victory! Blake the Conqueror. The Emperor Blake. The Mighty Blake, Warlord of Acorn Park and Ruler of the Western Marches as Far as the Bandstand.

I was allowed off the lead this morning and was having a snuffle about the park, picking up the news, when Scottie came at me like some moth-eaten, white missile, growling, 'I'll huv yer goolies off, ye dirty wee mongrel.' I had completely forgotten the lamppost/pique episode, but I am a highly trained dog of war. In surprise attacks like this I always remember the wisdom of Marcus Aurelius, who said, 'Execute every act of thy life as though it were thy last.' Rearing quickly up on my hind legs, ears raised, teeth bared, I dropped on him from above, a growling thunderbolt, which was more than a match for the old boy's wheezy violence. In a matter of seconds his little tartan doggie coat was spattered with his own blood. This stirred his Highland spirit and with a bark of 'Stitch this' he was at me again. I ran rings around him, snapping at whatever parts he was too slow to defend, and he was soon on his back with my teeth at his throat.

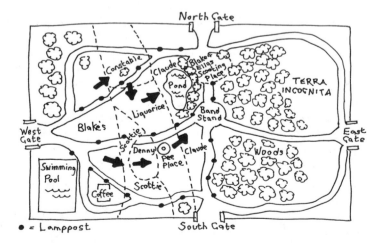

12

A triumph! His territory now belongs to me.* Growling, he admitted it, just before the Owner yanked me away by the collar. Scottie's doddering old human got there about the same time and there was a furious argument about vets' bills with my Owner saying that he'd seen Scottie go for me so his owner could pay his own bills and get his mutt a muzzle and some sessions with an animal psychologist while he was at it.

So, as Julius Caesar said on crossing the Rubicon, '*Alea Iacta Est*,' (the die is cast). My territory is doubled much sooner than I had planned. There were a lot of lampposts to mark on the way home.

* The conventions are strict on this point – to the victor the spoils – but I'm going to let Scottie keep the little patch of wasteland behind his house. It's useless to me and it's where he takes his evening dump. Generous to the defeated, you see.

Friday, January 18

Gave the postman a satisfyingly nasty turn this morning by forcing my nose through the hole in the door, giving it a bit of serious menace, wrinkling the muzzle, baring my fearsome teeth, low but heartfelt growling and all that. I hate that postman. Who does he think he is, pushing his paper rubbish into people's dens day after day when they're enjoying a quiet snooze? He does it to taunt me because he knows I can't open the door. The Owner hates him too, every day he races down before I can get to work chewing the paper up and then looks at them, moaning 'Bills, bills, bills. . .' Who is Bill? And why is the postman putting all his crap through our door? The Owner should block up that hole, it just encourages him.

Strolled into the park feeling like Napoleon Bonaparte during one of his triumphal entrances into Paris. Took great care to ostentatiously mark the borders of my new territory and strolled around looking noble and victorious. No bitches around, but probably just as well because I couldn't help a small scoot of conquest on my new turf. The Owner must have been in a good mood too, serious stroking action tonight. There's nothing to relax a dog like a full body massage.

Saturday, January 19

Feeling full of pep and vim today after an epic sleep and Hallelujah! Dottie was in the park. I've had my eye on her for a while, she's pedigree Dalmatian and too posh to sniff the likes of me, but what a scent – urine like expensive perfume – and she was looking sleek and gorgeous even at this time of day, trotting around on my territory as if it were hers. With class bitches like this you shouldn't just go straight for the bum, so I stood staring at her until she came to me.

'It's Blake, isn't it?' She spoke to me. I nearly widdled with excitement.

'Rrrright. And you are Dottie.'

'Tell me, how big is your pack?'

I resisted the temptation to make the obvious vulgar reply. Damn, I'd been distracted by the glory of my victory over Scottie and hadn't considered the recruitment of a pack. If you want to impress foxes like this you've got to be Top Dog, and have a pack to be Top Dog of. Luckily for me, her human called her at that moment and she was off like a rocket. As you'd expect, she's got exquisite manners. I watched her spotty bum disappear with my tongue hanging out. I have to get a pack, and quick.

Sunday, January 20

The Owner was out all day. I hate being stuck inside on my own, but used the day wisely by drawing up a list of dogs to join my pack, meanwhile absent-mindedly chewing the leg of some old chair out of habit and boredom. That's one resolution down but, in my defence, when will the idiot learn to leave me a bone? Even one of those tasteless chew toys would help. Preferably one that looks like a cat. Anyway, these are the prospects:

Scottie (already a *de facto* member of my posse)
Denny the Flea (has a small patch of territory by the dog toilet that will be strategically useful)
Liquorice (quite a big territory, but he's a big black lab and

looks to be quite useful in a fight – I'll have to start training for this one)

Constable (negligible territory, but he'll make up the numbers; also, he's a 'best of breed' winning Old English sheepdog and star of numerous TV commercials. It will give the operation a bit of style having a celebrity member)

Claude (a big, chunky boxer with prize territory around the pond – he'll be my biggest problem)

A pack of five (five and a half counting the Owner) should give me the kind of princely standing Dottie will respond to. I'll start with a *blitzkrieg* campaign on Denny and Constable's territory, and draw up a strategy for Liquorice and Claude.

Monday, January 21

That chair turned out to be a family heirloom and the Owner flipped when he found it all chewed up. Not only was there a psychotic moment with the Rolled-up Newspaper, but he then went and made a spreadsheet detailing all the things I've ruined and their replacement value. Top of the list is that crunchy mobile phone that he *still* hasn't forgotten about. He stuck the list on the fridge, and apparently I've caused well over £1,000 worth of damage so far. There's a graph with a line at the £1,500 mark, which says 'NEUTER.'

Short, moody walk and just the usual unidentifiable meat product in 'tasty marrowbone jelly' for dinner, with no leftovers. This is serious. Until he calms down I have to stick to that 'better behaviour' regime. Quite aside from the pain and humiliation of being emasculated, I'd lose my land and any chance with Dottie too. Plus, I hate it when he makes that sad face at me. In an effort to cheer him up I spent the night sitting quietly at his feet. Close to the fire, obviously.

Tuesday, January 22

Obedience classes again and Molly showed him what anyone living in a modern capitalist society should already know, which is that I will do better work for a fair wage. There's a complex economic model that we canines use. It calculates if the reward on offer is greater than the effort of the job multiplied by the loss of face involved in taking orders. There's also a random element, the 'do I feel like it?' factor. I believe it's a similar system to that used by Parisian waiters. Taking into consideration my renewed effort to be a better dog, today's fee for a prompt 'sit' was one medium-sized meaty treat. (If you want to maintain decent service a tip doesn't go amiss either; a nice pat or a bit of stroking is always welcome.) I get food, my *numero uno* favourite thing, and he gets to feel in control for a couple of seconds. It's not rocket science.

The Owner was feeling so chuffed with himself that he asked Molly for a date. Imagine my surprise when she said yes. I mean, for Dog's sake, he looks like he needs a fortnight in a grooming salon. This could be serious, but despite my New Year's Resolution it might not be so bad having him date a dog lover.

Wednesday, January 23

As it turns out, Old English sheepdogs aren't very aggressive or bothered about territory. A show of teeth was all it took for Constable to turn over his lands today, after which I laid down the rules of belonging to my pack, as set out here:

Rule 1: Submission and respect to be shown to yours truly at all times.
Rule 2: All bitches are Blake's by right of conquest.
Rule 3: Pack dogs are required to spar with Blake on a regular basis to help keep him in shape.
Rule 4: Blake will be first to sample any food left in the park or elsewhere on his territory.

Constable didn't seem to be very interested, just woofed a bit and wandered off. Still, it's a start. I now have a pack of one dopey showbiz dog with a coat you could hide a haywain in.

Thursday, January 24

Scottie was even less enthusiastic about joining.

'Yer pack? Whut wud I want tae jine yer pack fer, yer traitorous fleabag?' was his response to my invitation.

'Because, as a conquestee, you can't actually refuse and if you try I'll rip your other ear open,' I growled. A successful general can't afford to have dissent among the ranks, after all.

'Och, well if ye put it like that whut choice do I huv? I suppose I'll join yer pathetic pack, though at my time o' life I wus hopin' for a bit o' peace 'n' quiet.' He looked thoughtful for a second. 'There's sich a word as "conquestee" then, is there?'

Two. It's like the Magnificent Seven in the park at the moment. Flushed with success I re-marked Denny the Flea's patch by the toilet with my own scent on the way home. I must say it smells a hell of a lot better than his.

Friday, January 25

I've been getting to know my pack a little, as successful management is all about getting the best from your people. We've always been on bum-sniffing terms, but being their Pack Leader is an entirely different kettle of moist beefy chunks in a rich gravy. Scottie is your basic West Highland Scots terrier. White, fluffy and canny. Likes digging. Greyfriars Bobby was a Westie, so I hope Scottie has the same level of loyalty. He's old and he tells me that he has great wisdom, but I think he might be just a little senile. For some reason he's started calling me 'Grasshopper' and telling me I need to stand on a tree stump with three of my legs in the air. I think he's taken it upon himself to become my ancient, mystic mentor, though frankly I'd rather be mentored by a tin of beans. According to him, I need to learn to fight with my mind, not with my paws and teeth. That can't be right. I've made him my beta male anyway. He might be a little crazed, but the alternative is Constable.

Saturday, January 26

I tried having a conversation with the Old English sheepdog today, but it's not easy. I told him that Scottie was going to be my lieutenant, thinking that he'd be upset at being passed over for promotion, but he didn't seem upset at all. Stupid, yes. Upset, no.

'So, when is he moving in?'

'What do you mean?'

'Well, if he's going to be your lieutenant he must be moving in next door to you, on the left-hand side.' Constable explained this to me slowly, as if I were an idiot.

'I don't think you understand, Constable. Being lieutenant will mean Scottie is my right-paw dog.'

'I see, it's a riddle. Wait a moment . . . So he'll be living on your left and also be sitting on your right paw. So you must be facing the wrong way. Is that it?'

'No, no, you've got it all wrong. I mean I'm going to make Scottie my number two.'

The rest of the conversation is probably best forgotten. For the record, dear diary, I have an uneasy feeling that Scottie, my second in command, is one or two biscuits short of a treat and, whatever planet the rank and file are on, it's not the same as the rest of us occupy. Being a celeb, he's probably on drugs or something.

Sunday, January 27

A great morning, running with the pack. From a distance I bet we looked inspiring and fearsome streaking across the frosty grass. In the distance I could see Dottie watching us and I barked a greeting to her, but it looked as though she was on the lead. It's probably for the best as right after I spotted her, Scottie had to stop for a rest and Constable got hair in his eyes and ran into a bench. They may not be ideal pack material, but every great leader had to start somewhere, though I'm betting that Genghis Khan didn't begin his career swarming across Europe with just an elderly Scottish nutcase and a weirdo so shaggy that Genghis never knew which end to sniff first.

Monday, January 28

Not a bad day's work. Threw myself bodily at the door when the postman approached this morning, making it rattle in its frame. I'm sure I heard him yelp. Brought down the coat rack on the Owner's head in my excitement to be out walking, then nearly dislocated his arm on the way to the park. Mine and Ella's schedules overlapped so I romanced her with a nose up the bum for half an hour, and the rest of the day was spent in gainful employment chewing the Owner's underwear, which he leaves conveniently in a basket for me. After barking insanely at every passer-by on the street outside I got a decent-sized meal that barely touched the sides. Then there was the early-evening stroll after which we settled down in front of the television and I spent the next few hours trying, with varying amounts of success, to climb into his lap. It's a game we play. The loser is the first to have a temper tantrum. I always win.

Tuesday, January 29

These obedience classes are great. I get to act however I like and the Owner can't lay a finger on me. Today, I decided that I was bored with the whole thing and refused to co-operate. According to Molly, dragging your dog around like a sack of potatoes is not a valid training technique.

Wednesday, January 30

Met up with the pack in the park today for another training session. I'm starting to understand and respect Scottie's fighting systems. I thought that 'fighting with the mind' was some kind of stupid Eastern metaphor, but apparently it's all about 'sticking yer heid oan thum.' Not a combat practice much used by dogs, but very popular in Scotland. Watching Scottie demonstrate by jumping up and head-butting the place where he thought Constable's knees might be was enlightening, though obviously it works better when your enemy isn't a huge, walking mophead.

Thursday, January 31

The Owner was working in his office for most of the day. He's getting ready for some big human work thing next week. After a tolerable breakfast of some new brand of dog food that's not quite as bad as usual, mixed in with various stuff that's been sitting in the fridge for too long, I joined him, used his feet as a pillow and chewed on a big elastic band I found on the floor, farting now and again for the sheer hell of it. When you don't have keys to the car and a pocket full of credit cards, life can be a little dull. Still, it's definitely easier now Molly's getting him to be a good boy. Eventually the band went the way of all things left within my reach, which is to say down my throat.

FEBRUARY

Friday, February 1

I may never recover from the shame. The Owner was up early for more of the physical jerks, but took me to the dog toilet for my morning ablutions first. I crouched up to answer nature's call and at first everything was fine, I passed a satisfyingly sized stool with the skill and nonchalance of the professional toilet hound. But, when I got up to  leave, the damn thing followed me. Worse, Dottie chose that moment to arrive and was watching fascinated as I chased my own tail while my doings bounced up and down from my bum like a bungee-jumping Snickers bar. After what seemed like an eternity of confusion and embarrassment the Owner turned up to see what the gathering crowd was watching. By this time I was panicking and he had to chase me round the toilet, cursing as he trod in mound after mound while trying to catch me. Then he had to kneel down and pull a length of stretchy brown bunting out of my backside like a magician pulling handkerchiefs out of a top hat. When it was finally out I gathered what was left of my dignity and went to hide under a bush until the Owner came to take me home. It didn't take long; he seemed to be in a hurry to get to the shower.

Just to add to the humiliation of Dottie seeing my disgrace, Denny was there too, straining at the lead to get at me. It didn't seem the right time to settle border disputes though.

I never thought I'd say it, but thank Dog the Owner was there.

Saturday, February 2

Very depressed. Luckily the Owner had to go out early so there was no park visit and I didn't have to face anyone. Instead, I spent the morning curled up with my nose up my sore bum, keeping a low profile. When the Owner went out I pawed open the fridge door and helped myself to some comfort food. There are times when you just don't care about the consequences. Of course, he didn't understand that I needed the paté, cheese, ham, yoghurts, salami and potato salad for purely medicinal purposes, and I was literally in the doghouse for the rest of the day. Breaking the eggs and spilling milk on the floor was accidental, but if he had an ounce of initiative he could have scraped it up, added a bit of flour and made pancakes. That's another £20 on the fridge spreadsheet. I couldn't even muster a howl.

Sunday, February 3

Had to go back to the park today while the Owner did his keep-fit stuff. I wonder how you can 'keep fit' when you're not fit to begin with? In his case it would be more accurate to say 'sustain fitness level at slightly asthmatic and overweight.' Still, he seems to enjoy it and it makes for less of the 'training' sessions I've had to endure recently. I stayed close at first as I still didn't feel like meeting any of the pack, and discovered that there's some fun to be had in getting tangled up in his legs while he does the gawky human version of running. After I'd tripped him three times he made it pretty clear that I was *canine non grata*, so I trailed off to hide in the woods by the pond. It was a shock to find Ella already there and I was about to turn tail and flee when I noticed she was scooting. A bitch after my own heart, and one not in any position to laugh at me while she was inelegantly dragging her bottom around the park. So I walked over instead.

She heard me coming and tried to run, but I called her back with a bark. After a bit of initial embarrassment I admitted my own addiction and we spent a happy half-hour scooting together down the bank to the lake, like two dogs having a sledging race. There were occasional breaks to check each other's grass stains. Yum.

Monday, February 4

Did I say it would be OK to have the Owner date Molly? How wrong can you be. All afternoon it was Blake sit, Blake stay, Blake put on a tutu and dance the lambada. Then I got tied to a lamppost while they had coffee, and she calls herself a dog lover. I nearly hanged myself trying to bite my own tail.

When we finally got home she told him that I had 'dominance aggression' and instructed him on how to stop it. This means taking all my stuff away – chew toys, blanket, bed, everything I own – and intensifying my training, making sure he stays in control at all times. Apparently, I have to earn back my things. I am at a loss for words. I thought she was nice, but it turns out she's a complete human female! She even gave him tips on 'reacclimatising a dog to sleep outside.' This has to stop.

Tuesday, February 5

More obedience classes. After yesterday's betrayal, is it any wonder I was less than well behaved at training school? Besides, I can't really understand what the fuss is all about. So I ran three miles across country with a small, incontinent poodle called Snowy in my mouth. So what? I'm under a lot of pressure and a show of high spirits is only natural. When the Owner finally caught up with us I got a kick in the tail. Molly saw and they had a bit of a row about it, then Snowy's owner joined in with a few words you wouldn't expect from a respectable senior citizen. According to Molly I will end up psychologically disturbed if he keeps whacking me. I think he felt quite sorry about it as he bought me a chewy poodle on the way home. I took great pleasure in shredding it while thinking of Molly. A plan is forming though – if they have a row every time I misbehave . . . Well, I'm sure a dog of my creative resources can incite a little discord.

For dinner he made me medallions of filet mignon in a light wine and caper sauce with sautéed potatoes and julienne carrots. Just kidding, it was bits of horse again.

Wednesday, February 6

The poor Owner's not making much of a hit with the ladies these last couple of days. Ella was in the park today and we were getting on famously. Rolling around in the grass, splashing in the pond, a quick scoot in the woods, it was all very romantic. So romantic in fact that I ended up on top of Ella for a quick tail-trembler. It was all going brilliantly until we were disturbed by her furious owner, a little blonde female who pulled Ella away from me by the collar. When my Owner turned up she started yelling at him to 'keep that disgusting sex-fiend mutt under control.'

I'm proud to say that he leaped to my defence, shouting right back that it was only natural if she let her bitch wave her backside around the park like some canine hooker. He'll make a good pack dog yet.

It was quite a quarrel and ended with them staring at each other while they snapped our leads on before stalking off. They got about twenty yards before they realised they'd put the leads on the wrong dogs and had to come back, muttering apologies. Humans are crazy.

Basking in the afterglow I was too happy to care really, even though the Owner was muttering that he'd a good mind to take my balls off with the bread knife.

Thursday, February 7

I haven't written about pack activity for a few days, as there's not much to report. Either Constable or Scottie or both are usually in the park and there's usually a bit of sparring while I tell them my plans for Park Domination, though as sparring partners go they're not ideal. Scottie is trying to teach me the 'Yapping Teeth Tail and Paw Technique' and the 'Pose of the Fluctuating Wolf,' but he keeps falling over, and fighting with Constable is like wrestling fog. Underneath all that hair there might be a dog, but it's like finding a needle in a haystack. Sometimes I see Scottie in the wasteland at night when the humans take us down for a final pee of the day. They seem to have made up now, as our fight didn't cause Scottie any real damage. I haven't seen Denny the

Flea for a while, but the pack has reported back on Claude and Liquorice's movements. The trouble is that as my Owner works from home our visits to the park are erratic, and they're usually there about six in the evening when their owners get back from work. I've got a plan though. Denny first.

Friday, February 8

I've been had! The scheming Owner's been talking to Molly on the phone and she's been filling his head with psychology. He was calling for me in the park today just as I'd found a pile of interesting litter, including some sandwich boxes that were just begging for a good licking, so I ignored him with barely a glance. And then the devious, woofing human started running. Not toward me, shouting, as he usually does, but in the opposite direction. The wolf in me sat up immediately and said, 'Hello, that's prey, that is,' and before I knew it my legs had whipped into action, running the meaty feast down across the trackless, freezing landscape. I caught him easily of course and was barking a victory when he snapped the lead on, laughing at me. Of all the low-down, dirty, underhand tricks.

Dinner: A new brand of muck with added vitamins and minerals to keep me in 'tip-top condition.' It seems to be working already.

Saturday, February 9

Of course, I couldn't let yesterday's scam pass without some kind of retaliation, so while he was asleep last night I had a snuffle around the kitchen cupboards. Contrary to popular belief, opposable thumbs are not indispensable for opening the kind of cheap furniture the Owner buys. He's wise to me now and all the good food's kept in the higher cupboards, but I did find a box of little square things that smelled divine. Stock cubes, it said on the box, so I scoffed the lot. I don't think they agreed with me though. When I went to wake him up I came over all queasy and threw up on his feet as he got out of bed. All right, I can imagine standing in a pool of warm, runny vomit isn't the nicest way to start the day, especially when it's made up of the rubbish he feeds me, but was there any concern for a sick dog? Did he rush me into the ER for a stomach pump? Were there grapes, magazines and daytime TV for Blake? No, it was a dripping foot up the backside and never mind what Molly would say about the violence. Admittedly, the shiny scraps of foil wrapper stuck to his ankles might have given the game away.

I thought the day might be looking up when we finally got to the park and Dottie came over, to say hello. News of my pack is spreading. The joy as she finally deigned to go round to the back door for the tiniest of sniffs, and the horror as she backed away asking, 'Blake, do you often vomit out of your backside?'

Of course, the Owner had been kicking me with his vomit-slicked foot. I couldn't help a whine of humiliation, but she wasn't done yet. 'I thought the bouncing stool was amusing, but it seems your posterior is quite the talent. What else will it do? Can I pull a rabbit out of it?'

It was too much; I fled.

Sunday, February 10

All thoughts of Dottie-humiliation are banished now I run with a pack of three. Today will be remembered for evermore as Battle of the Dog Toilet Day. Denny surprised me during my morning ablutions and the scrap was epic. Underneath that matted coat he's a big dog, but the training regime with Scottie and Constable paid off. Back and forth across the arena we fought, like two gladiators in a malodorous coliseum. One moment I was on my back, the next he was. It was no-holds-barred claws and teeth as we rolled back and forth across Denny's filthy territory. With no owners in sight to stop us, the fight went to the finish, but finally he was prostrate below me, my mouth gripping his neck in a vice-like grip and Denny yelping in submission. Why couldn't Dottie have been around to see it? Still, she'll pick up the news from the lampposts.

Victorious, I instructed him on the Rules of the Pack and wandered off to wait as if nothing had happened for the Owner to finish gambolling about. Of course, today of all days he decides to develop a sensitive nose. While the fight might have left a trace or two of evidence stuck to my coat, I'm sure a quick brush would have removed it. The icy hose down and the broom he sweeps the back yard with were totally unnecessary. Even though he towelled me down afterward, I made sure there was plenty of water left in my coat to shake out over the sofa. He'll think twice before trying that again.

Monday, February II

Molly and the Owner went out last night, so I took the opportunity to get some decent sleep on his comfy bed. I'm not complaining about the basket, it's home, but you can't beat soft eiderdown and I couldn't help having a nibble on the corner of a pillow as I settled down for the night either. Usually, when the Owner comes home after a night out he'll just shove me to the end of the bed – it's one of his redeeming features – so it was a shock when I was dragged out of the room, by Molly. I'm starting to think she's actually evil. By the time I woke them up this morning (I was pleased to see they were both covered in feathers), my resolve had hardened. The woman must go.

Tuesday, February 12

It's obedience day today, so I started winding him up early by knocking the bin over while he was having breakfast (I went hungry meanwhile I might add, *Molly* told him that to show me he's the alpha he must always eat before I do). The plan was that by the time we got there he'd be at boiling point and lashing out left, right and centre, thus making Molly mad and causing a row that would bring their vile 'relationship' to a happy end. Reminding the postman of my ferocity was the work of a moment and I managed to get to the paper stuff first too, shredding it nicely as he tried to grab it from my mouth. At obedience classes I growled at Snowy (sending him into a state of panic during

27

which he wet himself), ate Molly's box of treats while her attention was distracted by Snowy's owner and peed on the same man as last time, who wasn't at all pleased. It goes without saying that I was as obedient as a looter in a riot zone. All to no avail. He was stern. He was upset. The teeth were gritted, the fists curled, but the worst he did was to stare at me and say 'Bad Dog'. To my shame, I whined and wagged my tail. To cap it all, Molly made it very obvious she was pleased with his behaviour. It's disgusting what humans do with their mouths. Don't they know how unhygienic that is?

It was chokey for me once we got home, all afternoon in the backyard prison. On the plus side, the chicken wire he patched the fence up with is coming away nicely. Next time, I'm out of there.

Wednesday, February 13

Yet another date with Molly, but it was a sunny winter's day and they were too busy wandering about holding hands and doing the mouth thing to crush me with their jackbooted 'heel.' I made myself scarce while the going was good.

All the owners must have come out to get some sunshine; for once the whole pack was there and Ella, too. Denny has fitted right into the pecking order with barely a growl. I've put Scottie in command of him, but as a sop to his pride, made him superior to Constable, who still seems to be having trouble working out what the word 'hierarchy' means. Denny had some mildly interesting intelligence to report, too. Apparently there's a new dog in the Eastern Park, a pit bull called Razor, who's terrorising the dogs there and setting himself up as a tyrant. I'm not worried, it's a big park and I don't have any plans to invade the East at the moment. I very rarely go over that far, and look what happened to Bonaparte and Hitler when they tried to invade Russia. Those that don't learn from history are doomed to repeat it.

Besides, pit bulls might be fearsome in a fight but they're as thick as the idiots who usually own them and he'd stand no chance against my strategic genius. I'm all for dogs, but I never understood who'd want one that would chew up a brick if it looked at them in a funny way. I'm not saying they're all bad, I've met a couple of neutered ones who were very friendly, but your pit bull is programmed for one thing – to rip other dogs to shreds. That kind of genetic inheritance is tricky to eradicate and can resurface at any moment, no matter what a 'Good Boy' the dog has been in the past. Given the right provocation it might still become a mincing machine on stubby legs with the temper of a minefield. A human can be tickling their tummy one minute and the next it's all 'Look, Mum, no hands.' Not their fault, of course, they've been bred that way. Dog knows why. I mean, what definition of 'man's best friend' includes 'must maim if feeling out of sorts.' My Owner's not the sharpest fang in the jawbone, but at least he doesn't expect me to be some sort of fear-inspiring accessory.

Anyway, I soon forgot about Razor. Having inspected the troops I left for the woods with Ella and this time no one disturbed us. Valentine's Day tomorrow, and Cupid was definitely smiling down on Ella and me as we scooted across the damp turf.

Thursday, February 14

Saint Valentine certainly loves me, or could it be that I am an irresistible hunk of canine? The bitches are falling at my feet at the moment. Today, it was Dottie's turn. She'd heard all about my expanded territory and had thawed considerably. For once nothing happened to embarrass me and Dottie succumbed to my charismatic generalissimo and Top Dogginess by indulging me in some mutual sniffing. Her backside smells as sweet and interesting as something dead in the road. I am in love. I could just eat every one of her adorable little spots.

I've written her a poem in haiku form. It goes:

> Arf arf arf
> Wurgh woof arf
> Arooo Waugh Woof!

It loses something in translation, but in human, it would read:

> Docking of the tail,
> Makes the spotted bottom more pleasing.
> Oh, that you were in season.

Friday, February 15

Now that the campaign is gathering momentum, I've been sniffing about Liquorice's territory and the pack has been reporting back on his movements. He's a big lad, and like all

Labradors he's got enough lunatic energy for about three dogs, plus he's fiercely protective of his patch, so it could be a dangerous campaign. Luckily, 'Danger' is my middle name, or would be if I had a last name.*

If Liquorice has any weak points it's his bouncy friendliness. He can't resist running around saying 'Hello' to anything that moves and he's got the natural cunning of a chew toy. I've seen him jumping up excitedly at a concrete bench, so I'm thinking that if Scottie and Constable create a diversion with a nonaggressive incursion and

Denny attacks from the left flank then peels off at the last moment, in the confusion I can sweep in from the rear like the Assyrians falling upon Byzantium. A classic Doberman Pincer movement. It should all be over before he can say 'Pearl Harbour.' It'll need the whole pack though, so the timing is crucial. From now on all the troops are at battle stations until the optimum moment presents

itself. As the clouds of war gather we must be ready to unleash Hell at a moment's notice. Hopefully, there will be more of these sunny weekend afternoons.

* Maybe I could adopt it. Blake Danger has a nice ring. Blake Danger: Dog of War. A name like that is made for the history books.

Saturday, February 16

The Owner forgot to buy any tins of food so I survived the day on those cardboardy biscuits that tear your gums up with a tin of Spam that had been in the cupboard since we moved in. Actually, it was surprisingly good. Like ham, but spicy. Yum. Signalled my appreciation by falling asleep on him and farting like a steam train all the way through *Star Trek*. When he's talking to Molly you'd think he watched nothing but European art-house film and new works by interesting Japanese directors. If only she knew he's got every episode of *Battlestar Galactica* on DVD.

Sunday, February 17

High hopes for a new brand of dog food we were trying out today, called Mr Spew or something like that. The packaging promised great things: 'delicious 100% beef chunks in a rich gravy' and 'improved, unbeatable flavour your dog will love.' It was just as crappy as the cheap stuff though. These food manufacturers rely on the dog's lack of access to a good lawyer to flagrantly flout the trading standards laws. It makes you sick. Literally.

Monday, February 18

There was a small contretemps over breakfast this morning (his fault for leaving food on the table when the phone rang) and without trial I was sentenced to another day of backyard stir. Ten minutes was all it took for me to tear through that chicken wire, then I was through to next door where they have a proper garden. It isn't a big space, but much better than our concrete yard with a couple of dead pot plants.

I had planned to have a stroll round the neighbourhood, marking a few lampposts, checking in with the local cats, nosing through the bins: taking the air and seeing the world sort of thing. But who was to know that just over the fence would be such a paradise?

After chasing their disgusting tabby up a tree, I noticed that someone had been digging recently and there were all these interesting-looking plants standing around in fresh earth. There must be some terrier in me because I was overcome with the urge to see what was underneath. An hour later I could tell you all about roots, worms and crunchy sticks. Then I found some old shoes on the back step. Not hand-stitched Italian leather exactly, but the aroma! These were shoes that had been lived in. By a large family of blue cheeses from the smell of it – Stilton, Roquefort, Danish Blue, the whole clan. Gourmet shoes like that come along once in a lifetime and I savoured them all morning.

Of course, the Owner had to ruin the fun. I was just getting to the sole of the second one when his stupid head popped through the hole with a little gasp of shock. It was obvious from the tone of his voice that once again he'd taken umbrage, so I tried to make good my escape, but found that the gate was closed. I was trapped and the Owner was already climbing over the fence, all red in the face and shouting things at me that I cannot bring myself to repeat. I suppose it wouldn't have been so bad if the fence had been stronger, but as he reached the top it started wobbling, with the Owner flailing around on top like King Kong on the Empire State Building. Then it collapsed, dumping him into a water feature that frankly should have been cleaned out long ago. I took the opportunity to slink into my kennel and look innocent.

The neighbour choose this inopportune moment to return from work, and a hush fell as he found my Owner trying to hide by ducking his head under the water. I expect he was planning to use a reed to breathe through until the danger had passed. No reeds being available, he eventually had to come up for air among the lilies, all draped with bits of weed. He looked like an idiot.

Judging from his reaction, I guess the neighbour is a bit myopic when it comes to seeing the funny side, or that he'd had a bad day at work. He shouted a lot and brought up the howling incident once or twice. The Owner, who by now had blue lips and was shivering, finally mollified him by offering to pay for all the damage and spend the weekend making repairs, then he dragged me into the kitchen by the collar and slammed the door on me. Whining pitifully was no help at all. He was very quiet all evening, but there was no Rolled-up Newspaper. Neither was there any dinner. I have decided that checking through the bin tonight might be a bad idea. Something tells me that my testicles have never been more at risk. Perhaps it was him tearing the graph from the fridge door, screwing it up and throwing it in the garbage.

Tuesday, February 19

Except for a surly walk to the wasteland and back with just enough time to relieve myself, I spent the day chained like a . . . well, dog . . . in the now high-security back-yard Alcatraz. Just me, six foot of unchewable stainless steel, a handful of dry biscuits for dinner and next door's tabby grinning at me from the shed roof. No fetch, no basket, no warm fire, no toys, no stroking and no weekly obedience class. Not even a harmonica, though I wouldn't dare to play it with the neighbours poised to lynch me. A few bars of 'Missing Balls Blues' might have softened his human heart; whining, tail-wagging and the occasional hopeful bark certainly didn't get me very far, even though I laid it on thick.

Wednesday, February 20

I was finally let back into the kitchen last night for an inadequate dinner, then Molly came over for a conference. The Owner ranted about me for hours and was all for castrating me on the spot, but dear, sweet Molly, the voice of reason, told him that at my age neutering was highly unlikely to make any difference to this kind of behaviour. She suggested much more intensive training and a couple of books on dealing with difficult dogs. From the sound of it, the Owner wasn't convinced. He said even a small change for the better would be worth the price of the operation and if I didn't calm down he'd have to think about re-homing me. How could he? After all we've been through together. He's not perfect and I know things have been a bit rough – mistakes made on both sides – but he is my Owner for Dog's sake. That's a binding, unbreakable contract between human and canine, in sickness and in health, for better or for worse, until death us do part. Even after that I'm supposed to spend the rest of my life sitting on his grave (though I'm not entirely sure that bit is obligatory).

Very, very depressed, I spent most of the night licking my public parts. It was scant comfort, but they could be snatched away from me at any moment.

Thursday, February 21

 I'm still on red alert, especially as the Owner had to get his wallet out at the garden centre and then spend the rest of the day fixing the fence and digging new plants in next door. The neighbour meanwhile regaled him with a horrible story about a dog he'd had as a boy who'd been a menace to society until the vet had his wedding tackle off, after which he'd been 'the nicest dog you could have hoped for.' I stayed in the kennel, curled protectively around the favourite parts of my anatomy and wishing the Owner would use the rusty trowel to unman the cat-owning psychopath.

Friday, February 22

Back to the park today, but only for extra training. On the bright side, he's stopped starving me and let me back on the sofa tonight. I offered my belly for rubbing and he sighed and said, 'What am I going to do with you, Blake?' Still, there was rubbage, pleasured moaning and a tail a-wagging.

Saturday, February 23

After last night's love-in he seems to be back to his usual self, though I had to endure yet more training and the retractable lead means I have a ten-foot radius of operations for the moment. I could see Dottie loping elegantly along in the distance and Scottie came over to commiserate, but not even the Eyebrows of Great Suffering or tangling the string around his legs every two minutes would move the Owner to unclip me. The fact that even Bonaparte spent time under lock and key on Elba consoled me a little. When I am released I shall ravage the Western Park like a forest fire.

Spent the evening alone, then Molly kicked me off the bed again. In their inebriated state they didn't notice me slink off with one of her socks, which I buried in a plant pot.

Sunday, February 24

While waiting in a queue for coffee this morning I couldn't resist having a sniff at the backside of the human female who was standing in front of us. Although I don't approve of human females as a general rule of paw, they do smell nice, and I can resist anything but temptation, as Oscar Wilde used to say. Anyway, I was up her skirt before you could say 'white cotton' and it was so good I went in for some deep nose action. This not only pushed her skirt up, revealing her haunches to everyone outside the coffee stand, but also made her jump about six feet in the air, landing in a selection of biscotti.

It was at this point that I learned that showing a female's undergarments to a coffee stall crammed with people is one of the endless crimes that comes under the heading 'Bad Dog'. How was I supposed to know? There are all these petty regulations, but no rulebook. I mean, if the Owner sat me down and said 'Rule number 3,287, clause c. The dog will not cause a human bitch's underwear to go on public display,' then I might have had pause for thought. As it was I got a Slap on the Nose (but not before I'd managed to snaffle a couple of biscotti in the confusion). Then the Owner offered to buy her coffee and now

35

they're meeting again tomorrow. Good Dog Almighty! Her knickers smelled much nicer than Molly's though, so I can understand the attraction.

Monday, February 25

Life is looking up again. It was another beautiful sunny day and at last I was let off the lead while he went to have coffee with the smelly underwear woman. I spotted Dottie immediately and bounded over to recite my poem. She liked it enough to let me have another marathon backside session and then we went for a pleasant stroll across my now vast domain, condescending to the underdog and generally mingling with the riff-ruff. Everything was going well until the Owner started running around shouting for me, forcing me to lope off in the opposite direction with Dottie in tow, but after a few short minutes more of honeymoon bliss Dottie ran away when she was called, damn her obedience. By this time the Owner was tearing round the park looking for me, but I waited for the right moment then went and sat by the gate, looking like I'd been there all afternoon, and gave him such an effusive 'welcome home' that he couldn't possibly have gotten mad with me. What with one thing and another I've been neglecting practice recently and I know he loves a few stone of slobbering, licking dog in his face, even if he keeps pushing me off and shouting. It certainly seems to put minor disobediences out of his mind.

Dinner was meat by-product again, but I'm in no mood to complain.

Tuesday, February 26

It's been over a week since there was any talk about vets or the dog's home and relations have been warming during the past few days, as symbolised by the nice bit of leftover lasagne I had for breakfast this morning. So, I thought I might chance my leg by resuscitating the plan to stir up a little bit of tension with the Owner and Molly. Only in a minor way, just to see if the ice would hold.

As luck would have it, when we got to obedience class she wasn't very waggy to start with. Snowy's owner and the guy with the wet leg have both joined a school on the other side of town, citing me as the reason. The Owner was quite cool with her, but he was right; if she's setting herself up as some sort of dog expert then she ought to be able to control the animals in her classes. After that it was easy: she put her coffee mug down on a chair, I 'accidentally' knocked it over with a wag of the tail, the Owner gave me an offhand Slap on the Nose and suddenly I was in the middle of World War III with all its Mutual Assured Destruction, cities razed, nuclear winter and – hopefully – radioactive fallout.

We left before the class started.

Wednesday, February 27

While I've been romancing Dottie and Ella, it seems the Owner's been no slouch either. 'Faye' with the smelly bum has landed. Coffee in the park turned into a drink in a bar by the smell of them when they got back to the den, disturbing my well-deserved snooze. Even if she did help save my testicles, I'm still not happy about Molly, and whatever the risk I'm not putting up with the inner sanctum of my territory being invaded by every passing human in a skirt just because the Owner's under the misapprehension that losing a couple of pounds makes him some kind of Don Juan, so I was immediately on the offensive. Credit where it's due though, she's a worthy adversary. I barked and growled at her and she just played with my ears and called me a 'fierce doggy.' I squeezed between them on the sofa and she made a fuss of me. I even lifted her skirt and sniffed her bum again, as she disliked it so much at the coffee stand. But this time she just giggled and I got another Slap on the Nose from the Owner.

Short of actually biting her I was out of options, figuring that even a warning nip might sour relations again. Forced to cease offensive manoeuvres for now, I contented myself with lying by the fire looking at the pair of them reproachfully until their blah, blah, blah about art and books sent me off to sleep. While I was in this weakened state she started rubbing my tummy. The horror of waking up to find yourself on your back with your feet waving in the air, drooling while the enemy makes free with your underside! I yelped in confusion and leaped on the sofa again, in a determined assault designed to separate them. This was when the Owner uttered the horrible, horrible words, 'I think he likes you,' which, as anyone knows, is more or less an invitation to move in. Worse was still to come though. Due to her being freshly bathed and wearing some filthy perfume that hurt my nose, I nearly missed it until she was almost out of the front door to catch a taxi. The unmistakable stench of cat.

Thursday, February 28

Talk about hangdog. The Owner spent most of the day chatting on the phone to either Molly or Faye, when he should have been working and paying attention to me. In vain did I rest my head on his lap, I just got pushed away or a perfunctory ear scratch at best. Whining and barking got me shut in the kitchen. So I was fairly preoccupied when we arrived at the park, walking to heel perfectly without even realising it, and desperately trying to think up some plan that would end these sordid affairs.

After the inevitable training session I did get to run around with Ella for a while. I've been such a Good Boy for the past few days that the retractable lead has been unclipped for now. When he saw whom I was sniffing he went into a bit of a lather, but Ella's owner assured him that this time I'd been a perfect gentleman, then they started laughing and apologising to each other. Humans are crazy.

Friday, February 29

Just me and Denny in the park today. It seemed like a good idea to continue with the training, but after watching him scratch himself I decided against it. I could almost see his coat moving with parasites; and whatever his owner feeds him, it obviously disagrees violently with him. There's nothing wrong with a good fart, but the gasses that Denny manufactures must be making a small but significant contribution to the world's environmental problems.

MARCH

Saturday, March 1

Another wonderful morning with Dottie, though we only got ten minutes of overlap in our humans' schedules, and we wouldn't even have had that if I hadn't studiously ignored mine. I met her owner today, a funny-looking man with a moustache and a flat cap. Seeing his dog so happy, running around with a mate, you'd have thought he'd be overjoyed, but he just shouted, 'Oi, shoo you dirty mongrel, get away from her,' at me. I've heard that some owners can be overprotective of their bitches; I'm sure he'll warm to me when he sees how much in love we are.

Sunday, March 2

Ella's owner is much nicer than Dottie's. Obviously, my suave charm works better on female humans, because now when Ella and I play together she always says 'Hello' and gives my ears a scratch. I wish my Owner were a female. For a start he'd smell a lot better and secondly he might be a better cook. I'm not complaining about the occasional steak, not that I get much more than the odd bit of fat, but frankly everything else he cooks tastes worse than some of the stuff he feeds me. No wonder there's always so much of it in my bowl.

Whenever I'm with Ella, I forget about all my problems with the Owner and all the cares of ruling a vast empire. If she were a pedigree like Dottie I'm pretty sure I'd choose her instead, but a Top Dog has to have a Top Bitch and Dottie can trace her ancestors back to a strangely marked wolf called Spotted Jim.

I haven't mentioned Dottie to Ella, but I'm sure she understands the position. Dogs have evolved out of all that monogamy stuff, of course. Wolves mate for life,* but your modern canine is pretty progressive when it comes to sexual matters. I, for example, would get down and dirty with a wooden spoon given two minutes notice and a steak dinner to get me in the mood. Bitches are slightly more choosy of course, they like to know who's behind them during the act of love. I suppose it's all part of ensuring the best genetic heritage for the pups. Not a problem when you're the Genghis Khan of the Western Park.

* And look where that's got them. To the point of extinction.

Monday, March 3

Not much to report today. The Owner had gone to bed leaving the bin full to overflowing and came down to find it on its side and empty. Needless to say, the sentence for this petty crime was unduly harsh and after a short walk to the wasteland I was left to rot in chains all day.

Tuesday, March 4

The Owner must have made it up with Molly on the phone. It was back to obedience school today, and once again the humans were pressing their mouths together. If they just tried the bottom sniffing I'm sure they'd find it much more satisfying. Thinking of Dottie's or Ella's rich, information-packed glands got me all hot and bothered, which gave me an idea. Perhaps if Molly could see that the Owner was already taken, she might be less interested in him. Accordingly, I spent the lesson humping his leg at every opportunity. She affected not to notice him battling me off, but underneath I could tell she was seething with jealousy.

Wednesday, March 5

As it was a nice day the Owner decided to drive us out to the forest for a long walk. A great idea, spoiled by his insistence on dragging Molly along. The smell of small, crunchy wildlife was everywhere and it took me approximately three seconds to lose the humans. The trouble with wildlife, however, is that being tasty and defenceless it's used to being hunted and is very good at hiding, so after a couple of fruitless hours I made my way back to the car for an afternoon nap while the humans continued crashing through the brambles shouting my name.

It's good for them to get some exercise in the healthy fresh air. Not that they appreciated it much. You'd think it was my fault that the Owner fell into a muddy ditch lined with thorny bushes.

Thursday, March 6

Mine and Ella's humans got chatting again, so we took the opportunity to sneak off to our scooting place by the pond. Unfortunately, we had hardly had time for some gentle foreplay before the peace was shattered.

'Oh my God, your dog is a total sex pest!'

This was followed by the Owner saying, 'You try living with him, my leg's a constant victim of sexual abuse. I'm thinking about putting it into therapy.'

'Why do they do it? It's not as if Ella's even in season.'

'You have to understand, Samantha, with Blake it's a compulsion, an addiction. Ella's just been unlucky to become prey to his depraved sexual appetite, like my poor leg.'

'Is there any hope, do you think?'

'I've considered that question from all sides and I think the only hope for me is to have both legs amputated. For Ella, I'm afraid it's already too late.'

Even though they were laughing, I still got pulled off and clipped on the leash.

Friday, March 7

I've neglected the campaign, understandably given the major events over the last few days, but with just me and Scottie in the park it seemed like a good time to have another nose about Liquorice's and Claude's territories. Very strong territorial markings, but prime land of rolling fields dotted with very peeable trees and, past the woodland, the Eastern Park beckoned. It made a dog think. Scottie was less than enthusiastic though.

'Are ye sure ye want tae take these wee bits of land?'

I just growled a little to indicate my firm resolve, Top Dog and all that, but he's been a staunch number two since I took his territory so I let him have his say.

'Only, ah reckon ye can take yon Liquorice, the plan's gude and ye are in bonny fettle, but Claude is another matter. Ah've been around yon park fer more dog years than I care to recall. Ah've done mah share of soldierin' and ye jest dinnae get intae a scrap wi' a boxer unless ye can help it. And then there's yon new dog, Razor.'

I gave him the Eyebrows of Puzzlement.

'Smell on the posts over the way is that he's a wrong 'un. Nae right in the heid. We're all bad dogs from time tae time, but a wee bitty o' pee on the carpet is one thing, this is another box o' treats altogether – ye're not talking aboot a Naughty Boy here, yon pit bull is a killer.'

You don't get to Scottie's age without learning a thing or two, so I cocked my head, interested, as he went on.

'Noo Claude's territory is a fair buttress between oor lands and the East, so if the filthy pit bull's got an idea tae come West it makes sense tae let Claude take the brunt, dinnae ye think?'

Saturday, March 8

I spent the night mulling Scottie's sage advice. My thoughts are best summed up by Shakespeare, who wrote, 'Cowards die many times before their deaths: The valiant never taste of death but once.' To win the whole park, from road to glittering road, has never been done before. If I could do it then future generations would howl about Blake the Conqueror, Blake the Mighty. Russia might have done for Bonaparte and Hitler, but they were both losers anyway. No, my gaze has settled on the East and the park will tumble before me. There are bitches over there that I've never even heard of. Some of them might even be sexier than Dottie.

Sunday, March 9

The day started out well with a good run (from now on I'm in deep training), but went downhill after that. I was starving after my exertions and the Owner ignored my polite whines and begging, except to give me the corner of a sandwich that wouldn't have filled a shrew in its entirety. And it had coleslaw in it. Finally I had no option but to damn the consequences and eat something out of the gutter; something that is Best Forgotten. The Owner went a bit pale when I licked his face after, but not as pale as he was by the time that Faye came round for dinner. I was a bit peaky by then, too, and where the smell of steak would usually have me drooling, by now it just made my plumbing creak and gurgle like the *Titanic* sinking.

I have to hand it to the Owner, he struggled on dogfully right up to the moment that the food hit the table. Unfortunately, at that moment I let off a fart, the smell of which would have made a health inspector condemn the whole street. While Faye leaped for the kitchen door, the Owner ran for the toilet at a pace that I've never seen him match in the park. Just then, to my complete surprise, my sluices opened uncontrollably and I disgraced myself in quite a violent manner. Though it felt good to be empty, the resulting slick would have put a holed oil tanker to shame. It was a major disaster. We're talking sea life flopping helpless and the ecosystems of entire coastlines damaged beyond repair.

With the Owner welded to the toilet, Faye was left to clean up the mess, and even though I was probably on the very brink of death I winced when she blamed the steaks. There followed a strained conversation through the toilet door, after which she got her coat and left. A few hours later the Owner crawled into bed. Not that he stayed there.

On the bright side, I can't see Faye sitting by the phone waiting for another invitation.

Monday, March 10

My powers of recovery are truly amazing. By midnight I was feeling a lot better and with the Owner safely locked in the toilet my thoughts turned to those juicy steaks. Surely he'd forgive a little mess in the cause of not letting such prime cuts of beef go to waste?

As it happens I needn't have worried – at half-past seven the back door was opened by fanatical obedience girl. With only moderate recriminations Molly swept up the spill from the bin, clipped on the lead and we were off to the park. I guessed that he'd called her from the lavatory late last night pleading emergency.

All the way it was 'heel, heel, heel' and annoying tugs on the lead if I attempted to investigate an interesting smell. It's pathetic really, like a obsessive-compulsive disorder. The woman is a control freak, though admittedly she's a pro at the praise and stroking thing. But really, for Dog's sake, can't she just enjoy a stroll in the park and let me do my own thing? Is there any real need for me to sit down two dozen times in the space of ten minutes? I might be more willing to play along if I could see some sort of reason for it. As it is, after today I'd be a contender in the World Sitting Championships.

When we got back she noticed that the table was still set for two from last night. There was a sharp intake of breath and then she went to wake the Owner up. The following conversation was as entertaining as chasing rabbits. My favourite lines were: 'She's just a friend'; 'Do you often put candles on the table for friends?'; 'Honestly, there's nothing going on'; and, probably the best, 'I just feel sorry for your dog, what hope is there with an idiot like you for a role model.'

Two cats with one bite! I shall certainly be resorting to the diarrhoea option for problem-solving in the future. After the door slammed I celebrated by ripping up Bill's paper rubbish unmolested for once, then unearthed Molly's sock and gave that a good chewing too. I even had a little scoot of joy on the carpet, which was justified in the circumstances as being symbolic of our freedom from tyranny. With the Owner single again I can refocus on bringing the park under my iron paw.

Tuesday, March 11

I love the rain, it's so good to be wet and muddy. Though the Owner was still looking a bit under the weather, I was right on top of it. With Molly huffing out of our lives, he had to drag himself out of bed, and even though we only got as far as the wasteland with him clutching onto fences for support I made the most of it, getting drenched, rolling around in the mud and scooting through puddles. Obviously, obedience class was out of the question. What a shame, just when I was getting on so well.

When we got back to the den, he did his best to dry me off with an old towel, but wasn't very effective and his walls got a new spattered-mud effect. It's my favourite thing. I get to be destructive and he can't say a thing about it. Shaking mud out of the coat and getting dirty footprints everywhere is all part of the dog package. You can't give a dog the Rolled-up Newspaper for obeying instinct, though I think he would have liked to.

Thankfully, he managed to feed me, though there was a little retching, then he laid down on the sofa in front of the fire to watch his *Star Trek* DVDs. Around him the room filled up with the smell of wet dog, the happy aroma of bachelorhood.

Wednesday, March 12

Still raining, though today we just walked the streets with the pooper-scooper in hand and me on the retractable leash. I was dragged away from every puddle. Sometimes, I wonder if my Owner is the Anti-Dog, placed upon this world for the sole purpose of ruining my fun.

With nothing else to do all day I had to content myself with barking at the postman (who cursed at me through the letterbox), licking myself and scratching my ears. Then I fell asleep on his feet while he was working. Just enjoying the combined heat of the computer thingy and his legs; in no way was this needy or affectionate behaviour. That said, I didn't mind at all when he leaned down and patted me occasionally.

For dinner, a bowl of the usual, and then he tried to give me the bit of plain fish, which was the first thing he'd had to eat in two days, but apparently still wasn't feeling up to. Fish! Is my name Tiddles? Do I bounce around chasing butterflies? Do I wear a collar with a little tinkly bell?

I ate it of course, but frostily.

Thursday, March 13

Last night it froze and started snowing. Fantastic! Not quite as good as mud of course, but fun all the same and not even a misery like the Owner could resist a romp around the park. It was late when we got there, so all the pack's owners must have been and gone already, leaving me in his company. He must have been feeling better because he threw snowballs at me. I retaliated by jumping up and stealing his hat. Then we stopped at the coffee stand for hot chocolate and he shared his Danish with me. Single life definitely agrees with him.

Friday, March 14

Liquorice is vanquished. Now I know how Wellington felt at Waterloo. My strategy worked like an electric tin opener.

Another six inches of snow, arriving during the busy hour between seven and eight, and a spectacular dawn ensured that the park would be busy, and sure enough the pack was assembled by the dog toilet, waiting for my arrival. Across the park I could see a black dot that was Liquorice, rushing about and raising white clouds while simultaneously trying to make friends with a snowman.

Not losing a moment, I reviewed the troops, checking tags were shined, tongues lolling eagerly and ears pricked. Then I sternly reminded them of the seriousness of our mission. Constable was reluctant, asking why we'd want to attack Liquorice, who is 'like, a really cool dog, right'. I'm beginning to suspect that he's some kind of peacenik. However, I ensured him that it was for Liquorice's own good to be brought under the protection of the pack in these trying times and he seemed to accept that, though Scottie winced a bit. Denny scratched himself, but went off to take position without complaint and Scottie took charge of Constable, marching him off to their decoy engagement like a seasoned sergeant-major. I chased my own tail, closer and closer to the enemy territory, looking as unthreatening as possible.

As Scottie and Constable engaged, Liquorice went crazy with welcome as expected, jumping about three foot in the air and yapping excitedly. My troops behaved impeccably – running around, sniffing him and, at the appropriate moment, parting to let him see Denny bearing down growling furiously. This was the moment. I began my own silent, stealthy run across the snow, closer and closer.

Liquorice was confused, looking from his 'friends' to Denny streaking in on his left flank. He never even noticed me. Just as he'd decided that this was a real threat and had taken up a defensive position, crouching and snarling, Denny whirled away, leaving Liquorice spinning round and exposing his right flank to my headlong charge. I crashed into him like the Light Brigade riding over the Russian defences in the Crimea, rolling him in the snow and growling a warning against resistance that turned into a bark of triumph as we came to rest with me rising above him, teeth bared.

'All right, all right, I get it. Nice tactics, lovely. You're the boss, OK. Let's be friends.'

I released him, and he streaked away, whining for his owner.

After I congratulated the pack on a job well done, I turned to face Claude's territory. The boxer was watching nonchalantly, but turned and trotted away when I barked a challenge.

Saturday, March 15

There is nothing in life so satisfying than scent-marking new territory – a dribble of urine here, a stool there, a deft scratching to spread the smell around a bit. Each squirt and secretion packed with pheromones telling the world that I am Top Dog. As I had the park to myself, a tiny scoot of celebration on my new patch was in order. I must be careful not to let it become a habit again, after all a dog in my position can't afford to show any chinks in the armour.

Sunday, March 16

A dismal show from the Owner today. How can he ever expect to be taken seriously as an alpha when he runs crying to the phone after only five days without a female. Fortunately, Molly was having none of his weak excuses and lame protestations that Faye was just a 'friend.' She just hung up on him and eventually stopped answering the phone.

It would be a different story if he got himself a pack and could claim a significant portion of the park as his territory. If he wants the bitches to sit up and beg, he needs to have a little more self-respect. I bet that Captain Kirk he loves so much never phones his mother to moan about his love life.

There's a tasty mouthful on every cat though. It was comfort food all the way tonight, and guess who was on hand to snap up cheese-stuffed pizza crusts and leftover garlic bread?

Monday, March 17

During my daily tour of the territory I picked up the fresh, unmistakable and heavenly odour of Dottie. From the smell it seems that oestrus is not far away. That methyl p-hydroxybenzoate the bitches start producing twice a year really gets me drooling; it's the olfactory equivalent of a lap dance or a dose of ground rhinoceros horn. I'll have to start getting the Owner out of bed extra early from now on so that I can be sure to be around when she comes into season. With great genes like this, it would be a crime not to sire a litter or two, and a dash of Dalmatian would make a nice addition to the Dog knows how many breeds I have sloshing around my DNA. It's quite possible that by impregnating Dottie I might even complete the set and my pups will have a combo of everything, except pit bull of course – we mixed-breeds have to draw the line somewhere.

Tuesday, March 18

Dottie was in the park this morning and my nose does not lie, her season is on the way. If everything goes well a couple of months from now I could be a family dog, though obviously not in the sense that I'd be suitable to have around young children, unless they were plump, tender and juicy, of course.

Talking of which, chicken scraps for dinner tonight with

roasted potatoes and some vegetables that gave me such serious wind that I was dragged out of the room. If his nose was 44 times more powerful he might not have so much difficulty in picking up all the joyous aromas of a meal well digested and infused with the mucus secretions of a finely tuned gastric system.

Wednesday, March 19

Dragged the Owner out of bed at the crack of dawn with some nicely judged barking and a little wet-nose work, subtly suggesting that bounding around the park might be a lot of fun on a frosty morning. Credit where it's due, he really seems to be learning. Although he's been a bit morose the past couple of days he took the hint and slipped on his sweaty running outfit.

No sign of Dottie unfortunately, but had a good run round with the pack. Liquorice is going to be an excellent training partner. He can go from lying on the ground to three foot in the air in about half a second and dodges and weaves like Muhammad Ali in his prime. It would have been easier to concentrate on the workout if Scottie hadn't been running around us shouting instructions like, 'Keep your guard up, Blake,' and 'That's right, Licky, jump six foot to the left for no apparent reason, that'll fox him.' Even so, I was panting so much at the end of it I thought my tongue was going to fall out.

Thursday, March 20

Still no Dottie, but Ella was in the park today and we had an invigorating early dip in the pond together chasing some species of migrating water fowl that picked the wrong pond to rest in. Even though the birds got away it was an exhilarating chase and Ella looked great with wet fur clinging to her, so it was a shame that our owners interrupted, panting and complaining to each other about the cost of having carpets professionally cleaned. Still, there was some joy to be had in waiting for them both to clip the leads on before shaking ourselves vigorously. I love the smell of wet human in the morning.

Friday, March 21

Missed the postman again due to the early-morning run, but managed to get some excellent menacing on at two stray Jehovah's Witnesses who came knocking while the Owner was in the shower and who proved quite persistent in the face of some barking that must have registered on the Richter scale. Wearing just a towel and dripping all over the carpet (an act of pure hypocrisy when you consider how much he hates me doing it), he opened the door just a crack, while restraining me from savaging the desperate old women who were assaulting my den. Not to be stayed in my mission from Dog to see them off, I immediately got a nose and paw around the door, forcing it open and taking his towel off in my struggle to be at the invaders. He tugged at my collar with one hand while the other couldn't decide whether to slam the door, cover his anatomy, pick up the towel or slap me on the nose.

You have to wonder about Jehovah's Witnesses. I've gotten pretty good at judging his moods, but I would have thought that even a cat would realise it probably wasn't the best time to ask him if he had considered letting God into his life. I guess when you're full of the Holy Zeal being fed to the wild animals must seem quite attractive. Their Lord saved Daniel from the lions after all. Perhaps they were banking on Him working the same trick with me. If the Owner had let go my collar for a moment we could have put their belief to the test, but unfortunately it seems that his certain knowledge of Blake is greater than his faith in the Lord.

After a minute or two of this, the elderly humans must have realised that I wasn't about to lie down meekly at their feet and my ferocious windmilling paws might send them to witness Jehovah a bit sooner than scheduled. Either that or trying to convert a naked man struggling with a large enraged beast might prove an uphill struggle. Whatever the reason, they eventually started backing slowly down the path, but not before attempting to press some literature on him, which I snatched and shredded.

I was expecting the Rolled-up Newspaper, but all I got was a pat on the head while he laughed. I mention this only as it illustrates how unpredictable he is, and thus how unsuitable for the role of alpha.

Saturday, March 22

Finally caught up with Dottie, who is indeed tantalisingly close to ovulating, and in a flirtatious mood. She let me have a lingering sniff and lick, by which time my libido was steaming, but ran away laughing when I tried to mount her. Instead, we wrestled back and forth across the park, nearly but not quite Doing It once or twice, the little tease. Such was my white-hot passion that after she was called away I had to relieve my ardour by humping the Owner's leg again. He's not exactly Marilyn Monroe and, considering he hasn't been getting much recently, I'd have thought he would be grateful for the attention. If his idea of sexual reciprocation is squawking, flailing and trying to throw his partner off, is it any wonder women keep leaving him? All in all it was an uncomfortable scene, the more embarrassing when I realised that Ella had arrived and was watching with her head tilted to one side in bemusement.

As the Owner grappled with me Ella's Samantha human ran by and called, 'It's so good to see an openly gay, inter-species couple enjoying themselves on a spring morning.'

Sunday, March 23

Molly finally deigned to speak to the Owner today on the phone, though thankfully she still wasn't friendly. By the sound of it she was still blaming him for losing some of her best customers and generally being a cheating, lowlife scumsucker. Much as I'd like to agree with her character analysis, he had coffee with cat-owning smelly bum today and spent the whole time moaning about Molly, which was odd behaviour, even for him, if he wants to get anywhere with her. Faye was all sympathy and told him to keep at it. Female humans, like their canine equivalents, apparently like a dog to chase them down occasionally. Perhaps he doesn't have sexual designs on Faye after all. That would be an uncharacteristic flash of sense for him, bearing in mind her foolish predilection for feline vermin.

Anyway, Molly eventually admitted that Faye might not be moving in on her territory and even grudgingly conceded that she might have overreacted, but she still wasn't happy about her missing customers. The Owner swore that if she could give me private training once a week in exchange for dinner he'd get them all back, but I don't know how he's going to manage that given his marked reluctance to fight, which must be a major drawback when he needs other humans to be submissive. It's a shame, as he would stand a good chance against Snowy's owner. The skin on her face is all loose and wrinkly like a Shar Pei. Plenty to get his teeth into.

Monday, March 24

A great workout with Liquorice today, in training for Claude. We chased each other up and down the park like greyhounds. By the end of it I was totally pumped and couldn't have kept my tongue in my mouth if it was slathered in barbeque sauce. A fighting machine in his prime needs to get plenty of refreshing sleep, too, so I spent the afternoon on my back under the Owner's desk, dreaming of running down a herd of postmen, Jehovah's Witnesses and door-to-door salesmen. My legs may have twitched occasionally.

 I woke up with food high on the agenda, which came as no big surprise, but the Owner is still under the impression that he can force me to wait until he's eaten before I get my share. Fortunately, I am a master of the art of begging. During Stage One I sat by his chair dripping great strings of saliva into his lap while he tucked into his microwave 'healthy choice' risotto for one. Once I had his attention I started shuffling the eyebrows around in the Look of Great Pleading while whining gently and fondly pawing at his knee. Such was the power of my Big Brown Eyes that he finally sighed and scraped half the risotto into my bowl, at which point I dropped the charade of affection. If he wants me to be a Good Boy then he really ought to stop rewarding my bad behaviour.

Tuesday, March 25

Books on dog behaviour and training should be outlawed, they're all part of the conspiracy to keep me in bondage. Yesterday he bought a new book called *How to Screw Up Your Dog's Self-Esteem*, or something like that, which is full of information that, in my opinion, should be classified. For example, today we started playing my favourite game – the Owner throws a stick then I run around him with it in my mouth making him chase and threaten me. Then I let him get one end of it and we have a tug of war while I growl. No more though. First off, he did the running away thing, and schmuck that I am I fell for it again, bounding right up to him like a good boy. Then this so-called book informed him that if he pinches the tips of my ears I will immediately drop anything in my mouth. I feel violated. After this happened about thirty times I stalked away in high dudgeon.

As Francis Bacon once said, 'Some books are to be tasted, others to be swallowed, and some few to be chewed and digested.'

Wednesday, March 26

Dottie is a dish seasoned to perfection, put on a high heat and cooking up a Blake-flavoured litter thanks to yours truly, the park's very own Casanova.

She was waiting for me when we arrived this morning and snapping and growling at the other dogs who were flocking around her. Why her owner let her off the lead in that condition is a mystery, but one that no dog in the Western Park this morning was about to ponder. I could smell her from miles away, oozing ripe sexuality, and I strained at the lead more than usual in anticipation. Even Scottie was trying to get in for a sniff, which was fairly optimistic of the dirty old dog considering their relative sizes and his age. Given the chance, he'd still need a stair-lift to get up there. My own human was oblivious (it's amazing, I would have thought that even monkey boy with his pathetic nose could smell her). He just slipped the lead off, grateful that his arm was still attached, and loped away for his run without bothering to look back. I sprinted straight over, barking orders at the dogs who surrounded her. They scattered instantly. After a quick nuzzle of welcome we loped off to a patch of bushes so as not to be disturbed. There was more nuzzling and some blissful sniffing after which I put an experimental paw on her spotty shoulder. Finding no resistance, I gave her another little lick – the tender, considerate lover – gently assumed the classic position with my front legs wrapped around her shoulders and went at it like a pneumatic drill on Viagra.

Afterwards, we were tied together for about twenty minutes, during which we basked in the afterglow and I growled at a couple of interloping chancers who were snuffling around the bushes. Then she gave me a last sniff and wandered off to find her owner, who was reading the morning paper on a park bench, none the wiser.

Spent the rest of the day congratulating myself on what an irresistible figure of a dog I am and naming puppies in my head. The males should have traditional heroic names, like Fang or Claw, while the girls should be more soft and feminine. I like Analie, Sphincterina or Bumhola.

Thursday, March 27

I was hoping for an encore today, but it looks like Dottie's owner has finally caught on. She was on a tight lead and I got water squirted in my face when I went over to present my compliments. As a rule humans are harmless, and it's altogether too much hassle to bite them unless you want to take the trip to the vets from which there is no return, but I could have happily gone for the jugular on this one. Dottie and I are like star-crossed lovers, cast asunder by the cruel winds of fate. Or something like that. She must have realised that it was a lost cause as she trotted along at his side with haughty pedigree composure and barely a glance at me. The way she smelled and twitched her beautiful backside made me momentarily consider the tender charms of the Owner's leg again, but I dismissed the temptation and took advantage of Constable instead. He is in show business after all.

Friday, March 28

I am in disgrace once more, even though it's all the Owner's fault. Usually we take an evening stroll down to the wasteland so that I can relieve myself before digging in for my restoring eight hours, but last night he was up until late rattling the computer and then fell asleep without a thought for my bladder. A couple of hours later nature was calling as persistently as a team of telemarketers on commission.

I've been accused of a lot of bad behaviour, but I've never been one to deliberately pee in the den unless there's a pressing reason. I tried whining by the door, but he was dead to the world. In the end I had to resort to full-on barking while trying to stop the little squirts that kept escaping onto the kitchen floor. It woke the neighbours, but still took half an hour to get him out of bed, cursing and shivering in his shorts. Is it my fault he slipped in the wee and cracked his head on the kitchen table? Can I be blamed for the crockery that broke on the floor? He finally managed to skate across to the door to let me out and I was off like a whippet, sluicing down the nearest lamppost. Then he called me.

Now I'm back on the chain gang, starved and excluded from the den, convicted of a crime I didn't commit. After all, he owed me a trip to the wasteland, and if he wanted to come running around after me in a dressing gown in the middle of a cold March night, that's his decision. Can I be blamed if his shouting and whistling woke up the street again? It's a total miscarriage of justice.

Still, a dog of my resources is rarely beaten and I have noticed that though the chain is impervious even to my jaws of steel, the post that he's attached it to is a bit rotten. Fortuitously, chewing is what I do best.

Saturday, March 29

No park, staple rations and another day chained with only the wooden box I'm supposed to call home for shelter. Actually, it's not that bad now I'm used to it. It keeps the weather off and the Owner thoughtfully put some bedding down.

It would be quite acceptable if I didn't know that only a few yards away there's a sofa with my name on it and a blazing fire. With nothing much to look at I entertained myself by howling a new kennel-house blues tune I'm writing called 'When a Dog's Gotta Pee.' I've gotten as far as the first verse, which goes:

A dog's gotta pee, every evening without fail,
And if you done forgot it, then fetch your mop and pail.
Cos' a dog's gotta pee, every night at around nine,
And when he gets that pee, Good Boy that sure feels fine.

Sunday, March 30

I think the Owner's realised that he was at fault the other night. I got a kind of apology, in the shape of 'Blake, you can really pick your moments, but it's not your fault I've got to work so hard at the moment,' and a longer walk than usual in the wasteland. Met up with Scottie and discussed the further expansion of my territory. Our conquest has been too slow recently; now is the time to strike at Claude. I can sense Scottie is reluctant, but I'm unstoppable at the moment.

The park was empty today, but while the Owner had coffee and dull relationship chat with Faye I surveyed Claude's territory again. Soon it will be mine.

Monday, March 31

After a Herculean struggle to get me in the back of the car we set off for destination unknown today, with me signalling my displeasure by tearing up one of his road maps while he tried to steer with one hand and grab it off me with the other. Imagine my horror when we arrived at a courtyard where an obedience-training session was in progress. I thought he'd seen the error of his ways and put all that unpleasantness behind us.

No amount of barking and trying to squeeze myself under a seat would deter him from dragging me out of the car, so eventually I gave in to the inevitable and bounded straight into the thick of it. Immediately recognising something that looked and smelled familiar I gushingly reacquainted myself with the man with the lamppost leg then, spotting Snowy, I bounded over, snapping playfully to remind him of our trip round the countryside. He wet himself on his owner's foot and tried to climb into her handbag. I've missed the little tyke.

In spite of the Owner's wretched attempts to train me in the park, I was a bit rusty and the rest of the lesson didn't go too well. The trainer, Steve, had his head in his hands at one point. The Owner happily, and loudly, told him that if we put in the effort week after week it would pay off in the end and that I seemed to like him much better than Molly on the other side of town who had kicked us out of her class. In fact, it went so badly that after the incident on the obstacle course I was expecting to go straight back into Alcatraz when we got home. Instead, I got a steak. Humans are crazy.

APRIL

Tuesday, April 1

Now I see the black depths of his twisted mind. Yesterday was all a ruse, an evil ploy, a perverse stratagem to win Molly back, and I've been duped into playing a part in my own downfall.

The horrible obedience junkie called last night. After yesterday's class Snowy's owner and the man with my favourite leg both phoned her to ask if they could be readmitted to the class. And after that there was a flurry of calls from other people at Steve's school who suddenly also wanted to switch. Apparently, I am the cause of this exodus. The impertinence!

The control freak was, of course, delighted. I could hear her on the other end of the phone telling the Owner he was a genius and thanking him profusely. I'm to have private lessons each week, after which they're going out to dinner. I sulked the sulk of a dog whose trust has been well and truly molested.

Even though this means Molly's temporary return, if I'm honest there was a very small part of me that wagged with delight at such a brilliant subterfuge, well executed. He might one day make a good member of the pack and I may even promote him above Constable, provided that he doesn't pull any tricks like that again. In the meantime I need a plan of my own to sever their relationship again. Diarrhoea served me well last time, I wonder if another bout might turn the tide?

Wednesday, April 2

Most of the pack was in the park today, so I had plenty of backup when I went to deliver Claude an ultimatum: join the pack or be prepared to fight for his territory. Claude just growled and walked away, so war it is, and with victory the whole of the Western Park is my dominion. To be honest, I'm a bit nervous; his sleek coat is all packed with rippling muscle and he's got a chest like a bull elephant. Plus he's nowhere near as dim-witted as Liquorice. It could be a costly campaign.

Spent an hour or so in training with the troops, during which I got a mouthful of Denny's coat, which was like sucking on a toilet brush. Luckily, for dinner there was reconstituted animal by-product, coloured and pressed into shapes that are presumably meant to resemble chunks of prime meat. These dog-food manufacturers aren't fooling anyone, though it still tasted marginally better than Denny.

Thursday, April 3

Bored out of my mind this morning. There is a howling gale outside and the Owner just about managed to get me to the end of the street before he was forced to abort the walk. I was happy enough, being a rugged all-weather, all-terrain kind of dog, but the Owner was being blown all over the place. His own fault for adopting a non-streamlined, upright stance. He'd have been all right a bit closer to the ground and with four legs keeping him steady.

Friday, April 4

Another day of foul weather and just enough time to relieve myself. With lots of pent-up energy and limited space, the only option for occupying my time was to chew something tasty and try and think of a way of beating Claude. I stole a sandal from the Owner's wardrobe, figuring he won't be looking for it for a while with the weather like this, and lay behind the sofa pondering tactics while I got to work on it.* Not even my brilliant military brain could come up with a fail-safe plan that would work against Claude though. The only thing that came to mind was 300 Spartans beating down a mighty army of 10,000 Persians at the Gates of Thermopylae. Or Rocky Balboa triumphing over all odds to beat Apollo Creed. It looks like it's going to be a vicious fight that only a body of steel and a stubborn refusal to admit defeat might win. Sometimes, it all comes down to muscle straining against muscle. All fired up with the Eye of the Tiger, I started throwing the sandal round the room and pouncing on it, pretending it was Claude.

Spent the afternoon banged up and had to hide from the rain in the kennel.

* Of course I could have selected any one of a number of chew toys, but there's a tangy flavour to a well-worn shoe that's tough to beat.

Saturday, April 5

Weather still horrible, but he got bundled up in just about every item of clothing he owns and at least we made it to the wasteland and I got a chance to pick Scottie's brain about Claude. He said he knows a few tricks from the old days that aren't much used now and he'd have a think on it.

I miss running around the park, Dottie, Ella and the pack, and I'm completely fed up with the Owner, who's even more of an ogre than usual. I try to have a simple conversation with him about how frustrated I am being cooped up; just a little whining, barking and pacing his office floor, and what do I get? Curses and being shut up in the kitchen. I sometimes think he likes pressing those little buttons and staring at the screen more than he likes me.

Sunday, April 6

Day four of storms, torrential rain and minimal walks, but at last the penny seems to have dropped on the chewing issue. With Molly's advice he went out last night and came back with the biggest bone I've ever seen. It must have come off an animal the size of a zeppelin, and it still had scraps of meat clinging to it. Apparently butchers just give them away if you ask nicely, but it never occurred to him that a tasty bone might pip even a hand-stitched Italian leather shoe in the flavour department. Sometimes it's tough to under-stand him, but then I remember he's as dumb as a box of hair.

Despite the weather I had a fantastic day rolling around the kitchen floor with my new best friend, Mr Femur.

BLAKE

Monday, April 7

Back to the park at last, though only Denny was around. With the Big Fight looming I made the best of it and put in an hour's hard training and sparring. The Owner did the same, though not by wrestling with Denny, lucky him. He's probably trying to look his best for Molly tonight, much good may it do him, for the Blake brain never fails and I have hatched a doozie of a plan. It's not elaborate, but will rely on a steady application of pressure, using Molly's own psychological conditioning principles to turn the tables on her. I have high hopes that it will yield the required result.

All the training made me hungry and I have to bulk up, so I stole a croissant off one of the tables when the Owner went to meet Faye. To be fair, the man at the table didn't look that interested in it, and how was I to know he was saving it for a friend?

When we arrived at the one-on-one obedience classes, Sergeant-Major Molly said that it was best to go 'back to basics' as I was obviously confused. For an hour she held me while the Owner said 'Blake, come' from further and further away, then she'd let me go and I'd go and collect my treat and enthusiastic stroking.

My conscience felt a bit queasy at my complicity in such an obvious attempt at brainwashing, but when all is said and done a meaty treat is a meaty treat. According to Molly he has to keep feeding them to me every time he wants me to go back to him until I have the whole 'come' thing down perfectly. I should be able to string this out for months, if not years.

After praising me highly for my success at assimilating the advanced learning that 'treats are good', they dropped me off at the den, gave me even more food and then left me and Mr Femur to spend a worthwhile evening communing together until they'd had dinner.

Tuesday, April 8

Stage One of the plan went perfectly last night. I have noticed that humans do not appreciate a dog's flatulence as it deserves, and I have also noticed that the quicker I eat my dinner the more I fart, so yesterday I inhaled my food in one breath and then clenched until they came home.

Once they were settled on the sofa, I placed myself at their feet – the Good Boy keeping them company – and then every time they went to press their mouths together, quietly let rip a belter so rich in texture and flavour that it had them choking and reaching for the windows. A few more dates and she will start unconsciously associating the act of kissing the Owner with gagging, retching and rushing for the door. I am a genius.

I supplemented the evening's farting by ensuring that neither of them had a good night's sleep, carefully measuring out subdued but insistent whining and barking to suggest I was concerned for the Owner's safety with a stranger in the den, while being careful not to go over the top. Even Molly's 'psychological' reasoning over breakfast sounded strained and they both looked haggard, which was excellent. A couple more nights like this and the idea of a date with each other will fill them with horror. The irony of their congratulating themselves on making me 'come.' If only they knew that I was playing them like a virtuoso of human manipulation.

Molly had to go off and teach her new enlarged class, so we had the day to ourselves.

Wednesday, April 9

The plan seems to be having an effect already! Molly phoned to cancel their date last night, saying she was too tired. The Owner seemed relieved. All this is superb news. If I keep the screws on she should be history sooner than I thought. I spent most of the day snoozing and dreaming of Park Domination, with every dog for miles around queuing for the distinction of sniffing my urine. The trappings of power.

Thursday, April 10

The big fight with Claude has been weighing heavily on me recently and I needed to motivate myself, so with the Owner trotting around in the sunshine I went East to remind myself of the expanse that my Empire might one day encompass. There's a lot of woodland over there and I was having a sniff around when I came across a Pekingese hiding in a clump of brambles. On my trotting over to say 'Hello' and pick up any news, the little dog flattened her ears against her head and drew her lips back in a savage snarl. Classic fear aggression. I could have chomped her with one bite of course, but the odd thing was it didn't seem to be me she was afraid of, she was just scared in general.

It didn't take long to find out why. The scent of pit bull was all over the place, and a nastier, more arrogant smell has never crossed my nostrils. If this is Razor then it's no wonder the Eastern dogs are running scared. Frankly, I was quite glad when I heard my name being called in the distance. I didn't need the promise of a treat to get me out of there.

Friday, April 11

Met up with Scottie this morning, who'd been considering the big fight and had a couple of excellent ideas. After we'd discussed tactics our conversation turned to my experience over in the East yesterday.

'Aye, it smells like yon Razor is a bad doggie all right,' Scottie said slowly. 'Whut them dogs need is a proper Pack Leader.'

'Well, after I've taken the East they'll have one,' I shot back, smarting at the suggestion that I wasn't a 'proper' leader.

'Och, yer still planning on goin' East, are ye? Well, I suppose that once Claude's oot of the way Razor'll come lookin' fer ye soon enough and frae whut I hear he'll tear ye a new hole.'

'And what would a "proper" Pack Leader do about it?'

'Och, yer not a Bad Boy, I'll give ye that, but yer only in it fer the personal glory. Back in the days when bein' leader meant somethin', it was all about makin' sure the pack wus healthy and protected, with enough food tae go aroond. Yer territory wus as big as it needed tae be and no bigger.'

'What's your point?'

'Well, ye dinnae care aboot protectin' the pack, we're jest here tae make ye look like ye're Top Dog.'

If anyone but Scottie had said that I would have taken a good-sized chunk out of them; instead I replied coldly, 'When I've given Razor a beating we'll see who's a good Pack Leader.'

'Och aye,' he said morosely, 'ye can show them by takin' all the bitches, eatin' all the food an' wanderin' around like Lord Dog Almighty.'

My respect for the elderly saved him a broken neck.

Saturday, April 12

Oh, Dog. I was having a well-deserved sleep this evening and something bit me. Denny's given me his fleas. I am a fleabag. What are the bitches going to say? I mean, it's hardly suave, is it? 'Hello darlin', have a sniff of this, it's teeming with parasites.' Dottie will never let me anywhere near her sweet behind again. Ella will spurn me. I had my first fight with Denny well over a month ago and the female flea will start laying up to 40 eggs a day just 48 hours after finding a new host. There could be thousands of them on me, by now – I'm a walking housing estate. The shame of it.

Sunday, April 13

After considerable panicked thought I realised that the only way to get rid of the fleas is with human help. This means the Owner has to get them too. Now I'm not allowed on his bed any more I had to exercise all my powers of stealth, but opened the door of his room without him noticing and spent the afternoon asleep on his pillow.

Got a Slap on the Nose for my pains, but it was half-hearted. He never hits me with as much gusto as he used to. Even so, I really hope a load of the little buggers crawl into his hair while he sleeps tonight.

Monday, April 14

The fleas seem to be multiplying rapidly, I swear I can feel them laying eggs all over me, their vile transparent larvae burrowing into my follicles and the adults making merry on my blood like miniature Vikings in Valhalla. My skin is crawling. I must be allergic to their disgusting saliva because I scratch all the time.

Obedience this evening (Lesson 2: Remedial Sitting) followed by another night in with Mr Femur, who's now losing his appeal somewhat having been chewed and sucked dry of any flavour.

Tuesday, April 15

The Owner finally noticed. He was sitting with Molly watching some yawn of a movie about a male and female human falling in love. It's a bad sign when he forgets that he's trying to impress females and stops making them watch foreign films so I was fairly morose, sitting at their feet trying to squeeze out a fart or two and scratching constantly. I must have disturbed a small colony behind my ear though because a couple jumped out into the bowl of popcorn.

Molly squealed and immediately burrowed into my coat, then started looking at the carpet. Eventually she looked up and said the magic words.

'Your dog has a severe flea infestation.'

Naturally, there was no hint of sympathy from the Owner, just his usual stream of curses. Molly, to her credit, was fairly sharp with him about not keeping an eye on my health or grooming me often enough, and even he had the decency to look embarrassed, though he didn't go as far as admitting that he doesn't even own a dog brush and his 'grooming' routine mostly involves throwing a bucket of cold soapy water over me occasionally.

Wednesday, April 16

As luck would have it, Molly refused to spend last night in a 'fleapit' and spent the rest of the evening standing over him while he loaded up the washing machine over and over. Then she made him promise to give me a thorough treatment before our next training session and spray the house before inviting her back. It was almost worth hosting a flea metropolis to see the expression on his face when she left. I'm beginning to see another way in which a stake might be driven into this unnatural relationship.

Thursday, April 17

Spent most of the day at the launderette as his geriatric washing machine couldn't cope with the volume and leaked all over the kitchen floor in the night. Even my bedding got a wash, which is a shame as I'd been working on that smell for months and now I'll have to start over. By lunchtime he finally got round to ridding me of my unwanted visitors. First there was a bath with some vile-smelling liquid. As a matter of principle I struggled dogfully as he tried to lift me in. I'm not a small animal and it was entertaining making him stagger around the bathroom with a heavy armload of writhing, barking dog in his arms, but I was feeling good about being rid of the flea circus so I let him know it was only in fun by giving his ear a good licking – I know he loves that because he always makes the cutest little barking noises. After a bit of splashing about in the bath, I condescended to let him shampoo me, then jumped out and shook myself all over his pristine bathroom and managed to spray as far as the entry hall before he caught up and assaulted me with the towel. Then came all kinds of potions and powders and finally a thorough brushing, which was a novel experience and not an unpleasant one.

By the time we made it to the park I was as clean as I've been since the day my old mum licked the placenta off me. What was a dog to do but celebrate by heading straight for the pond and splashing about like a hippo at a mud-wrestling club?

Friday, April 18

Molly is over again tonight and I am planning just the tiniest nose about in the garbage. Mostly, just checking to make sure that nothing's going to waste, but also as an experiment in the second prong of my Molly-busting attack. I have a hunch that there could be a way to intensify the campaign.

Saturday, April 19

Once again the Owner took exception to the trail of chicken bones, paper towels, empty tins and potato peelings across the floor, even though it must have taken all of fifteen seconds to clear up. I avoided both the Rolled-up Newspaper and the Slap on the Nose under Molly's watchful eye, but had to endure a couple of hours in the backyard, exclusion from the den being all the rage as a punishment these days. It was worth it though. Before he had a chance to chain me up, Molly the 'dog expert' had already started yapping about ways in which my bin-diving behaviour could be modified, and I was gratified to see him roll his eyes as he dragged me out the back door. It's a look I've seen many times before and I'm pretty sure my expertise on his behaviour is greater than Molly's on mine. It means, 'Oh, just shut up and leave me alone.'

Sunday, April 20

It was a cold, wet day in the park, with just Claude and me staring at each other and growling across my territory like two gunslingers, our ears and tails pointed, walking slowly towards each other with the stiff-legged gait of dogs on the very edge of extreme violence. He went for the leg-cock, but I got there first, jetting a stream of pheromone-enriched urine into the dirt. Then he came at me, teeth bared and ears swept backward.

It was like being run down by a bulldozer, and he kept me pinned down while trying to find somewhere on my twisting body where his teeth could find purchase. I may not be as big as him, but I'm supple.

Remembering Scottie's secret weapon, I managed to wriggle out from under him, pounced on his rear end and got my teeth around his testicles in a vicelike grip, snarling, 'Stitch this, ye ugly, creepin' blasted wonner,' through a mouthful of impressively sized boxer balls. The line comes from the Robert Burns poem, *To a Louse*. The Scottish have a great turn of phrase.

Claude was nonplussed for a second – it's difficult to keep on the right side of plussed with your maracas enclosed in jaws of steel – but in an unexpected move that must have hurt him bad he rolled and turned, bringing his head up to my flank and allowing him to sink his teeth into the base of my tail.

While all this was going on, somewhere at the back of my brain the sounds of human barking registered, but it was not until now that I realised that the Owner was dancing around us, screaming at me to 'Leave It.' Obviously, that wasn't going to get him anywhere, but then another human arrived, shouting, 'No, no, don't shout at them, they'll turn on you. Grab his back legs.'

It's a base human trick. To stop dogs fighting, silently grab their back legs off the ground and separate them. In an instant Claude and I were being pulled away from each other like two battle-ready wheelbarrows, still eager for action, but unable to get any purchase on the ground or twist round to make our owners let us go.

Leads were snapped on and the two owners quickly checked us for damage as best they could, shouting apologies at each other, then we were dragged away. I am now languishing once again in the backyard penal complex. The Owner is Not Talking to Me, no matter how much I wag and give him the Big Brown Eyes of Repentance. If only he knew how much it hurts to get the tail going at all. And all for an enforced stalemate. Now I'm going to have to do it all over again, and Claude will be expecting Scottie's little surprise next time.

Monday, April 21

Bar a night on the cold kitchen floor, I have been doing stir for over a day. At mealtimes the warder brings round a handful of dry biscuits and for half an hour I get walked up and down the street on a short lead to relieve myself.

It's a harsh regime, but I'm working on an escape attempt. The post to which I am chained is nearly two-thirds of the way through now and there's definite give when I pull on it.

Tuesday, April 22

Bad news all round today. There was a walk to the park and Ella was there, but I was on the lead (not even the retractable one) and he pulled me away sharply when she came to say hello. To make matters worse, there's some sort of locking device on the fridge door and when, in despair, I went to investigate the bin, it gave my nose an electric shock. The Owner has wired it up! I swear that every time he heard me yelping he laughed the maniacal laugh of the criminally insane.

To make matters worse, today's 'lesson' with Molly consisted of her sitting and talking at the Owner about how to make me more obedient by impressing upon me that he's the alpha. I sniffed around the courtyard, bored. She's been studying books about being a 'dog whisperer' and apparently the key to having a well-adjusted dog is understanding its behaviour and methods of communication, not giving in to its demands, rewarding good behaviour and firm (but non-violent) action if necessary. At worst, the Owner is allowed to shake me by the scruff of my neck for major transgressions, but she mostly recommended staring me down and growling at me as a Pack Leader would in the wild, which just shows what she knows. In the wild I would sink my teeth into him if he pissed me off. He doesn't realise how much slack I already cut him because of his dexterity with the tin opener. All Molly's blah, blah, blah sounds like touchy-feely psychobabble to me. If he really wanted to impress, shaking her by the throat would be a great start, but at least it looks as though he's going to dispense with the Rolled-up Newspaper indefinitely.

After an hour of this New Age claptrap she said that it was no good doing it in fits and starts when he remembered to, he has to adhere to the new regime all the time. Give me strength, as if I haven't got enough problems without having Sigmund Freud on my back all day and night. He must be blind if he can't see that the den is so much more harmonious when there aren't any women around. I really need to step up the campaign to separate them.

Wednesday, April 23

I am still suffering from cruel mistreatment and torture by electric bin, but things are looking up on two counts. First, the post in the back yard is getting nearer breaking point, and once it snaps I shall be away from here for ever.*

Second, the Owner is such an idiot that he keeps forgetting that he electrified the garbage. I was gratified to watch him get half a dozen shocks over the course of the evening. As the old saying goes, 'He's crapped in his own bowl,' and it brought a smile to my face for the first time in days to watch him scream and jump six foot across the room every time.

* Or until the following mealtime, whichever is shorter.

Thursday, April 24

The Owner finally relented and let me off the lead in the wasteland this evening and I was allowed to run off with Scottie while the two owners stood around chatting. The first thing I did was ask him if he had any other old techniques I could use in my next round with Claude.

'Then ye havenae heard? Yon Claude wus attacked by Razor yesterday. Word is, he wus rushed intae the vet, but it's touch an' go. Liquorice wus there and tried tae help, but Razor took a bite oot a him too. Claude wus in a bad way when Razor's owner finally dragged him off.'

He paused for a second to let this sink in, then continued. 'O' course ye ken that this means Claude's territory now belongs to yon mad pit bull, so even if he survives it won't be him ye're going up agin.'

I wasn't going to let Scottie see it, but for the first time since I heard Razor's name I felt fear. It was fifty-fifty whether I'd beat Claude and if the pit bull could take out him and Liquorice together so easily and savagely, it looked like my territory could be trembling on the brink of disaster.

Scottie looked up at me sagely. 'Time tae start bein' a proper Pack Leader, I reckon.'

Friday, April 25

With the retractable lead still being strictly enforced in the park today, I couldn't even check my own territory for the new markings that would tell me if Razor intends to come West. If he does then I'll need a plan of extraordinary brilliance to combat him. I've already started formulating a couple of strategies, but I want to think about the battle plan from every angle before committing myself. Like Lord Nelson, I like to have every possible eventuality covered. This will be my ultimate challenge. To win will be to rule the entire park. To lose is unthinkable.

Saturday, April 26

While minding my own business last night, I happened to paw at a new pair of training shoes the Owner bought recently. I wasn't going to chew them, just checking out the smell. When he saw me, he started with the growling like Molly told him to. It was hilarious, the first laugh I've had in days. He's got the accent all wrong, and his vocabulary is dreadful. What he actually said was, 'Sniff my mange, rabbit leg.' Sometimes he is so cute I could forgive him anything, so I spent the evening snuffling his groin to show him that I know he's not all bad.

Sunday, April 27

Claude is out of intensive care and his owner brought him to the park for the first time since his fight. He's in a terrible mess with stitches all over his hindquarters and on his head and one of those funnel things around his neck. Although it made him look as though he's been poured down the drain, even from a distance he looked sad and broken and I didn't have the heart to laugh.

Our owners started a conversation by shouting at each other across the park, but when they saw that we weren't growling at each other, gradually got closer, feeding us both treats all the way until we were within sniffing distance. Now he's been dispossessed of his territory there's no reason for me to fight with him – not that I would in his condition. Rule number one: you can't kick a dog when he's down. The owners soon got on to the subject of Razor, and so did Claude and I.

'I heard about the fight, Scottie says that you fought like a wolf. I can vouch for that from personal experience.' I was being supportive and magnanimous, of course.

'All I know is that I can handle myself against any dog I've ever met and I didn't stand a chance against Razor. He's a beast.'

'No hard feelings about our little skirmish, then?'

'None, though if things were different I'd be having a quiet word with you about chewing on my prize assets.'

'Sorry, I had to have something up my collar.'

'Understood. So what are you going to do when Razor comes looking for a fight? You know he's been re-marking all your territory, right?'

I didn't and this was very bad news, but I bluffed it out, the dog of destiny, supremely confident and unshaken.

'I'm not too worried, I've got a few tricks and the pack is five by five behind me.'

'You mean that bunch of flea-bitten geriatrics and misfits you hang around with? You'll need more than that and a bit of dirty street fighting.'

'Well, seeing as you're not a big Razor fan, why don't you join us?'

'You know as well as I do that's not how it works.' He looked back at his haunches. 'Besides, do you think I want to go through this again? As it is Razor would tear another chunk off me if he knew I was talking to you.'

Our conversation ended about the same time as the humans. They were saying something about the police not caring if no dog had died and no humans had been hurt. Nothing sensible as usual.

Monday, April 28

As the famous military strategist Sun Tzu once said, 'Make it impossible for an enemy to know where to prepare . . . release the attack like a lightning bolt from above the nine-layered heavens.' I've pondered the Razor problem and I think that it will be solved by a surprise attack of such ferocity that he'll be running with his tail between his legs. I'm a big dog, I've been training hard and am in the best condition of my life. My previous opponents have all been honourable and I've gone easy on them. Well, I've tried the noble approach; now it's time for shock and awe. Once Razor's seen the extent of my arsenal, I'm betting he'll whine like a puppy for mercy.

This is the plan. I will attack Razor on his own turf when he is expecting it least. My mistake with Claude was to give him a chance to prepare. If I'd have hit him when he wasn't expecting it, like Liquorice, then things would have gone very differently. I'll have the pack deployed at strategic points to deal with any dogs who might want to wade in, but with his reputation for terrorising the troops, I am banking that when they see their Pack Leader in difficulties they'll not lift a paw. Once he's beaten of course they will all switch their loyalty to me and can serve as an elite bodyguard under Scottie's command, protecting me from any retribution if he's not already learned his lesson. One decisive victory will swing the balance of power throughout the whole park.

Now the threat of my fighting Claude has disappeared I was allowed off the lead again today, and angrily re-marked my territory until I ran out of pee. The nerve of that pit bull. I can't wait to sink my teeth into him.

Tuesday, April 29

All is prepared. Scottie and Denny are spreading the word among the pack. Denny saw Liquorice back in the park yesterday and he's healing well. I'd like to be able to spare him from another battle so soon, but he's keen to be in on it. That bounciness hides a courageous heart. Now all there is to do is wait until the pack is assembled and go East. Until then, all dogs are on reconnaissance and intelligence missions. I want to know when Razor comes to the park, where he pees, bitches he consorts with, everything.

Scottie took me aside in the wasteland later and warned me again not to fight Razor, but I ignored him. He may have been a fighter in his day, but sometimes his constant questioning gets my hackles up. A good general needs to be bold and decisive as well as tactical.

Wednesday, April 30

The Owner was ambushed by Dottie's human today. He took her to the vet a couple of days ago and the man in the white coat confirmed that she is expecting our puppies. However, instead of celebrating the happy event and offering me a cigar, he started jabbing his finger at my Owner and shouting that he'd seen Dottie and me running around together and that if she gives birth to mongrels that look anything like me then he'd be leaving them on our front step.

Sometimes the Owner impresses me with his *savoir faire*. He coolly responded that if the red-faced human allowed his bitch to run around the park in season then what else did he expect? Dottie's owner immediately came back by demanding why I hadn't been neutered, and mine asked why Dottie hadn't been.

'Because she's a pedigree dog, for goodness' sake. We can trace her ancestry back through ten generations and when we breed her the puppies will be worth a fortune. It looks as though you can trace your dog's family back to an unfortunate liaison between a Shetland pony and a dishrag.'

'Well, Blake's not the only non-neutered dog in this park,' the Owner replied with chilly aplomb. 'And though I haven't noticed any other pedigree Dalmatians, I have seen plenty of other mutts sniffing about your bitch, so it looks as though the precious aristocrat likes slumming it and *you* had better get used to the delights of raising mixed-breeds. Perhaps next time you should make sure she has some condoms in her diamante clutch bag. Either that or keep her on the lead while she's on heat. Now, if you'll excuse me, Blake and I were enjoying a peaceful walk.'

74

At this point he was enjoying a hitherto unprecedented rise in my regard, but when Dottie's owner was safely out of sight he grabbed me by the scruff of the neck, looked me in the eye and said, 'If I get any more dogs like you dumped on me, then I will definitely be having your balls off.'

Which was a nice way of congratulating a new father-to-be and completely killed the warm glow I was feeling for him. Over the last couple of months his threats have lost their punch though. I'm starting to think he can't stomach the thought of having me done. Underneath that sadistic exterior he's all soft-hearted and cuddly. No wonder he can't pull off the whole alpha thing.

May

Thursday, May 1

It's an outrage. I am being psychologically controlled like a lab rat. All week the Owner has been growling and staring at me in a most disconcerting way. Once the initial humour value wore off it just jangled my nerves and I'd end up doing what he said just so he'd stop making a spectacle of himself. With all the making me sit for every little treat, pretending to eat out of my bowl before I get a look in and making me walk to heel by tugging at the lead whenever we're out for a walk, I wouldn't be surprised if he was making an attempt on the title of Most Irritating Owner of the Year. But the upshot of all this sorry behaviour is much more worrying. At today's obedience classes I *came* without even the promise of a treat, *sat* for nothing more than a pat and a 'Good Dog' and even went *down* on command.

I blame the fact that it has been a difficult week and I've been preoccupied, but even so this is the thin end of the wedge. Next he'll be making me drool when he shows me a raspberry Pavlov, or whatever it is humans do in these twisted experiments. I'm sure mazes come into it somewhere.

Now, not only is my status in the park under threat, but there's an attempted coup in my own den. I have to reassert myself, and as soon as possible.

Friday, May 2

Walked straight into more trouble today. Ella, it seems, is an old-fashioned girl who likes a dog to be monogamous. Dottie's scent markings have spread the news of her happy condition around the park, and Ella's enquiries have led her to the news that I am the father. She was furious. In vain did I point out that dogs are not bred to mate for life, and she was equally unreceptive when I said how much I enjoyed her company and our scooting sessions and what a shame it would be if a little thing like my impregnating another bitch get in the way of our fun.

As she was walking away I tried reasoning with her, by pointing out that as the Top Dog around here it should be an honour for her to allow me to service her. She turned round growling and snarled at me.

'Dog, you don't think that's the reason I ran around with you, do you? You males are all the same. It's all about how much territory you have. For your information, I liked you because you made me laugh. Now I just think you're a brainless, macho idiot with balls on your brain. Your owner would be better off having you castrated, you might turn out to be a good dog.'

'Yeah, well there are plenty more bitches in the park,' I barked at her retreating backside, which, I noticed for the first time in ages, is beautifully soft and fluffy, like she's wearing sexy white fur knickers. Admittedly, it wasn't the best retort ever delivered and probably won't be included in any anthology of Blake quotes.

With a last angry bark, she yelped back, 'That's if you're capable after Razor's finished with you.'

Saturday, May 3

I've been really low since Ella dumped me, just lying around looking up at the Owner pitifully and whining quietly. He's not the world's greatest agony aunt, but at least he stroked me and asked if I was feeling OK, which was oddly comforting. I didn't really think about it too much at the time, but Ella is really good company. Much more fun than Dottie, though she hasn't got as much class.

Sunday, May 4

Never let it be said that humans don't have their uses. Seeing I still wasn't my usual bouncy self we stopped at the butcher's on the way home and the Owner went and found a replacement for Mr Femur, who really has been losing his youthful allure recently. Mr Fibula on the other hand is nubile, sleek and full of fleshy promise. Molly came over and after the humans ate I also got leftover steak without having to beg for it. If being quiet and relatively obedient bears such fruits, perhaps it might not be such a bad thing if I let him call the shots every now and then. Not in an alpha way, just purely as a commercial transaction of services for goods. I can still be Top Dog. After all, even Napoleon compromised sometimes.

I was so replete and entranced with Mr Fibula's many attractions that I allowed the two humans an evening off from my relationship-wrecking flatulence. It was, however, a very pleasant surprise to see that after a few glasses of wine both of them consistently forgot about the killer garbage bin and electrocuted themselves seven times in total. Humans must be really stupid – I haven't touched the thing since the day after he powered it up, but he manages to shock himself at least four times a day. I don't think I'll ever tire of hearing him scream.

Monday, May 5

I tried to reason with Ella again, but she just ran in the opposite direction whenever I approached – even her human seemed perplexed. Samantha was talking to the Owner when I found him and gave me my usual scratch behind the ears.

With amazing perception for a human she said, 'Ella doesn't seem to want to play with you today, have you been upsetting her? I bet a Bad Boy like you has been seeing another bitch, eh?'

The Owner chipped in with, 'That Dalmatian's owner thinks his bitch is expecting Blake's puppies and threatened to dump them on me. I can't believe he let her wander round the park on heat.'

'Well, you could have Blake neutered.'

I bristled. I hadn't expected such filthy talk from a human I liked so much.

'Yeah, I keep thinking about it, but it doesn't just magically make them into good dogs and besides, though he's a complete pain, I kind of like him the way he is.'

Samantha redeemed herself by kissing my forehead and saying, 'He is a lovely dog, it would be a shame to change him,' which is probably the first time anyone's ever thought that, let alone said it out loud. Give her an evening with my internal gasses and she'd be singing a different tune.

'What about Ella, is she fixed?'

'No, I can't bring myself to do it. She's so good and so beautiful that I'd like to breed from her one day. I know there are too many mixed-breeds in the world already, but she's one in a million.'

These sentiments reflected my own exactly. How could I have been so stupid?

Tuesday, May 6

Scottie was in the wasteland last night and I decided to confide my bitch troubles in the old terrier.

'Och, if it's advice oan matters o' the heart yer wantin', ye've come tae the right place. Scottie the Bonny Boinker, they used tae call me in me younger days.'

Looking at the mangy geriatric, it was difficult to imagine him as a young Lothario, but I suppose every dog has his day.

'So, what should I do about Ella and Dottie?'

'Well, I'd forgit aboot the Dalmation if I were you, yon Ella is far more the type fer you. Nice buttom she has, too.'

'Yes, but Ella's not speaking to me and Dottie's expecting my puppies.'

'Aye, the bairns . . .' Scottie paused for a moment, then continued, brightly, 'Like as not yon wee uns'll all be given away, and many a dog's come frae a broken hame. Me oan father only knew mah mother for aboot twenty minutes, and look how bonny I turned oot.'

I looked, and coughed a little. 'But how do I get Ella to speak to me again?'

'Och, get away wi' yer. Romance the bitch, ye great fool. Howl at her, recite her poetry, bring her awld food ye find in the bin and lay it at her feet. Let her know how ye feel.'

I nodded. It was worth a try.

'But by the by, ah hate tae remind ye, but as yer number two ah should bring yer attention to the fact that there's rather a pressin' matter in the form of a rabid pit bull awaitin' yer prompt attention. Ah tell ye once an' fer all ye need tae work out a tactic tae keep him away frae oor side o' the park wi'oot fightin' the lunatic.'

Wednesday, May 7

Scottie was right last night of course, about my needing to concentrate on the Razor problem at least, but not about avoiding a fight. Today might have offered an opportunity to launch the attack on the East, but it was raining and the park was almost empty. My Owner seems to be the only one for miles around who makes an effort to walk his dog in the rain, probably because he knows how animated I get around the den if I'm denied the daily scamper. On reflection though, every day that passes lulls Razor into a deeper sense of security and the extra time will come in handy for further recon missions.

When we got home I had a bit of fun by making him stand outside for ten minutes yelling, 'Shake, dammit, Blake!' He even started to mime shaking, doing a twist that Chubby Checker would have been proud of. It was so humorous I gave him the Eyes of Bewildered Affection until he gave in and opened the door. Then I shook mud and rainwater all over the den.

Thursday, May 8

I am now graduated into 'advanced' obedience training with Obergruppenführer Molly, whose definition of the word 'advanced' differs from mine by some margin. We are now studying 'leave it,' 'take it' and 'stop'. Oh, the dizzy heights of academia. She says that she is very pleased with my progress and the Owner's, though back in the real world all he's actually accomplished is to make it harder for me to satisfy my natural urges. What with the Electric Garbage, the lock on the fridge door, regular spells chained up outside (that post is going soon), all his shoes locked in the wardrobe, food put beyond my reach and the lovely Mr Fibula keeping me occupied, there's very little to tempt a dog. Obviously, I've still managed to purloin the occasional biscuit and sandwich when the Owner has one of his many bouts of absent-mindedness, but otherwise I've had to satisfy myself by intensifying my feud with the postman and farting at Molly. Having said that, when Razor is extinguished, the Owner and his wretched female are in for a shock.

Friday, May 9

Clear blue skies this morning and the Owner dispensed with training today so that he could lope shambolically round the park with the grace of a wino after a particularly heavy binge. I immediately went undercover, slinking through the woodland with the uncanny stealth of a deerhound to spy out Razor's territory. At my side Constable, Scottie and Liquorice completely ruined my secret-agent vibe by having an argument about the best kind of treat (Constable and Liquorice favouring savoury meat or cheese snacks while Scottie was a confirmed choccie drop addict, which would explain the state of his teeth).

Razor wasn't there, but I did notice an area of dense bushes close to a meadow that was particularly ripe with his stink. An ideal place to strike from. Mentally, I made charts and maps of the area, noted troop placements and sketched out the order of attack.

Saturday, May 10

Just when I should be concentrating on winning the largest empire the park has ever seen, the Owner keeps making me revise what we've been learning with Molly. Humans are so inconvenient. I was so bored it was a welcome distraction when a whole load of human runners in a big pack ran past. I wonder what the collective noun for joggers would be? A 'pant' of joggers would be appropriate, or maybe a 'wobble' or a 'perspiration.' Either way, all dressed up in their colourful tight Lycra with the inevitable trickle of sweat dripping between their buttocks, they looked and smelled like a herd of gaudy caribou to me, so I spent a stress-relieving fifteen minutes chasing them across the park. I had separated an old and infirm one from the pack and would have brought her down, too, if the Owner hadn't thrown himself on me in the nick of time.

Sunday, May II

Saw Dottie today, but her owner is keeping her on a short lead and shouting obscenities at any dogs who come near – especially me – which is like barking after the cat is treed, but humans and logical thought don't really mix. By my calculations the puppies should be due in about a month, but I can't afford to be distracted now. If my offspring are to have a stable empire to inherit then I need to focus on the campaign. Despite what Scottie says, I hope they go to local owners. Even if Dottie and I are estranged then it would be good to see them grow up and keep a fatherly eye on them.

Monday, May 12

I'm getting impatient to be at Razor, but we have to choose exactly the right moment to strike. In the meantime, I'm staying on top of the training. With no members of the pack around today, I had to content myself with running flat out in huge circles, jumping benches and attacking litter that was blowing across the park. It's not the best way to keep in shape, but I did subdue a plastic bag with considerable skill. I think I'm ready.

Tuesday, May 13

A late walk today as the Owner was busy on the computer all morning. Despite the discomfort of a bladder stretched well beyond its recommended capacity, this proved a useful delay as

I managed to catch my first sight of Razor from a reconnaissance point on the edge of the woodland. Oddly, he was trotting obediently alongside a big human, looking affable and harmless. When he was let off the lead he just bounded around like any other dog. From all the reports, I expected to find him ripping a bloody path through the children's play area. Although he looks compact and well muscled, he's also less than half my size so I'll have a weight and height advantage. I'm still on my guard – after all, he did see off Claude and Liquorice – but I'm starting to think that a lot of his fearsome reputation might be down to propaganda and deceptive scent-marking.

Wednesday, May 14

Ella is still ignoring me, though our two owners now spend a lot of time running around in circles with each other. Sometimes I think that dogs and humans aren't all that different. It would be nice to see them enjoying a scoot down the bank to the pond though.

I found half a sandwich for Ella, but she turned her nose up at it, and I declaimed a little poetry I'd written especially, likening her backside to a sweet-smelling powder puff. Without being too immodest, it was almost Shakespearean. Nothing made any difference though. Will anything melt her cold bottom?

To add insult to injury, when I finally gave up I found the two humans wandering round the pond laughing at my unfortunate rubber-band incident. How insensitive. After a couple of turns they went and had coffee while Ella and I were tied to the same lamppost. I tried to nuzzle her, but she sat rigid and refused to even glance at me. Pitiful whining would not crack her stony heart.

Thursday, May 15

Scottie cornered me in the wasteland after more bloody obedience training this evening and started giving me an earful about Razor, but I was able to quiet him with an affectionate sniff and just the hint of a growl.

'Scottie,' I said, with the calm of Sir Walter Raleigh playing bowls while the Spanish Armada heaved to, 'I have everything in hand, and there's no need to worry your fluffy white head about it.'

He wasn't to be silenced so easily though.

'Whut the Pussy are ye talkin' aboot, ye mixed-up mongrel? Yer goin' tae git seven flavours o' meaty chunks knocked oot o' ye.'

'Not so,' I continued, letting the mongrel crack slide for the moment. 'I have seen Razor and am confident that the assault I have planned will bring him to his knees.'

'But . . .'

'No buts, Scottie. Razor is essentially a small dog – no offence – and while he might have been lucky against Claude, I have seen him trotting tamely around the park like a lapdog and I'm beginning to suspect the pit bull reputation owes as much to hearsay and bad press as it does to fact.'

'Yer a tin opener short of a dinner, ye fool. Ye said yersel' that pit bulls are a catastrophe waitin' to happen.'

'I may have misjudged. I'm still wary, but what else is there but to attack?'

'Can ye no' see it's impossible? I'm ainly tryin' tae spare ye a hidin' cause ye're no a bad wee doggie.'

'Well, maybe I'm following your advice for once. If Razor's as bad as you think then maybe I won't stand by and watch my pack picked off and brought under the iron paw of a psychopath. If you're right then none of us are safe until he's dealt with, and if you're wrong then taking him down will be as easy as chasing a cat up a tree.'

'Aye, there's something in whut ye say, I suppose, and I dinnae have a better plan. Ye'll let me fight at yer side though.'

'No, I've been thinking about what you said about protecting weaker members of the pack and I don't want you in the front line at your age. You can still be useful though. There's a little Pekingese I want you to cover. Besides, it's got to be one on one or it doesn't count.'

I might as well have tried to steal his bowl of haggis for all the thanks I got for my new policy, but if he doesn't want dogs to take advice he shouldn't go around dishing it out. I was insistent and as I'm Pack Leader there is very little he can do about it.

Friday, May 16

More marking on my territory. I am having to drink the pond dry in order to maintain my own perimeters. Razor will suffer for his impertinence!

Saturday, May 17

Liquorice has gone over to Razor and while his old territory is still technically mine under all the conventions of war, it is covered with new markings, placed with such careless arrogance that they invite a swift and merciless military response. Constable saw the whole thing from a distance, but due to being on the lead was unable to help, though he did bark in support. Apparently, it was a short tussle with Liquorice still recovering from his wounds and the cowardly Razor merely holding him by the throat until Liquorice submitted.

You can imagine my feelings about this direct incursion onto my territory and an unprovoked attack on a member of my pack, but I steeled myself to stand firm until the time is right. I was half expecting Razor to move quickly and Scottie agrees that this is an obvious move to draw my forces onto a battleground of his choosing. If that's the extent of his strategy, we shall prevail, even though we are but four dogs against a superior force. A dog like me loves those kind of odds.

Sunday, May 18

The Owner is going shopping with Molly after her class this morning (hopefully she'll force him to buy some clothes that'll make him less of an embarrassment) so just a quick run around the park. Nevertheless, I managed to review the troops and make a few last-minute changes to the plan. Tomorrow, if all goes to plan, we launch Operation Beard.*

* My choice of name and obviously referring to the fact that no Razor is required by the owner of a beard. I thought it was quite witty but the pack just looked blankly at me when I announced it.

Monday, May 19

It looked as though good fortune was smiling upon my ragged band of soldiers assembled by the dog toilet this morning. The sun shone brightly, ensuring that all the owners wanted to spend as long as possible in the park and Scottie was able to report that Razor had been spotted entering the Northern Gate a few minutes earlier. Timing was of paramount importance, so after a few well-chosen words to stir up the lads' blood we deployed quietly to the East, into the woods.

The enemy pack was congregated in the meadow, as expected, with Razor at the centre. With a final quietly growled word of encouragement to the troops, they left to take up their positions and I slipped away through a stand of trees that curled round to the East of where Razor was holding court.

I watched for a few moments until Razor squatted to answer the call of nature. The time had come. With a silent prayer to Fido, the Dog of War, I began my charge, downhill from the East with the sun behind me as Razor dribbled out what was obviously his second or third stool of the day. The window of opportunity wasn't big, but my thunderous gallop carried me to him before he had managed to squeeze out the last shred and I descended on wings of fury, scattering his pack before he knew I was there. When my teeth closed around his neck I tasted the leather and steel of his studded collar and, for one brief moment, victory.

This was the signal for my troops to launch their attack. The confused barking around me said that Scottie, Denny and Constable were indeed streaking out of the woods to hold off any interference.

From the corner of my eye I saw Constable baying theatrically at a seemingly terrified Claude and Liquorice while Scottie chased off the Pekingese easily. Denny was wrestling with a Jack Russell who seemed to be the only member of Razor's pack who was putting up any fight. I had other problems though. Instantly my teeth had touched his neck, Razor exploded into a twisting, snarling ball of terrifying violence. He seemed impervious to pain and I was being slowly forced to relinquish my grip on his neck as he thrashed about and began clawing painfully at my underbelly while his gnashing bear-trap teeth got closer and closer to my leg.

Letting go, I threw him as far as possible, but he came straight back at me, his huge mouth open like the jaws of doom. I just had time to raise myself up, in order to drop on him like a hammer. I might as well have dropped on an anvil. Razor was interested in one thing only – attaching himself to my flesh – and as I came up again he jumped and found the back of my neck with his teeth. I fell back and pinned him under me, but my struggles couldn't tear me away from fangs that tore through skin and were beginning to grind into my spine.

In fact, things were going quite badly when Scottie entered the fray. In a flagrant disregard of my orders he was dancing round Razor's head like a dog twenty years younger, trying to distract the pit bull. To no avail. Razor increased his grip on me and in desperation Scottie put the bite on one of his ears, with all the effect of a mosquito chomping into a rhinoceros.

As my mouth opened in a howl of pain, panic and – yes – submission, another dog sprinted in from nowhere, growling like a cement mixer. Suddenly the bone-crushing grip on my spine was released. The new dog shouted a muffled 'away' and as I struggled to my feet I saw Ella with her jaws sunk in Razor's belly as Scottie struggled to pull his head away from her by the ear that he still held.

I shouted back 'Now!' and Ella and Scottie simultaneously released their grip and bounded away, with me close behind them and Denny and Constable retreating on our heels.

As we left the pit bull behind us at top speed I heard a human voice laughing and shouting, 'Razor, stop playing with your food.'

Tuesday, May 20

The Owner's sympathy on finding me dirty and bloodied yesterday was astonishing in its absence. Luckily, he hadn't seen what happened and assumed that I'd been attacked, but there was still a trip to the vets to contend with. I have a mortal fear of these quacks – after all, a human wouldn't trust a dog to perform surgery – but on this one occasion I was all fought out and dispensed with the usual hysterical barking and trying to escape. In fact, I was as docile as a pup.

As the vet cleaned up the blood and pronounced my wounds 'not too bad' he also asked if I was often involved in fighting and what age I am. According to him, intact dogs around the age of two are more prone to dominance fighting. Then he said that if the behaviour proved persistent, the Owner should think seriously about having me neutered.

Well, according to me, intact human males about the age of 35 are prone to talking complete drivel, so why doesn't he go get himself neutered. How do these people sleep at night?

The Owner told him that there was a pit bull in the park that had attacked a couple of dogs recently. The vet shook his head and said he'd seen the results.

I've been curled up in my bed ever since, and was thankful that we only went as far as the wasteland this morning. All I can think about is that I was within a breath of submitting to Razor. If it hadn't been for Ella I'd now be at the bottom of someone else's pack with not a square foot of territory to call my own. And I didn't even get a chance to thank her. Or Scottie.

Wednesday, May 21

Fortunately, the Owner seems intent on keeping me away from other dogs for the moment. I cannot face the park right now. Instead I wander listlessly around the wasteland for half an hour before returning to him as soon as he calls. The rest of the time I spend in bed replaying the battle in my head. Even Mr Fibula holds no joy for me now.

Thursday, May 22

As I'm healing quickly, it was back to school today. I resigned myself and let them get on with it, but even Molly noticed I was not my usual dashing self, so the Owner drove us all out of town for a long walk in the forest again, this time with me on the retractable lead. Obviously, I wrapped it around as many trees as

I could, but without much joy. As I nosed around, I wondered if the hobo lifestyle would suit me. If I finish that post in the back yard I could be trotting along country roads, taking shelter in barns and stealing from the hen house by nightfall. Never again would I hear the name Razor.

Maybe some day another human – a generous butcher with a friendly bitch, no neighbours and a less uptight attitude to shoes – would take me in. Yeah, and maybe I'm Champion the Wonder Horse.

Friday, May 23

Molly came over and brought a new friend with her. I was grateful for the kindness, but couldn't muster the usual welcome routine, which I always give her because she gets so frustrated when she can't stop me. Nevertheless, I was feeling unusually cordial towards her.

I could see that Mr Tibia is a little minx, teasing me with his shreds of raw flesh and scraps of tendon, but an experimental lick turned to ashes in my mouth when she sighed and uttered the unforgivable words.

'You know, I really hate the idea of attempting to change a dog's behaviour with castration, but I thought you should know that inter-male aggression is the only form of behaviour where it has been proven to have some worth. There's a 60 per cent chance that it would stop Blake fighting and if you give him the female hormone progesterone, too, it's more like 75 per cent. It wouldn't help with the protection aggression though, so the postman would still get it in the ear every day.'

Oh My Dog. Good Boy is not enough for her. She wants to turn me into a Good Lady Boy. As if making a eunuch of me wasn't brutal enough, now she's seriously proposing surgery and hormone therapy to turn me into a bitch against my will. I knew it: all the dog-loving, bone-buying, training-with-love-and-affection is a front. Underneath it all she's a hardcore militant feminist who probably keeps a trophy jar of preserved testicles.

The Owner's response was hardly more encouraging. He pointed out that it had only been a couple of fights, that I was perfectly friendly with Claude now and that in all likelihood I had been attacked by 'that mad pit bull in the park.' Then he paused, and said, 'But if there are any more fights I'll seriously think about it.'

Saturday, May 24

There has been no more transgender talk since last night, but I know it's on his mind now and I'm monitoring the situation closely. With all this and the disastrous fight against Razor still lying heavily on my mind I am sunk in depression. If I launch another attack, I'll be munched up properly and if I survive then I'll be carrying my genitals home in a paper bag, barking in a high-pitched voice and wearing pink bows in my coat.

Sunday, May 25

Back to the park today, though I stuck close to the Owner at all times. Dog knows why, I mean what's he going to do in a Razor attack when he can't even stop me from chewing his ear at will? For once he seemed quite pleased of the company, especially as I ran alongside him without tripping him more than a couple of times.

We ran past Dottie and her owner, and the latter looked at me as though given the smallest window of opportunity I might try and impregnate him as well. He should be so lucky. My Owner gave him a cheerful wave and told him that Dottie was 'blooming.' Actually, she's pretty big, but when I looked at her I couldn't help wondering if she would ever attack a pit bull that was about to kill me. She might glower, or even go as far as to be extremely sarcastic, but I just can't picture her as a snarling bolt of spotted wrath. Still, she is to be the mother of my children – even if that now gives me a peculiar feeling of regret – and I owe it to them at least to pull myself together.

Monday, May 26

Razor counterattacked when I left the Owner's side this morning to try and find Ella. Less than a minute later I was dripping blood and barely conscious. By the time the Owner found me Razor was already gone, taking my dignity and my territory. It's all over.

Tuesday, May 27

I am home from an overnight stay at the vet's surgery. I have lacerations to my face, one of my ears is in tatters and I'll be limping for some time to come. I also have to wear a white plastic cone for the next few weeks, though right now I'm beyond caring about the half-dog half-lampshade look.

Before surgery, the vet asked if I should be neutered at the same time. The Owner went purple and started shouting that he wasn't going to have me castrated just because I'd been mauled by a savage beast and that if anyone should have their balls removed it's the owner who can't or won't control his murderous dog. I've never seen him so incensed, even after I ate the special edition box for his *Star Wars* DVDs. I whined softly and licked his hand to try and calm him down, and looked up to see that there was water coming out of his eyes. I've never seen this side of him before.

Wednesday, May 28

Dazed and confused. We took a couple of painful turns up and down the street today, but only so I could relieve myself. It's hard to take in that these few lampposts outside the den are all that remain of my once-mighty territory.

The Owner is feeding me prime beef, not that crap processed stuff, and making sure my water bowl is always full. He even leaves the radio on in the kitchen for me, which is quite soothing. None of it can take my mind off the fact that my empire lies in dust.

Thursday, May 29

I can't remember too much about the fight itself, apart from the fact that it was only a fight if you count howling in pain while being ripped and mangled by the canine equivalent of a chainsaw. I was trying to find Ella and it was much earlier than Razor is usually there so my guard was down. Then the pit bull came at me from out of the woods like some deranged whippet. I had no time to defend myself. I tried, I gave everything I had, but he was unstoppable. The only option was submission, and even then he didn't stop chewing on me and flinging me around like a toy for some time after.

Friday, May 30

Spent all day in my basket again, steeped in pain that I hardly notice when I think about my defeat and all that it means.

Saturday May 31

As I lie here surrounded by chew toys, bones and all the things the Owner has brought in to try and cheer me up it occurs to me that I might have been too hard on him. He may not be the juiciest chunk in the tin, but he's taking care of me, even though I'm a loser. Is this what Scottie means by being a proper Pack Leader?

I tried to get onto the sofa this evening, but my leg's too stiff. Instead, the Owner lifted me on gently and I showed my gratitude by snuffling whatever parts I could reach while he stroked the few bits of me that aren't held together by stitches. If I had a pack left he would definitely be up for promotion.

June

Sunday, June 1

The leg is slightly less stiff today and the pain has receded a little. Psycho Molly came round this evening, bringing doggie chocs. Some reports suggest that chocolate might help relieve depression, so I instantly prescribed myself the whole box.

I would have thought that my reduced state might have melted even her maniacal heart, but no. After putting on a show of concern she started on the castration speech again.

This time, I was gratified to see the Owner clench his knuckles, as he replied, 'If anyone else tells me to have the dog castrated, I am really going to lose it. He's not aggressive, he's just a bit cheeky and I've decided for once and for all that I'm not going to have him done just because he's got character. I love him just the way he is.'

Molly had the sense not to press it, but I could feel her eyes on my testicles whenever she thought he wasn't looking. Ignoring the pain I curled myself around them as best I could with a big plastic ruff around my neck.

Monday, June 2

Feeling physically better today and we even made it as far as the wasteland this evening. I was dreading seeing Scottie again, especially as he immediately confirmed all my fears. The whole park has formally recognised that my lands now belong to Razor, while Denny and Constable both went over without a fight. I can't say I blame them. Scottie has yet to capitulate, but is sticking close to his owner and trying to stay clear of trouble.

'At mah age I dinnae think ah can submit tae a monster like that. Ah heard that even after ye surrendered he niver stoaped chewin' oan ye.'

I looked away and whined in shame. And then Scottie said something that made me realise that I had been wallowing in self-pity when of course I should have been planning like mad.

'Och, dinnae be like that aboot it, it happens tae all o' us once or twice.'

I was stunned. It was like a cat had fallen out of a tree right in front of me. 'You mean you've lost territory and won it back before?'

'Aye, o' course,' he looked at me quizzically. 'Ye didnae think this wus over jest because ye got a couple o' flesh wounds, did ye?'

My respect for the feisty little fellow was growing rapidly, and what's more he was correct. After all, did Napoleon mope about on Elba? Did Ghengis pout when imprisoned by the Turks? On the other hand he was forgetting something fairly crucial. 'But look at the state of me, I can't go through this again.'

Scottie looked me hard in the eye. 'Ye dinnae listen properly, that's yer problem. I telt ye, yer always lookin' fer a fight, but there's more than one way tae eat a cat.'

'Is there?'

'Well, actually no. I jest made that up. Ye put it in yer mooth, chew an' swallow, an' that's aboot it really.'

'Not the cat, the fighting, you old idiot.'

'Och that,' Scottie sighed. 'Tell me, huv ye nevir heard o' Quintus Fabius Maximus?'

Tuesday, June 3

Scottie must be the most devious West Highland Scottish terrier the country has ever produced. If he wasn't my number two already then I would have promoted him on the spot with all due ceremony, marching bands and probably some kind of specially minted medal for services rendered.*

During his short history lesson, Scottie told me the story of the Roman dictator Quintus Fabius Maximus, who led the Republic during the Second Punic War after Hannibal invaded Italy. This Quintus human waged a war of attrition, wearing down Hannibal's forces and morale while helping protect Rome's friends and never being caught on the field. Fabian Strategy has been used successfully by weaker forces ever since.

For all their tartan doggie jackets and chasing haggis around the mountains, these Westies are surprisingly learned. It was a very illuminating lecture. In fact, Scottie's little speech has shown me that Razor is bloated on victory, overconfident and overextended across the whole park. Not only that, but his pack dominance relies on terror. Strategically and politically he is in an extremely vulnerable position.

We are now two dogs of destiny, thrown together in our defiance of the wicked oppressor and shining like a beacon of hope and liberty throughout the park. Before we get started with all the defiance though I've got to get this damn funnel off my head. Align me correctly and I could receive radio transmissions from distant galaxies.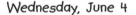

* Not that it would mean much right now, my number two being a position that currently holds about as much cachet as being my . . . well, my number two.

Wednesday, June 4

The Park Animals Resistance Party, or P.A.R.P. – that is, Scottie and I – will wait until I am fully healed before launching operations, though obviously we will both perform as much covert reconnaissance as is safe at the moment. Time is on our side and there's no harm in allowing Razor to become comfortable and negligent.

We have also decided that we will secretly put out word of our underground movement. A few words of rumour in the Razor camp might start to make his pack question the totalitarian regime of their leader. We need a dog who is not immediately connected with my old pack to help. Scottie suggests Ella. She is perfect.

Thursday, June 5

In recognition of his efforts as Florence Nightingale I have raised the Owner to beta male. Officially, only the alpha remains above him. Given his unfortunate human condition and the unlikelihood of his ever siring pups that wouldn't be tied in a sack and thrown in the river immediately, it's a purely honorary position and Scottie is still my actual second in command.

Nevertheless it's deserved, though to be honest he's starting to get on my nerves again already. With returning health my appetite's coming back and at the very time I need to ensure a speedy and complete recovery he's put me back on the horse's willy and gravel diet. I tried to supplement it by grabbing at a ham sandwich today, but encumbered by the huge salad bowl around my neck I got in all sorts of difficulties. The way he laughed you would have thought it was the funniest thing ever.

Friday, June 6

Everything is healing well, and the vet is satisfied with my progress. For once no mention was made of my nether regions, though I could tell the sadistic scalpel jockey was straining to whip them off. Although I have to wait another week for the stitches to come out I'm feeling a bit more limber and the Owner and I had a slow walk around the park this afternoon. I was kept on a short lead, but would have stuck close anyway.

Dottie and her owner walked past, both with their noses in the air. Maybe she'll be different after the puppies are born. The appearance of a dozen or so cute little balls of spotty fluff is bound to bring out her gentler nature. In the meantime, I'm really missing Ella, and I haven't even had the chance to thank her for saving my life yet.

Saturday, June 7

At last I think I've made some progress with the Molly/Owner situation, and for once being a bad dog has paid off.

She had offered to cook lunch for us, but must have been handling a bitch in season just before we arrived, because for once she smelled divine, and I mean grrrrr. Like a sex explosion in a pheromone factory. I would have dived on her as soon as we got out of the car, but the Owner held me by the collar, presumably thinking I wanted to give her my customary unwelcome welcome and not wanting me to rupture my stitches. I didn't have to wait long though. She started explaining to the Owner how she had been checking dogs' nails all morning and bent down to have a look at mine at the same time that he let go of my collar. I was on her quicker than you can say 'Tom Jones,' knocking her onto her hands and knees and humping away at her jeans at a blistering pace while barking with delight at this unexpected slice of heaven.

As Molly screamed and tried to shift my weight, the Owner calmly reached into his pocket and pulled out his mobile phone, which is also a camera. Amazing the things these crazy humans think of, though I've always wondered why adding a tin opener never occurred to these so-called 'egg heads.'

He eventually got about thirty seconds' footage of Molly flailing about on her hands and knees with me riding her like a sex-mad rodeo star wearing a large white traffic cone, but unfortunately Molly finally fought me off. The Owner was enjoying himself hugely and already playing the scene back, motioning a mussed Molly to come and see. She must not like that kind of movie though because she just tossed her head and stamped off, shouting that there wouldn't be any lunch after all.

Sunday, June 8

The Owner has been phoning Molly all day, but apparently the explanation, 'It just looked really funny from where I was standing and I wouldn't have let him hurt you,' isn't the grovelling apology that she was looking for.

Monday, June 9

This funnel is driving me nuts. Not only can I not scratch my wounds, which are now itching constantly, but it's really beginning to cramp my style. I woke up this morning with the realisation that I've been neglecting the postman recently, and I don't want him getting too complacent. However, my attempts to give him the full treatment were thwarted. The barking was good, and nicely amplified by the big loudhailer I'm wearing, but forcing my snarling muzzle through the hole in the door was a disaster. I just resembled a large toilet plunger that had been fired at the door and couldn't even get close.

The Owner's hysteria was totally inappropriate behaviour for a probationary beta.

Tuesday, June 10

Molly still isn't talking to the Owner, which is just dandy with me. With that going well, mine and Scottie's audacious plan to take back the park, puppies on the way and my wounds almost healed I'm beginning to get the spring back into my step and am feeling particularly well disposed to the Owner. Maybe now the psycho testicle thief is gone I'll even get my old place on the bed back. If I could just see Ella life would definitely be looking up.

Wednesday, June 11

At last, Ella was in the park and I was able to catch up to her while our owners took a stroll together. I started by thanking her for her help during the first fight with Razor, which seems so long ago.

'I didn't really do that for you, I just hate Razor. He's a killer and I was in the right place at the right time . . .'

I wondered hopefully if her being there had been coincidental, but decided it was probably not a good idea to question it, settling for a lame, 'Well, thanks anyway.'

'It didn't do any good though. Look at you. All I did was delay the inevitable . . . I'm sorry to hear about your territory, I know how much it meant to you, being Top Dog and all that.'

'That's OK, Scottie and I have got a plan to get it all back and put Razor in his place once and for all. Actually, we could really use your help.' I told her about P.A.R.P.

'Why would I help you?'

'I thought you hated Razor?'

'Yes, but I'd just be helping to replace him with another "Pack Leader" whose only motive is his own power. In my book the Pack Leader watches over and protects his pack.'

'But that's not fair, I'm not a killer. Quite noble actually, when you get to know me.'

For the first time she laughed. 'Yes, but the point is that you don't actually care about getting rid of Razor in the best interests of the other dogs in the park, you just want your territory back. You don't care about all the other dogs.'

'That's not true,' I found myself saying. 'I care about you very much.'

Ella turned and looked at me strangely, then trotted off toward our scooting place by the pond. I cursed the retractable lead that stopped me from following.

Thursday, June 12

Thank Dog my stitches came out today. Everything is still stiff and I wouldn't want to get into a scrap with a Chihuahua at the moment, particularly as I still have to wear the damn funnel for another week, but I can feel my health returning.

The next problem is getting the Owner to let me off this leash. I'm going to be no good to P.A.R.P. if I have to haul a gangly human around with me. That mixed-breed terrier Stubby who captured a German soldier during World War I probably wouldn't have managed it if he was dragging around some idiot wearing a *Happy Days* T-shirt with a picture of the Fonz on it. At present I'm hoping that walking to heel and acting like a civilised pet will build his confidence that I have fully succumbed to the Molly obedience brainwashing. You never know; after all, there's a sucker born every minute.

Friday, June 13

Ella and I were together again as our owners met for another walk around the park, but she wouldn't listen to my protestations about P.A.R.P., though at least she is talking to me again. Even so she's very cool and keeps asking how Dottie is, the last thing I want to discuss with her.

Saturday, June 14

Saw Scottie this evening and mentioned the problem in getting

Ella on board. After I explained her reasoning, he licked his genitals for a moment before talking.

'Aye, the lassie's got the measure of ye.'

'What are you barking about, you fluffy old fool?'

'Well, it's the same as I telt ye. Ye're ainly in it fer the personal glory. I'm backing ye up because I come from a time when loyalty to a Pack Leader meant something and I dinnae like that Razor any more than I do yon Tiddles, but the lady's nae got reason to help ye.'

'All right, I do want my territory back, but I also want to stop more dogs being chewed up like me, Claude and Dog knows how many others over on the East side.'

'Plus she's still smartin' aboot you and yon Dottie, o' course.'

I hung my head. 'So what can I do about it?'

'Talk to the lassie agin, and keep talkin' til ye've convinced her yer no' a Bad Dog.'

Sunday, June 15

Every time I think I've gotten rid of Molly she just pops straight up again, like a cat in a bathtub. She came over tonight because like a fool the Owner begged her to come and make peace. His abject apology for laughing at her when he should have been helping was pathetic to behold, though she eventually climbed down off her righteous indignation enough to admit that she had been with a bitch on heat shortly before the scene took place and it was no wonder I got a bit randy. As part of his reparations she insisted on watching while he deleted the little movie from his phone. As he's already sent it to everyone in his address book he didn't seem to mind that much.

Monday, June 16

Off the lead today, but I was kept well within eyesight with the Owner calling me back for treats every now and again, just to make sure that I wasn't being shredded. Obviously, the first thing to do was check out the scent grapevine. It made my blood boil to sniff Razor's fresh territorial markings masking the smell of my old ones, but I resisted the urge to retaliate. As a founder member of P.A.R.P. I must be covert, like a ghost in the park, spreading fear, mistrust and dissent.

Tuesday, June 17

First chance of a proper workout for weeks. No sign of Razor, but being a pit bull he's probably heard the phrase 'destroyed by a police marksman' a few times and won't be stupid enough to attack me when there's a chance a human might tangle with him. For the first time I realised I have no doubts that I absolutely trust the Owner to wade into a scrap on my behalf. It was a good feeling. Not that he'd be much good at the actual fighting with those pathetic little teeth – he hasn't got a canine worth mentioning in his entire head – but having him around is like an insurance policy. I loped along at his side like a Good Boy, stretching out muscles that haven't been used for a while, and was also surprised to find that he's got a fair turn of speed himself these days. Also, he isn't wheezing any more and he's quite sleek. All the running and the pull-ups on the swings must be doing him some good. One day he might even be a beta to be proud of. There were a couple of Razor's pack in the park, including Liquorice who should be a good candidate for switching his allegiance to P.A.R.P., but I don't want to show my paw too soon.

Wednesday June 18

Being off the lead again gave me a chance to talk to Ella properly, and I took Scottie along to help argue the case for P.A.R.P.

'I understand that you want to get rid of Razor, but I don't get how you're going to do it.'

'I told you, with covert military action, guerrilla warfare, and by eroding his political support. By the time we've finished with him he'll be running around the park all on his own, the leader of a pack that won't go near him and the ruler of territory that no longer exists. He may think he's the Top Dog, but no one else will.'

'But how are you going to actually achieve that?'

'We'll start slowly, spreading rumour to breed

dissent while re-marking tiny patches of territory in random places.'

'Aye, and ah'm gaunnae dig a network o' booby-trapped tunnels beneath the length an' breadth o' the park.'

Ella and I both gave Scottie a look and he shuffled about.

'Well, it worked fer the Vietcong,' he barked defiantly.

'Well, you get started on that, Scottie, and when you're finished perhaps could you build us a battalion of heavily armoured vehicles and a couple of short-range thermonuclear missiles.'

'And what do you expect me to do?' Ella interrupted.

I ignored Scottie's muttering and told her that she would be our agent, infiltrating Razor's pack and telling his followers that a day was coming when Razor would be defeated and every dog in the park assured of his or her own territory, of which P.A.R.P. would ensure the autonomy.

She looked surprised at this. 'But what about your territorial ambition?'

I laughed. 'I've decided that that little clearing by the pond where we go scooting is all I need.'

Thursday, June 19

Ella agreed to join P.A.R.P. and has already performed her first mission successfully. At 11.07 this morning she rendezvoused with a known member of Razor's pack, a border collie called Barney, who was carefully selected as having no ties to my old pack while being known for his gentle nature and liberal views. Luring him into the scooting place with her feminine wiles, Ella conveyed the message of liberation. Then she showed him our sign – the muddy pawprint of freedom.

Though Barney probably won't tell him directly, it is only a matter of time now before Razor hears and comes looking for P.A.R.P. Scottie, Ella and I have devised an early-warning system that will allow us to elude him and his running dogs.

The first blow is struck. Long Live the Dog's Republic of Acorn Park! *Liberté, Égalité,* Woof!

Friday, June 20

No one has seen Dottie around the park recently, but fresh scent markings today say that the puppies have been born. I am a father. Ella congratulated me politely and I thanked her. I wish that she was the mother.

I suppose that it will be some time before the pups are allowed out in the park, but I hope that when the owners meet there won't be any red-faced shouting. It's a time for celebration, even if I'm starting to think that Dottie's as stuck-up and stupid as her owner. I wonder how many sons and daughters I have and what their names are. Perhaps they've called one of the boys Blake Jr. It would be nice if her owner brought some photos along to the park, but he doesn't seem the type really.

Saturday, June 21

The funnel is off! I can finally raise my head again in the park without anyone thinking I've tried to jump through a giant cupcake, and what a revelation on the way back to the den. As it was a warm sunny day the Owner opened all the car windows, so I stuck my head out. When the world is going by at fifty miles an hour it's like a kaleidoscope of smell. I spent the entire journey with my ears streaming out behind me, breathing in the whole town; the restaurants, the people, the other animals, the shops, everything. Amazing. As a special bonus it also meant I didn't have to listen to his Bee Gees greatest hits CD for the millionth time.

Sunday, June 22

Very Good News. Molly was over last night and going on and on about dog behaviour as per usual, like she personally invented the whole species. I could see the Owner getting tense so I let off a nice ripe fart just to thicken the atmosphere a bit more. She must be getting used to it by now because she just waved her hand under her crinkled nose and launched into a fresh rant about body-language signals that show a dog has accepted the alpha male or female as leader, 'fascinating' with a capital N.O.T.

I'd just decided that a strategic sleep might help blot out the drone of her voice when the Owner interrupted with a question I've been longing to hear the answer to since he first met her. My ears pricked immediately.

'If you love dogs so much, why haven't you got one?'

Molly dropped her interminable whine and then gave a nervous little laugh and started speaking again slowly.

'Well, I should have told you this some time ago, but I'm saving up to travel for a few years as a volunteer for animal charities.'

The Owner looked stunned. 'So out of consideration you wouldn't take in an animal, but that consideration doesn't extend to a fellow human being?'

'When I started seeing you it was just a bit of fun and when it got more serious I just didn't want to spoil it. And it has been a bit on and off, you have to admit. I would have told you soon and I'm not going for another six months or so.'

'I see, so this relationship has an expiry date and in all your incessant talking you couldn't find two minutes to pass on the one piece of information I might actually be interested in?'

'It's not necessarily an expiry date, we can still be together, just . . . apart for a while. And excuse me, incessant talking? I know you're upset, but . . . '

'I'm not upset, Molly, it's just that you've been going on and on and on about dogs all evening as always and haven't even asked me how my day was. Now I know the only reason you're not going out with Blake instead of me is that you wouldn't want to hurt his feelings in six months, I understand perfectly.'

Well, you don't have to be a meteorologist to see which way the wind is blowing (especially if it's my wind, which you could basically cut with a stick) and sure enough within ten seconds a storm was blowing through the den. After ten minutes Hurricane Molly howled through the front door and, hopefully, out to sea. Her parting words were, '. . . and for your information that vile-smelling, badly behaved, farting mutt of yours is the only dog I've never liked. If he was a person, he'd be you!'

As the door slammed, I barked happily and performed the Frisky Happy Dance of Good Riddance.

Monday, June 23

Molly came round to drop off a few of the Owner's belongings, but left again after yapping on the doorstep for only a few minutes while the Owner tried to look at her sternly. I might have ruined his air of stately granite resolve by barking and trying to get through his legs to see her off. I guess it's difficult to maintain a wounded but dignified façade when you're being pulled around the entrance hall shouting 'Down!' and 'Stop!' ever few seconds.

Afterwards, he seemed a bit misty-eyed. He even whimpered a bit on the sofa. It was the perfect opportunity to grab the detritus of takeaway curry from the table and chase those delicious silver containers around the kitchen floor with my tongue. For once he didn't seem that bothered, just scooped what he hadn't eaten (a lot) into my bowl and let me get on with it.

Tuesday, June 24

Tried my luck with climbing onto the Owner's bed last night and met with no resistance at all. In fact he seemed glad of the company and stroked my head until I fell asleep. At last, it's like old times again, just me snoring gently and the teasing perfume of his feet rising up through the duvet. I think he may have regretted letting me up when the curry made its presence known. I was shocked myself, but in a good way. A smell like that is almost rich enough to eat up all over again.

Wednesday, June 25

I think Scottie is finally going senile. As we prepared for our trial P.A.R.P. mission today he kept talking about 'Gooks,' 'Grunts' and 'Demilitarised Zones.' As we departed he said, 'Lock 'n' Load Point Man'. He thinks he's back in 'Nam, though as far as I know the closest he's ever been is peeing in the doorway of the Korean restaurant on the high street.

Nevertheless, it was a successful mission. After drinking as much as we could from the pond we crept through the ~~jungle~~ woods and slipped past a couple of Razor's pack who were strolling around the meadow. Then we streaked for the East Gate, which he uses every day, and combined our urine to create a powerful P.A.R.P. territorial marking around the gate where he's sure to smell it when he arrives.

Leaving our muddy paw-prints in the centre of the path, we were away.

Of course, by leaving our scents we have declared ourselves, but we know this park like we know our own, and each other's, bums. He may try to find us, but he'll be wrestling smoke.

On the way back to our owners, Scottie showed me his 'tunnel system,' a small hole scratched out by the pond with an old sock half buried at the bottom. He's convinced he'll be under the pond within the week and has plans for escape routes, food and equipment storage and medical facilities. Terriers!

Thursday, June 26

It worked. Razor is steaming with fury and after re-marking his own territory came after Scottie and me, who were safely watching from the woods. All he found were more P.A.R.P markings, which seemed to drive him insane, running around biting at his own stumpy little tail, barking his head off in fury and spraying urine everywhere he could. While he was at it, Scottie and I slipped past his pack again and with military precision peed around the gate area, but with a wider perimeter this time. As Mao Zedong so wisely said, 'The enemy advances, we retreat; the enemy camps, we harass; the enemy tires, we attack; the enemy retreats, we pursue.'

Undercover Operative Ella reports that after watching Razor's reaction yesterday, Barney sought her out and asked for more information on P.A.R.P. He also had useful intelligence. Razor's pack currently numbers sixteen, and Barney knows of another dog who he thinks is bound to be a P.A.R.P. sympathiser. There might be more, but the pack is scared.

We told Ella to set up an assignation with our new mole, and then she returned to lookout duty, relaying Razor's current position to us through a series of coded barks. We always managed to be on the opposite side of the park from him, marking more patches of free territory.

Friday, June 27

I allowed myself a little rummage through the garbage last night, just for old time's sakes, and because he never bothered changing the battery when it ran out. Tired of shocking himself every five minutes I shouldn't wonder. There's also the small matter of my needing new friends to play with. Since Mr Tibia, they've stopped arriving and the once lovely Mr T now has all the flavour and marrowbone goodness of a house brick.

The Owner's been lax around the house for the last few days and the bin was full to the brim with all sorts of interesting things. So much so that I got slightly carried away. By the time he woke up the kitchen looked like a landfill site with me on my back in the centre surrounded by plastic bags, cartons and wrappers. Anything with a bit of flavour left in it really.

It's been a while since I've driven him to the Rolled-up Newspaper, but this time he reached for it. I was surprised to see him hesitate, then grab me by the collar and haul me off to the back yard instead. Perhaps his behaviour has changed for good.

Either way, for the first time in weeks I was doing time again, but used my sentence wisely to get reacquainted with the post. Not long now. Next door's ginger tom sat and watched me from the shed roof, but I reckon with a scramble up an old packing crate, onto the water butt and onto the shed I can be across the fence and have that smirking pussy between my teeth.

Saturday, June 28

I'm getting a bit worried about the Owner. He doesn't seem to want to get out of bed, and for the past couple of days he's been difficult to wake and smells of drink. Our walks have been short and he's not running. As I've started chewing things again out of sheer boredom the mood in the den is rapidly deteriorating.

It's all Molly's fault of course, the same thing happens every time he gets mixed up with a female. A few days after they leave he starts getting all depressed. They should come with a health warning: May Cause You to Remain on the Sofa for Six Months Drinking Liquor and Watching Crap Movies. Remembering how he nursed me back from the jaws of death I made a concerted effort to cheer him up this evening. I'm sure that the majority of self-professed 'dog lovers' would find it pleasantly soothing, not to say uplifting, to have a large dog sitting in their lap, affectionately chewing their ear. I can only assume from his reaction that he's not as avid a dog fan as he thinks he is, which is a shame as my entire cheering-up strategy hinged on lap sitting and ear nibbling. I suppose I did make him spill whisky all over himself twice, but he should have been thanking me for saving him from his own self-destructive behaviour. To be honest there's not a lot else in my cheering-up arsenal. I am, after all, a dog of destiny, not some emotional crutch for old lamebrain.

Tonight, the bedroom door is closed to me. The batteries in the Electrobin machine have been replaced.

Sunday, June 29

Caught up with Scottie this evening at the wasteland. Apparently Razor has found and covered all our territory markings and is boasting that he has already crushed P.A.R.P. If we are to win this war I need the Owner in the park for at least an hour a day, and not just standing there watching my every move. Alone, there's not much Scottie and Ella can do. I have to get him out of the doldrums and back into his stinky trainers.

Monday, June 30

Hallelujah! No walk today, which I know is hardly cause for joyous celebration, but joyous, joyous day!

As I was curled up in the kitchen this morning, trying to ignore my protesting bladder, the doorbell rang. The Owner staggered out of bed and without thinking opened the door wide to reveal who else but the postman in all his quaking glory.

All trivial thoughts of bladders were vanquished as I crossed the den in two bounds and was on him before the hung-over *Homo sapien* could make a grab at me.

I'm not, and never have been, a biter of humans. As my mother used to say, 'Cross the line from Bad Dog to Mad Dog and you'll find a world of pain, but only for a very short time.' Fortunately, the postman has never conversed with my old mum and wasn't to know that I have never done anything worse than nuzzle the occasional earlobe. From two inches away, snarling and barking into his face, my fetid breath hot and jaws slavering type of thing, well I fancy I must have looked like a hound of Hell, come to savage him into the next life,  though the dramatic effect was somewhat lessened by the jet of excited urine that squirted over him. Mine, not the Owner's, though it would have showed some solidarity if he had joined in.

As it was I only got a second or two of decent face-to-face menacing before the Owner grabbed my collar and pulled me off. The lily-livered postman made a run for it, scattering letters behind him and throwing the parcel that he was trying to deliver at my head (I dodged it easily of course).

I'm back in Cell Block Backyard for my crime, but it was worth it. The delicious scent of the postman's fear is still lingering in my nostrils. They say that postmen always ring twice, but in his case I don't think we'll be hearing that doorbell again.

JULY

Tuesday, July 1

Made a concerted effort to get monkey boy back to the park this morning. A certain amount of scrabbling got his bedroom door open while the morning sun was streaming into his bedroom and the Cold Wet Nose of Rise and Shine persuaded him to open his eyes. There was no way I was going to allow him to roll over and go back to sleep so followed up by grabbing his trainers and delivering them straight to his pillow.

'Hello, Blake,' he said. 'This is a first, bringing me my shoes.'

You could have knocked me down with a rubber bone. Trust a human to misread insistence on being taken for a walk as a token of servitude. Nevertheless, there was no time to remonstrate now. I sat, to show him I was serious, but shuffled around like I was sitting on coals, while letting rip with a series of ear-splitting high barks. Success.

'All right, Blake, you've made your point, I suppose you have been neglected for a couple of days.'

P.A.R.P. is back in action, and as a small bonus I have saved the Owner from years of alcoholism, rehab and probably eventual death from liver failure. As I watched him haring around the park it crossed my mind that owning a dog really does enhance the poor human's life.

Wednesday, July 2

Thank Dog the Owner decided to take a lengthy run in the park with Samantha today, because Scottie, Ella and I had a clandestine rendezvous to keep. It was decided that the dog toilet would be the meeting point as it's out in the open with dogs and humans coming and going all the time, so our conversation would go unnoticed, hopefully.

The park was reconnoitred and Razor found absent, so at two-minute intervals we made our way to the toilet and began sniffing around at the undergrowth nonchalantly. Five minutes later Barney turned up, and had Constable with him. Great, it looked like one of P.A.R.P.'s first converts would be a dog who saw the world through a haze of white fluff, and I'm not talking about his floppy fringe.

Looking around to make sure that we weren't being observed I walked slowly up to them and there was some reserved, tail-erect bottom-sniffing. Formalities complete, I looked at them seriously.

'So you're both here to defect.'

'No man, I've already done my business in the woods. We came to get out of Razor's pack and join P.A.R.P.,' said Constable.

I was puzzled for a second and then the light of understanding dawned.

'I said defect, not defecate.'

'Oh, right. Yeah, there's definitely something wrong with him.' Scottie started licking himself to hide his laughter; Ella looked away.

'This is serious business, Constable. If you come over to P.A.R.P. it will mean running in the pack of danger, sniffing the backside of death.'

'Like a guide dog?'

'What are you talking about, Constable?'

'Well, they must sniff the deaf, it stands to reason.'

'That would be the blind, Constable.' I decided to cut it short. 'Look, are you both committed to defying Razor and helping to create a New Park Order where every dog has his own territory and can run free without let or hindrance?'

'Are they, like, friends of Raz–'

'Yes, we are,' Barney cut in quickly. 'Just tell us what to do.'

Thursday, July 3

The run yesterday must have done the Owner some good. His mood has certainly improved and we were out the door early so he could bound around with Samantha again. Since the birth of mine and Dottie's pups Ella has been slowly thawing and it's almost like it used to be, though there's no scooting, or any suggestion of any sniffing action. However, I think I'm gradually wearing down her resistance.

It's too early to see what effect yesterday's defection had, but it was decided that Barney would stay with Razor's pack for a while as our deep undercover espionage dog, while Constable, as a complete idiot with known connections to yours truly, probably wasn't safe. Accordingly, Constable was debriefed and added his urine and pawprint to mine and Scottie's by the gate. Barney was given our codes and told to communicate with us covertly, through Ella. As of now, they are having an 'affair.'

Friday, July 4

No word from Barney, but it's probably too dangerous for him at the moment; the smell on the ground is that after Constable's defection the pit bull is putting the bite on the rest of the pack, literally. Little does he know he's playing right into our paws.

Saturday, July 5

A close shave today, which is exactly what Constable needs if he's going to avoid being mauled. The idiot didn't see Razor approaching through his ridiculous haircut until it was almost too late.

Fortunately, the pit bull had failed to take into account Constable's owner, a mountain of a woman who wears green Wellington boots and a headscarf all year, and always carries an umbrella. As Razor stalked the sheepdog, growling quietly with his hackles up and revenge in his cold heart, this female Hercules came running up behind and caught him a magnificent kick up the backside, shouting, 'You leave my precious Constable alone, you vicious thug.'

As Razor turned on her, snarling, she gave him a whack with her umbrella, looking deep into his mad pink eyes with not a shred of fear. 'Oh yes, I know all about you, you little bugger, but touch my sweet pawpaw and I'll rip your balls off and feed them to you.'

It looked like a standoff until Razor's owner

ran up puffing, 'Oi, what's going on here? Why are you hitting my dog?'

'That's not a dog, it's an abomination. You should have it castrated and muzzled and preferably kept in a cage.'

'Them other dogs attacked him, Razor wouldn't hurt a fly unless he was provoked.'

Constable's owner shook her umbrella in his face, and shouted, 'If he comes near my dog again I'll provoke him right where the sun doesn't shine, so unless you want a dog kebab you keep your filthy mutt under control.'

With that she clipped Constable's lead on and flounced away, the umbrella held jauntily across her shoulder like a bazooka.

Somewhere in the back of my head an idea is stirring.

Sunday, July 6

An excellent adventure today. It was hot so the Owner left the back door open, thinking that the side gate and new fence would hold a dog of my incredible athleticism. Once he was safely in his office I 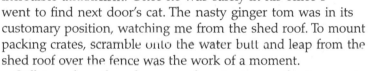 went to find next door's cat. The nasty ginger tom was in its customary position, watching me from the shed roof. To mount packing crates, scramble onto the water butt and leap from the shed roof over the fence was the work of a moment.

Still too slow though – scaredy-cat was up the tree again before I could sink my fangs into it. Barking at it to come and fight failed to prick its sense of martial honour, so I eventually took my paws off the tree trunk and had a look round. The ornamental pond looked very inviting in the midsummer heat. All the barking had put quite a thirst on me and what could be better than a refreshing dip. I've never been able to resist wallowing in muddy water; sometimes I wonder if in my patchwork genetic make-up there's a tiny bit of hippopotamus. I launched myself into the pond like the *Titanic* rolling down the Belfast slipway and was just enjoying a good romp about when I was disturbed by old killjoy's screams and the sound of him scrambling to get over the fence. Looking up at him as he made it to the top of the shed and prepared to jump, I could tell that I was in trouble again. It's like a dog can't do anything to enjoy himself without falling foul of that secret list of rules.

He looked in the kind of mood where the Rolled-up Newspaper, or worse, was very definitely on the agenda, whatever resolutions he might have made about abolishing corporal punishment, so after a last splash for luck I clambered out of the muddy hole. In my efforts to get out and away I admit I upset a small stone statue of a short human with a beard and fishing rod, and unfortunately that broke. Everything else that got damaged was the result of my clumsy oaf of an Owner lumbering around the garden trying to catch me.

To cut a long story short, a few minutes of enjoyable chasing later, the next-door neighbour's wife returned to find that the Owner has trampled over a lot of her husband's plants, while the contents of her washing line were now muddy and flapping around the garden. Some underwear was floating in the pond.

Obviously, a new human should always be treated to a proper welcome and I dodged around the Owner and launched myself at her accordingly. I may have been muddy, but shrieking was a bit ungracious, I thought. After all, it's not every pussy fancier that gets treated to a rough tongue in the ear.

From the sounds coming from next door as I lay here in chains, the bottle of champagne and bunch of flowers he took round didn't make her or her husband feel any better disposed towards us. It all goes to help corroborate my theories about cat owners.*

* Blake's theory of feline ownership states that humans choose their pets based on their own temperament. Dog owners are straightforward, trustworthy and loyal, whereas your cat people are cruel, selfish, conniving, preening simpletons who wash too often. In short, nine out of ten humans who express a preference for felines are deeply disturbed individuals. It probably won't be a popular hypothesis among cat fans, but the statistics can't be argued with.

Monday, July 7

I was eventually let into the house last night well after dark, but

I had to howl for a while and there was certainly no chance of getting on the bed. This morning the postman pushed something called a 'dry-cleaning bill' through the door and the Owner now seems more intent on this ludicrous obedience-training regime than ever, only without Molly I had to suffer his own useless attempts. He was sour, but at least the treats were good and plentiful. I played along while they lasted and then ran off to catch up with Scottie, who had just arrived. When I got there his owner was shouting at Dottie's and waving a fist in his face. Ignoring the spotty bitch and her red-faced human, I ran down to the pond with Scottie to check progress on his earthworks.

There wasn't much, except that the sock had gone. Scottie whispered that he had 'buried it elsewhere, fur tae keep it safe.'

He seemed nervous and about to say something else, but before he could bark it out, the Owner caught up with me and I was clipped and dragged off. Scottie got a pat, which was more than I did.

Tuesday, July 8

The Owner spent most of the day fixing all the damage he'd caused in the garden next door, while I lurked in the kennel on the chain. Nevertheless, I could hear the neighbour droning on about how great cats were, and had the Owner considered trading me in for a pet that would sit quietly on his knee all evening and not wreck people's property. What I'd like to ask is, has he considered toxoplasmosis? I bet he won't be loving his little tabby pal so much when his lymph nodes are the size of basketballs.

Obviously, I barked a lot, challenging the kitty supporter to fight it out, but like his stupid pet he didn't want to know.

Wednesday, July 9

P.A.R.P. is making excellent progress. Constable has been given his territory back and proudly marks it every day. He's turning out to be a surprisingly useful party member. Somewhere in that dippy head he's taken a real dislike to Razor. Ella had another rendezvous with Barney who said that something had happened between the two dogs, but nobody knows what. Whatever it was, Constable certainly kept Razor busy while Scottie and I spread the bouquet of P.A.R.P. around the park. Directed by Ella's barks he seemed to be everywhere, always just out of Razor's reach, but visible enough to keep him occupied while Scottie and I worked. Whenever Razor threatened to get too close, with a quick sprint Constable was back by his owner's side, his tongue hanging out and mocking Razor from a distance.

Thursday, July 10

Barney reports that he is now certain that another couple of dogs have P.A.R.P. sympathies. He is keeping a low profile as Razor is getting paranoid under the strain of keeping a constant eye on his pack, trying to sniff us out and re-marking territory. Although Razor appears to have no suspicions that we have infiltrated, Barney is playing a game as dangerous as fetch with a stick of dynamite.

Friday, July 11

A dog likes to be shown that he's appreciated and the Owner's usually pretty good at doling out the stroking, etc. For the last couple of days though there's definitely been a dry spell on that front, due to him still sulking over the next-door incident. We canines don't hold grudges* so I remonstrated last night with some insistent nuzzling and snuffling. For a while it was touch and go, but I didn't take 'down' for an answer and after a while he relented and let me put my head in his lap while he scratched behind my ears and stroked my head. I can wrap the stupid human round my paw.

* Hence the famous saying about sleeping dogs. Humans, on the other hand, would shave a sleeping dog's eyebrows off and paint its backside purple.

Saturday, July 12

Just me and Ella in the park today. She was briefing me on Barney's latest intelligence, and she looked so good being all brisk and businesslike that I couldn't resist going in for a sniff. It did me no good at all though. She just growled and whipped her lovely fluffy bum, with its oh-so-enticing glands, out of nose range.

'If you think you're sniffing that after Dottie, then you're even more stupid than I thought. Go find yourself some more *pedigree* bum.'

I tried to tell her that in the past few weeks I was a changed dog, that my nose belonged only to her and yearned to be as one with her most intimate regions, but she wouldn't listen. She just kept talking about Barney's new prospects – Liquorice and the Pekingese, who's called Chu Chu (stupid name, makes her sound like a steam train). He's grooming them ready to abscond from the Razor pack, but we are waiting for a time when their desertion will have the maximum impact on the rest of the pack.

Sunday, July 13

Something's going on. There's a suitcase on the Owner's bedroom floor filled with beach clothes, and he looks and smells more excited than usual. It probably means we're going on holiday, and Dog knows I've earned a break with all the training, fighting and politics of the last few months. I love the beach; all the dropped ice cream you can eat and a great big pond to splash in. I'll have to brief the ~~pack~~ P.A.R.P. members that they'll have to do without me for a couple of weeks. It could be a good time to turn the heat down anyway; hopefully if P.A.R.P. disappears for a while it'll make Razor even more paranoid.

Monday, July 14

I don't know what crime I've committed, but I've been sentenced without trial to incarceration in a maximum-security penitentiary; the kind of place that's surrounded by barbed wire and gun towers. All was going smoothly this morning. We had a run in the park as normal, and I told Scottie that he was in command during

my absence. He was about to tell me something, but then said, 'Nay, it's of nae importance, enjoy yer holiday.'

When we got back, the Owner loaded the suitcase in the car while I jumped around him, all excited for the journey and looking forward to smelling a few hundred miles of countryside on the way to somewhere exotic. Instead, we drove here and I was dragged out of the car into a tiny, white tiled cell with bars on the window and only a bed and a bare light bulb. They say 'if you can't do the time, don't do the crime,' but I didn't know that the penalty for a splash in the neighbour's pond and a couple of stolen sandwiches would be so severe. I would have thought a suspended sentence and maybe a little community service would have sufficed.

I fought as hard as I could, but all that training's put some muscle on the Owner and now I'm cowering in a corner, too scared even to whine. I've heard about these places. What if it's a life sentence and this is one of those 'rescue' centres? What if I get on the wrong side – the underside – of Mr Big? How could the Owner leave me to rot in some dungeon after everything we've been through together? He tried to calm me down before he left, but the warder (who reminded me distinctly of Molly) told him that it would be best to leave quickly and I would be fine in a little while. He threw me a couple of my favourite toys and shouted, 'Bye, Blake. Be a Good Boy,' and then he was gone.

Half an hour after he'd left I heard the cell door next to mine clang open and raised my head to see Ella being dragged into it, whining and barking. Her owner seemed distraught, but roused herself enough to pat my enquiring nose, which I pushed through the bars. Her last words were, 'Well, Blake, I'm going on holiday with your owner, so you can have a holiday with Ella. Look after her for me.'

Then she gave Ella one last stroke and was gone.

Tuesday, July 15

Day One at Stalag Woof. The regime is harsh and authoritarian. At seven in the morning it's a small breakfast in the cell, then a door opens allowing you out into your own small exercise area. An hour later, me, Ella, a neutered spaniel called Clancy, and a Yorkshire terrier bitch by the name of Susie were taken to a large fenced-in field and allowed to run around for an hour. After that, we were confined to our cells and small yards for the rest of the day, with just a large meal at three, some treats from a warder who comes round and makes a fuss of us and another hour in the field at six to relieve the monotony of doing stir.

Ella was very distressed without her owner, and I did what I could to comfort her. We have developed a simple method of communication, which just goes to show how canine ingenuity can overcome any obstacle. It involves barking at each other through the bars.

I'm trying to be strong for Ella's sake, but I don't know how long I can keep going in here. I hear her whining for her owner in her sleep, and I have to admit I miss mine too. I can't believe the two of them have absconded together. How did I miss that? I was too complacent after Molly, but usually it takes him months and months to even get another date, and no one but me has ever been mad enough to go on holiday with him.

Wednesday, July 16

Day Two at Stalag Woof. Ella looked at me through the bars today and asked if I thought the owners would ever come back. I choked back a horrible surge of doubt and assured her that they surely wouldn't leave us here for ever. Well, mine is more than capable, but her owner seems much more of a decent human. I keep thinking about everything I've chewed recently. Could that dirty pair of pants be the straw that broke the camel's back?

Thursday, July 17

Day Three in Stalag Woof. Ella's still very depressed so I wrote some jailhouse blues to cheer her up. It goes like this. To be howled in D minor.

> Done my business in a corner,
> It gets hosed down around nine.
> Got a chew toy and a tail to chase,
> I'm one lonely, down canine.
>
> Now no one's gonna pat me
> And my tail done lost its wag,
> Ain't no leftovers, no paw to shake
> 'Cos I'm a low-down doggie lag.
>
> There's arrows on my collar,
> A shackle on my paw,
> Ain't got nothing but the doghouse blues
> And urine on the floor.
>
> Ain't got nothing but
> the doghouse blues,
> Only Bad Dogs break
> the law.

By the time they shut the doors to our runs and turned out the lights the whole jail was howling along, even the little pug down the row who's got a voice like a drain. It seemed to perk Ella up a little anyway; she barked out some pretty good harmonies.

Friday, July 18

Day Four in Stalag Woof. The woman that brings round the tiny breakfast you get in here seemed a bit dazed this morning and was complaining about the 'terrible racket' we made last night. Some humans just have no taste. She looks like the type that only listens to crappy pop music. The midnight howl seems to have improved Ella's frame of mind though, we even had a bit of a chase and play fight in the meadow. Both of us are keeping in trim for our P.A.R.P. campaign. I didn't try for a sniff though – I may be cheeky, but grrr means grrr.

Saturday, July 19

Day Five in Stalag Woof. Since the door clanged shut, I've been looking for holes in the security around here. The other dogs on our row of the 'Sunshine Kennel' say that escape is impossible, but no prison is impregnable. There's also a rumour that there's a separate wing for cats. Probably the psychiatric wing.

Everywhere is fenced. I've toured the perimeter and it is well-maintained mesh with no weak points. Our pens have walls too high to jump and you couldn't get through the walls with a sledgehammer, let alone a rubber chew toy with a bell in it. Nevertheless, it's worth a try and I've put in a request for a poster of Lassie to cover the tunnel I intend to dig. Disguising myself as a guard is out of the question, and I don't have the materials to build an aircraft. If only Scottie were here. With his engineering skills we'd be halfway to Switzerland by now.

The only real opportunity for escape is during the walk down to the fenced meadow, when the only precautions the jailers have taken are leads. I've also noticed that there's a white van that leaves each day around the same time as we are taken to the exercise field. If I can wrench the lead out of the warder's hand, get in the back of that van and hide myself under some old sacks then there's a chance. Either that or I could just run like hell in the direction of the den.

Sunday, July 20

Day Six in Stalag Woof. I've discussed my plan with Ella, but she doesn't want to join me in my prison break. In fact she was quite terse.

'Blake, forget it. I'm sure our owners will be back in a few days and it's not that bad here. Besides, where will you go? Even if you could find your way back to your den, you'd only have to sit outside the door until your owner came back to let

121

you in. You might as well stay here where there's food and company.'

As I feared, her depression has quickly led to her becoming institutionalised. But not me. I can't stay when there's a war going on in the park.

There is an old Old English sheepdog called Sparky in the next cell who wants to come with me though, but he's like Constable's great-grandfather. Infirm, half-blind and as dozy as the rest of the breed. If a dog was ever misnamed it's him, though you have to respect the old boy's nerve. I told him gently that he should sit this one out.

I tested my plan by tugging smartly on the lead this evening, but the warder has a grip like Razor's jaws. What I need is a distraction.

Monday, July 21

Day Seven in Stalag Woof. Clancy has agreed to provide a diversion, so long as I take him with me. I agreed. Last night I said a long goodbye to Ella, who just shook her head pityingly and refused to talk to me. Sparky tried to change my mind one last time with an embarrassing charade involving him proving his eyesight was good by spotting a chew toy in the corner of his cell. His sight's so bad he didn't realise I'd already stolen it through the bars.

I was on my best behaviour all day, remembering how to react to all the Molly-taught commands that humans love barking out so much, and by the time the evening walk came around I was definitely up for 'trustee' status. As far as I could tell there were no suspicions of the breakout. It was time.

As the warder came to fetch us from our cells I behaved perfectly. The plan is that Clancy will be sick on her feet as we walk to the meadow (he's eaten something absolutely disgusting in preparation). When the warder bends down to check he's OK, her grip on the leads will naturally relax. Clancy and I will seize the moment and dash for the border, and on to freedom.

Hopefully, by tomorrow I will be back in the old park stealing croissants from the café tables and making Razor rue the day I returned to the front lines.

Tuesday, July 22

They brought me back in soon after dark. I was conscious but hurting all over.

The scam worked perfectly. Clancy vommed up a sticky mess right on cue and as the warder bent down to see if he was OK I was away with a massive leap. I didn't look back, but from the shouting and enraged barking I could tell that Clancy hadn't made it, poor blighter.

There was no point in going back for him, so I kept going, running like I was part greyhound, which I probably am. All was going well until I reached a road, which I ran into without a second thought, right in front of a car. It squealed, but hit me full on and I was thrown about fifteen feet into a ditch. The car didn't even stop.

The warder found me there a little later and lifted me into the back of the white van. I noted without enthusiasm that there were sacks in there after all. The vet came quickly and pronounced me 'shocked and bruised, but amazingly unhurt considering'. The warder said that she'd keep an eye on me in the night.

All the while Ella had been whining and pawing at the bars between our cells. Eventually, the warder looked at me, curled, bedraggled and miserable, then at Ella, and said, 'All right then, I suppose it can't do any harm for one night and your owners said you were good friends.'

The door to Ella's cell was opened and she slunk in gracefully, lying down next to me and snuffling. I fell asleep with my head in her soft fur, and only woke up a few hours later to feel her nose gently sniffing my backside.

Wednesday, July 23

Day Nine in Stalag Woof. The vet was right, thank Dog. There don't appear to be any internal injuries and a good sleep seemed to work out a lot of my aches, though I am still a bit stiff. I'm sure that having Ella sleeping next to me helped.

We are officially an item again, and I have promised never to sniff another bitch again, even if she has a pedigree as long as my tail. I don't know why I should, I've found the perfect mate and mating for life is very wolf. In the meadow today I had my first sniff of Ella in what seems like dog years and we even had a small scoot of celebration together. Neither of us care what Clancy or Susie think.

Thursday, July 24

Day Ten in Stalag Woof. Dog bless that warder. After making double sure that Ella wasn't in season she let us share a cell again. She said it was to keep us both quiet, but I'm starting to think that under that cold, hard human exterior beats the heart of a dog.

Ella and I whined a few bars of 'Doghouse Blues' and slept like one big furry rug.

Friday, July 25

Hurrah! Ella and I have been paroled, and without any extra time being added for my attempted escape. The owners arrived together, holding paws and looking tanned. They smelled of odd food. Ella instantly went crazy with happiness, bounding around and barking with her tail set to 'the clappers.'

I tried to be more dignified, but my reaction at seeing the Owner again came as a bit of a shock. I gave a display of 'welcome home' about which the critics will be raving for years to come: 'One of Blake's best performances yet. This dog really is at the peak of his career. Rich, enthusiastic barking that might very well have ruptured an eardrum or two and vigorous gymnastic jumping up. What other dog could lick two human ears during one aerial bounce? Yes, this Blake is definitely a Dog to Watch.'

It's good to be back in the den, though I noticed that the postman's been wreaking revenge by pushing a mountain of paper through the door. I must remember to have a word or two with him on the subject.

Saturday, July 26

The Owner's not as soft and warm as Ella, but I happily fell asleep with my head on his knee last night and later jumped onto the end of his bed, where I was allowed to stay.

Back to the park this morning and it looks as though things have been quiet since Ella and I were banged up. A nose around told us that Scottie had kept a couple of strategic patches fresh in the name of P.A.R.P., but beyond that Razor has made a comeback, though some of the markings seemed weak, as though he'd strained to get the last dregs out of his bladder. Good. Hopefully he won't be expecting a big offensive now. Time for Stage Two.

Mine and Ella's owners seem to be locked into some kind of romantic entanglement. They are now running together, but stopping frequently to touch and slurp at each other's faces. It's quite disgusting, but if it means that I can see more of Ella I have decided to let them get on with it for now, though I'm withholding a full blessing. However, Samantha's taste in dogs means she's scoring highly on my femalarometer already. Perhaps, in time, I could come to accept her as some kind of Owneress, second class.

Sunday, July 27

Scottie confirmed that all has been quiet in the park. He has managed a secret meeting with Barney though, and the news is that Razor believes the P.A.R.P. threat to have passed. He even sent his second in command, a German shepherd called Rudy, to offer Scottie and Constable an amnesty. They played along by asking Razor to present assurances of their safety.

He's very proud of the progress he's made on the tunnel system, it's now the size of a bucket. The sock is back. I could see the tip of it poking through the earth at the bottom.

The little Westie seemed quite nervous – perhaps he's tempted by Razor's offer. I told him he'd done a magnificent job to bolster his commitment to the cause.

Monday, July 28

It was a beautiful summer's morning; for once all members of the party arrived together and a conference was called by the dog toilet. Dangerous, but we have set the date for the mass defection as Saturday. Barney will brief Liquorice and Chu Chu tomorrow. The Pekingese will have a head start on account of her tiny legs, but Liquorice and Barney will declare their allegiance while Razor is at his ablutions and run for a safe house (Constable's owner) where he will debrief them and assign new territory. While Razor gives chase, Scottie and I will conduct a saturation marking campaign. And I do mean 'saturation'. We have a couple of little surprises lined up for Razor.

Tuesday, July 29

Ella and I were alone in the park this morning and in the midst of war snatched an hour of bliss. Returning to the Scooting Place, we dragged our bums around while the sun shone through the leaves and dappled the grass. After that we sniffed, mounted, rolled in the mud by the edge of the pond and generally made the place our own again.

It was all over too soon, the owners called and with one last affectionate sniff Ella was away. I, on the other hand, settled down for a snooze. It was a lovely day, and the Owner's used to waiting for a while.

Wednesday, July 30

Relations in the den have soured over the last few days and the Owner is up to his old tricks. I suppose I should respect his perseverance, but it's so difficult when he's constantly shouting his head off and marching around with a face like a cat's bum.

I think the root of the problem is interpretation. He sees the word 'come' as an instruction to be obeyed instantly while I understand it to be a polite reminder that he will be leaving the park in ten to twenty minutes and if I wish to leave with him then I might want to consider wandering over. These little problems with canine-human translation can cause so many difficulties.

To add to the problem, he's in a complete quandary as to how to react when I don't jump to his orders. His new book on 'dog whispering' has the following to say on the subject of discipline:

A dog should be punished instantly for any transgression or will not understand why it is being rebuked.
A dog should never be punished after obeying the command 'come' as it will begin to fear to return.
Always use exclusion to punish your dog and never physical violence.

In practice, this means I can return by whatever lazy, circuitous route I fancy, like an Italian on the way to work, and he is powerless to punish me. Even if he wanted to, how's he going to exclude me in a park?

He's settled for looking me sternly in the eye and saying 'Bad Dog,' over and over. I mean, please. He's used that so many times it's almost a form of endearment. If he really wanted me to sit up and take notice, he'd threaten to get Molly back. Of course, bigger and better treats might help, too. If he laid out a three-course meal before starting with all the 'come' nonsense he'd be surprised at the results it yielded.

Thursday, July 31

The Owner has been going out a lot at night and coming back late smelling of Samantha and rich food. This female seems to really be out to impress me, she's even taught him the art of the doggie bag. There's nothing a dog likes more for breakfast than the remains of pork chops cooked with apple and thyme with potatoes dauphinoise and seasonal vegetables. The presentation leaves a little to be desired of course; I bet the chef never intended it all to be smushed up together in a tin bowl. Nevertheless, whatever restaurant they've been patronising, it deserves a Michelin star.

AUGUST

Friday, August 1

Ella, Scottie, Constable and I reviewed the plan for tomorrow's defection one last time, which in practice meant explaining it to Constable again and making him repeat it back until we were sure he knew what he was supposed to be doing.

Samantha came over in the evening with a bag of clothes and brought Ella with her. After they'd both had a nose about the den (Ella pronounced that 'it smelled of human') we laid down in front of the fireplace (Ella and I, not the humans, though they would have been more than welcome to join us in a bit of licking and sniffing). I've never approved of the Owner inviting women back to the den, but Samantha is definitely welcome to come again. Usually my evenings consist of some synchronised farting and a bit of ear-scratching if I'm lucky, so it was wonderful to have Ella to talk to and play with all night.

Saturday, August 2

Everything went according to plan. Liquorice, Chu Chu and Barney are now fully pawed-up members of P.A.R.P. and have been assigned their own territory. Chu Chu left quietly five minutes beforehand, then Barney and Liquorice broke from the pack, shouting 'P.A.R.P. forever!' and making off through the woods by separate routes while Razor was mid-dump. Scottie and I were watching from deep cover and the pit bull didn't even stop to finish, but gave chase instantly, treating us and about six of his pack to the undignified sight of him trying to  follow both dogs at once while squirting faeces out at a run. He might be strong, but he's not built for speed and was easily outpaced. Constable reports that he eventually caught up after the three traitors were safely playing around his owner's feet and she saw him off with the umbrella, disgusted at his still dripping behind.

As soon as Razor was safely out of the way, Scottie and I began the second prong of our attack.

Seeing his owner talking on a mobile phone, we ambled up nonchalantly from behind. He was so engrossed that he didn't even notice as we simultaneously cocked our legs and claimed him on behalf of P.A.R.P. Not until our pee was dripping into his trainers anyway. Now that's saturation. After jumping up and leaving our muddy pawprints on his white trousers, we were off. Phase Two has begun.

Sunday, August 3

Very pleased with the results of yesterday's movements. With three new members, P.A.R.P. is growing, while Razor's pack has diminished to twelve. Being small, Chu Chu is not much of a military asset, but it is agreed that she will be closely guarded by whoever is available. Barney believes that a blow of this magnitude will inspire more defections soon, especially as morale has been plummeting to new depths in Razor's pack recently. Ella reported that the marking of his owner sent him into a fresh fit of rage and he is again taking it out on the dogs around him. I hope that he's not hurting them too much, but P.A.R.P. must be looking more attractive every day.

Monday, August 4

Tension is mounting over my lack of boundless enthusiasm for the word 'come.' I really don't know what he expects. If he wasn't so witless, he would see that I am a dog on a mission and my time is precious. With hostilities at a crucial stage, a growing membership to watch over, strategies to discuss and top-level scooting to be completed with Ella, something's got to give. Besides, it's not as though I haven't compromised again and again. I now 'sit' before every meal and I haven't chewed anything other than a few odds and ends that accidentally fell out of his wardrobe for weeks. Plus, there's the 24-hour guarding service I provide, not to mention finding time in my hectic schedule to stick my nose in his crutch as often as I can. You'd think he'd cut me some slack. But no, it's 'Blake, come, Blake, come, Blake, come,' morning, noon and night. Often for no good reason at all. It's time he faced up to the fact that his control-freakery is well out of control. I suppose it's my own fault for not spending the time training him properly, but hopefully if I studiously ignore his demands he'll eventually get the message.

Tuesday, August 5

The reason for Scottie's recent nerves around me becomes clear. With nothing much happening on the P.A.R.P. front, Ella wanted to join the humans on their dash round the park, so I went with her. We were about halfway round when we came across Scottie and his owner sitting on a park bench with a box. A box full of puppies. West Highland terrier puppies. With spots. There was a sign that read 'Free to Good Homes.'

On spying me Scottie looked extremely sheepish (which must be very easy when you're white and fluffy to begin with). Tucking his tail between his legs he crouched down and made himself look as meek and submissive as possible.

It took a while for me to comprehend what I was seeing, and I just stood surveying the scene with my tail wagging slowly and my mouth hanging open. Meanwhile, our two owners were cooing over the little balls of spotty white fluff. Ella and Scottie were both holding their breath.

Eventually, I walked over and looked down at Scottie with my lips drawn back.

'You sly old dog, and I thought you'd need a winch to get up there.'

Scottie relaxed a little and mumbled, 'Aye, well, I had to take a flyin' . . . leap, ye ken. And grip a bit tae stay oan.'

He looked down. 'Tae tell the truth, I'm not sure yon lassie even noticed.'

The three of us inspected Scottie and Dottie's progeny. They were adorable and we weren't the only ones who thought so.

Holding up a particularly spirited little fellow, my Owner turned to Samantha and said, 'What do you think? Shall we?'

She smiled at him and said, 'Let's talk about it.'

He can't even control the dog he's got, and he's talking about getting a puppy! And what's all this 'we' business? It sounds like moving-in talk to me. The last time that happened it was a complete disaster. The female in question lasted a week before she got tired of having to buy fresh underwear every day. I couldn't help it, it was just so tasty.

Wednesday, August 6

Another visit from Samantha and Ella last night and it didn't take long before there was talk of puppies, with Samantha asking what were, in my view, very sensible questions.

'But Blake runs rings around you, why on earth would you want *another* dog?'

The Owner looked vexed for a moment, then said, 'He is a handful, but he's also great company and despite all the trouble he gets me into there's never a dull moment.'

There followed some recounting of my recent adventures in which Jehovah's Witnesses, the neighbour and the postman featured prominently. The bouncing poo that wouldn't go away was also brought up again, as if I wasn't in the same room, listening.

'Besides, it wouldn't be my dog, I was hoping it might be *our* dog.'

'What are you saying?'

'You know, if we ever decided to sort of move in together.'

Ella's owner laughed. 'Was that an invitation?'

'Sort of. It feels like the right thing to do, I mean we'd be heartless to split these two up,' he said, pointing to Ella and me who were happily snuggled on the rug.

'Hmm, well I'm hardly bowled over by your charming proposal, but you might have a point, they do look good together. I tell you what, let's give it a month and see how we feel. I'm sure Mr McCormick will keep a puppy back for us until then.'

Oh my Dog. In a month I could be a stepfather, living in a den that's been invaded by a human female. Looking at Ella snoring gently, I realised I didn't mind at all.

Thursday, August 7

It turns out that Dottie's owner wants nothing to do with the puppies and threatened to drown them if Scottie's refused to take them. Rather than let them die he now has the eight little bundles in a big box on his kitchen floor. Scottie is delighted, but tired.

'It's no easy bein' a single parent at mah age. The wee 'uns are up half the night wantin' tae play, an' I just dinnae have the heart tae say nay tae thum.'

Mr McCormick is going to keep two, but has to find homes for the rest otherwise they'll have to go to the rescue place. Every dog knows what that means: an eternity of sitting in a cell, hoping that a human will come and find them, while getting less cute with every passing day. I wouldn't wish it on any puppy, even a pit bull, so have told Scottie that we will adopt one, at least.

This means that for the first time in my life I will have to use every strategy and wile to make sure the Owner gets together with a female. It's a daunting task. I'll have to quit farting for a start. Knicker-sniffing and chewing will be completely off the menu. I might even have to go as far as to maintain some semblance of good behaviour.

Friday, August 8

P.A.R.P.'s manifesto of democracy, fairness and tolerance is definitely having the required results. The pit bull was not in the park, but one key member of his pack was, presenting the party with an unexpected opportunity to launch the second wave of Phase Two: Ideological Warfare. Using the plucky Chu Chu as bait, Razor's second in command, Rudy, was lured to a clearing in the woods. Instead of a Pekingese though, he found himself surrounded by P.A.R.P. A ring of jaws.

The German shepherd sat and waited until I trotted out to face him. He seemed faintly surprised when I didn't attack, but gave him a friendly sniff and a lazy tail wag instead.

'You are in no danger here, P.A.R.P. is not your enemy,' I reassured him.

He grinned. 'I am not frightened of your little ambush. Ha, maybe you vould ask Chu Chu to tear out my throat, huh? Or ze miniature poodle zere . . .' He looked at Scottie, who glared. 'I tremble at ze thought zat he might sawage me.'

'Sawage?' I asked.

'Ja, sawage.'

'There will be no "sawaging" here,' I said firmly. 'We have a message for your Pack Leader.'

'Unt vy should I deliver zis message?'

'Oh, we don't want you to deliver it. You are the message.'

'I do not understand.'

'It's easy. Barney here says that he used to run about with you as a puppy and has seen you letting children play on your back and playing "fetch" until you're going out of your mind with boredom. He thinks you're a good dog who would like his territory back and freedom from Razor. We'd like you to join us. That's the message to Razor.'

'Unt if I refuse?'

I leaned forward and growled softly, 'Well, Barney also told me something else about you that I'd hate to have to spread around the park. Apparently, your owner's one of those weirdoes that likes cats *and* dogs. Barney says he's seen you lying around the garden with cats curled up asleep on your belly in basic contravention of the laws of Dog and Nature.'

Rudy cringed. 'I have considered your invitation to choin unt it is acceptable to me. Ich bin ein PARPer.'

Democracy, fairness, tolerance, and the occasional use of blackmail, just to make sure.

Saturday, August 9

Razor's response to his second in command's P.A.R.P. marking and pawprint at the north gate was swift, as we knew it would be. Fortunately we were prepared. Each P.A.R.P. dog is under orders to roll in muck and rubbish as much as possible in order to mask their scent. For Constable, whose owner is fussy about his appearance, this means he has to have a bath and blow dry every day, but as his owner changes his shampoo and conditioner all the time this isn't too much of a problem, so long as you don't mind him smelling like a hair salon. I must admit, his coat is luxuriant, soft and glossy while mine is dry and lifeless. He says it's because he's 'worth it.' I wonder if I could persuade the Owner to invest in some grooming products – after all, I'm worth it, too.

As Razor's pack streamed across the park, looking for vengeance, P.A.R.P. just melted away. All they found was an empty park and a lot of owners calling for their dogs.

Scottie, I noticed, made excellent use of his tunnel system, which is now big enough to hide him almost completely. Perhaps I was wrong to scoff at it.

Sunday, August 10

I tried to be a good boy, for the puppies' sake, but how can I be expected to resist a cat, just sitting in front of me washing its paws in a very provocative manner? I am now banged up good and proper. By the time I get out of this kennel, I'll be good for nothing except maybe a stringy main course for a family of Koreans.

The weather has turned from hot to baking, and the whole street seems to be on holiday, sitting outside and enjoying the sunshine. As most of the houses only have small back yards, a lot of people had deckchairs out on their little patches of front lawn. There were even a couple of barbecues going. Very nice. It was the smell coming from a few doors down that made me try the gate. If I could just get out then the Expression of Woeful Longing would be all it took to beg a sausage or two. As the Owner was asleep in a deckchair I could be there and back before he'd even noticed.

Incredibly, the gate was a doddle to open. Since the last couple of incidents the Owner is a stickler over letting me out, but seemed to have overlooked this rusty old exit. A paw on the lever and it swung straight out. Not one to look a gift bone in the mouth, I looked back at him dozing and set off down the road towards teriyaki heaven. I wondered if a fake limp would get me some ketchup too.

I got as far as next door when I spied my ginger nemesis. Now, there's a time for barbecue and a time for crunching on the bones of your mortal enemy and I was down the path like a whippet in a Ferrari. There being no tree to climb, the cat turned tail and fled indoors with me close behind it, mounting the stairs and taking refuge under the bed. Behind me I could hear distant voices. The next-door neighbour's wife saying, 'What was that? I thought I heard someone going upstairs,' and from further away, the Owner saying, 'Blake? Blake? Oh no, not again.'

What happened next is still too difficult to think about. Maybe in a year or two I'll be able to heal with the help of a good counsellor.

Monday, August 11

Still in the back yard. I've been here all day with only a bowl of water and a small bowl of the gum-ripping biscuits for sustenance. On the street outside I can still hear the occasional bellow of laughter. From next door, nothing but a sob now and then. The Owner won't even look at me.

Tuesday, August 12

Samantha arrived last night and at her insistence I was finally let back in. I slunk through the door and gave my best stab at submissiveness with the Eyes of Penitence thrown in for good measure. It did no good at all. The Owner was banging on about having to get rid of me, which he only ever does under great stress. Pretty soon he'd be telling the whole story, and as Ella was looking at me enquiringly I led her away to the kitchen to give my, more accurate, account of events. What happened was this.

The ginger tom was right under the bed and although I struggled dogfully I couldn't get anywhere near the spitting, hissing coward. However, my nose was twitching with a familiar smell that reminded me of chewed up underwear and Faye. It's the reason I always like to get under her skirt. I looked around. Puzzlingly, it seemed to be coming from a pink chew toy, about the same length and girth as Mr Tibia. It was clearly made to fit a dog's mouth perfectly, but what could a self-professed cat-lover be wanting with such an item? Even the biggest feline wouldn't be able to get its mouth round this, even if it were disposed to chewing.

I gave it a tentative lick and then a nibble. Sure enough, it fit my jaws snugly and tasted divine. Forgetting about the cat under the bed I figured that I'd probably be doing the neighbours a favour getting rid of it. Perhaps it used to belong to that poor neutered dog he said he once owned.

As I pulled it out from under the bed I heard the sound of heavy footsteps on the stairs. I wasn't waiting to be cornered by a raving pussy fanatic, so I dived out of the door and around his legs just as he reached the landing, my teeth clamped firmly around my new toy. There was a strangled gasp, but as I got to the foot of the stairs the neighbour recovered himself enough to squawk, 'Maureen, the door. Shut the door. Don't let him –'

But he was too late, I was past the shrieking woman and halfway down the path.

Passing their front gate, with them both now in pursuit, one end of the toy banged on the wall. I nearly dropped it when it started buzzing and wiggling. How brilliant, an interactive chew toy. The sensation was like having a small animal you'd caught shaking with fright in your mouth and struggling to get free. A rabbit, maybe. They certainly weren't getting this back. I fled.

With the bemused Owner standing at the gate I ran down the street with the two neighbours behind me. The old boy was shouting, 'Stop that dog!' and along the road people were coming to their fences to see what the commotion was about. I kept running in the hope of finding somewhere quiet where I could experiment with my new friend, who I'd already named 'Mr Wobbly' in my head. Behind me the neighbour was now screaming, 'Get that off him, it's mine, it's mine!' Then he stopped and changed it to, 'It's my wife's, it's my wife's.' She didn't seem to agree. Struggling to keep up she was shouting,

'It's not mine, it's not. I've never seen it before. Brian, leave it.'

The traffic at the end of the street gave me pause for thought. I didn't want to get hit by a car again. Instead, I crossed the street and ran down the other side, past people who were hanging over their fences and cheering me on. It was all too good to last. With a turn of speed I wouldn't have thought possible from him, the Owner finally caught up with me and forced my jaws open. My beloved chew toy dropped to the ground and the Owner picked it up gingerly, I guess because it was all covered in drool now. It was still throbbing and twisting though as he turned and held it out to the next-door neighbour, who had finally caught up with us.

'Errr, sorry about that. Here's your, ummm . . . thing,' he said.

For a moment I thought the neighbour would burst. He went a horrible purple colour. Then he reached out, took my chew toy and started beating my Owner with it. This seemed to excite it, as the buzzing got louder and the wriggling more pronounced. What a toy! I shall miss it.

I tried to remonstrate – he is my Owner after all – but I was held firmly by the collar and pulled across the street while he tried to protect his head from the blizzard of blows.

Along the street people were laughing and clapping. The neighbour's wife seemed to be having some kind of seizure on the front lawn. It seemed a lot of fuss over a chew toy.

When I'd finished the story, Ella looked up at the sound of her owner laughing hysterically from the other room while my human tried to quiet her with a 'Shhh, the walls are thin.' Then, after a while, he started laughing too.

Ella looked at me and shook her head slightly. 'Humans are crazy,' she said, which were my own thoughts exactly.

Wednesday, August 13

I finally got taken for a walk again. Although the Owner is still being stern with me, I can tell his heart's not in it any more. We stopped briefly outside the neighbour's house and he made a small move towards their gate, then seemed to think better of it and we walked on. I was mildly interested to see that their front garden has sprouted a pole with a 'For Sale' sign at the top. Now they know I'm after their cat they must be moving away for its safety.

I'm glad he's gotten over it as he bought an enormous steak for dinner and couldn't manage it all by himself. Luckily for him, my middle name is 'Fooddisposalunit.' It's German, from my mother's side of the family. She said that she had a bit of Alsatian in her.

Thursday, August 14

A council of war with Scottie this morning, who spelled out a strategic problem that we've avoided so far.

'O' course, ye ken that all this P.A.R.P. business is fine fer messin' wi' yon Razor's heid an' makin' a point, but even wi'oot a pack the territory still officially belongs tae him an' iviry dog in the park kens it. There'll be nae peace here until he's formally submitted.'

'Can't we just all ambush him at the same time?'

'Nay, 'tis not how it works, ye ken that already. It'll all come doon to dog on dog. A scrap that will define the fate o' all future generations tae come. The turnin' point for the whole o' canine history, ye might say. An epic battle o' tooth an' claw –'

'Yes, I get the idea, Scottie. Did you have any plans?'

'Aye, well, that Rudy looks right tasty, an' he's provin' himsel' a bonny dog.'

'But he has the killer instinct of an ant hill and he's already lost to Razor once, just like every other dog,' I sighed. 'I have been thinking of something, but I've not really worked it out yet.'

I told him.

'Aye,' he nodded like one of those odd dog things you sometimes see in the back of old cars. 'That'll be tricky to organise, but it could work right enough.'

Friday, August 15

Scottie's owner is having some success finding homes for the puppies. Constable is to be a stepfather after his owner found Scottie's old man sitting on a bench with the box of ankle-biters at his feet.

'Oooh, they're adorable,' she bellowed in a voice that the profoundly deaf could probably hear on the other side of town. 'What are they?' On being told the puppies lineage, she held one up and cooed, 'Ahhh, a Dalmaland Terrier, or maybe a Westation.' It's frightening to think that this headscarf-wearing freak is the biggest cannon in the P.A.R.P. arsenal.

'I must have one. Of course it's not a pedigree, like my little snookums Constable, but it will be excellent company for him.'

After looking closely at each puppy, like a used-car dealer at an auction, she finally picked a little male. 'I shall call him Prince Berkhard I of Dalmaland. Barkly for short.'

Poor little dog. It's bound to grow up with some sort of emotional disorder with a name like that and Constable for a role model.

Saturday, August 16

All has been quiet on the Eastern front for the past few days. Scottie is right, Rudy has been a Dogsend. I suppose he was closer to Razor than any other dog, and now he's free of the tyrant he is ever vigilant against him, spending most of the time patrolling the forest that separates the Eastern Park from the West. Always out of sight, but ready to bark a warning to the rest of us if any of Razor's pack dares try and cross the divide. Meanwhile, the pee offensive continues, but Scottie and I are racking our brains to plan the final downfall of the evil Razor.

Sunday, August 17

Ella is coming into season, but unfortunately her owner is more vigilant than Dottie's. For the next two or three weeks she's on a tight lead in the park for a quick bladder- and bowel-relieving walk only, during which I'm also confined to the lead like I'm some uncontrollable sex maniac. Having said that, the instinct does tend to take over. Denied Ella, and confined to a three-foot radius of operation, the Owner's leg is starting to look remarkably attractive again. I think it's the way his soft jogging pants cling sensuously to the flesh beneath. Yes, I'm going to have that leg before long. Ella will understand. It's not a betrayal if you're being driven insane with desire and you pleasure yourself with your owner's appendage. I'm sure that's in the rulebook somewhere.

Monday, August 18

I am banned from the bedroom again. He went out with Samantha and came back smelling all saucy. I could no longer restrain myself so tried to get it on with that hairy limb of his, but he wasn't having any of it. Eventually, I had to wait until he was asleep then let myself quietly into the bedroom. I must have been a bit rough because he woke up with my forelegs clasped around his waist just as I was reaching the moment of ultimate pleasure.

It was just a bit of fun, but he accused me of leg rape and said he felt soiled and dirty, which is just the kind of uptight attitude I should have expected. If he didn't want it why did he go to bed without a shower after stroking Ella? He's such a tease.

Tuesday, August 19

Ella's absence has left a hole in our security system. Vigilant though he is, Rudy cannot handle it alone, so the rest of the squad is rotating lookout duty. Today, Constable warned us of imminent air attack from a stray Frisbee, while Chu Chu had everyone running for cover after she was surprised by a squirrel. However, all seems quiet in the park at the moment. Razor has even stopped re-marking the West. In fact, it all seems a little too peaceful. Scottie is sure that 'The eye of Razor is upon us and dark clouds are massing in the East.' I just think his owner has been down the DVD rental shop again. Nevertheless, the calm is ominous. We've put the word out that the guard should be doubled. What we really need is another spy. Now that Barney's come over we have no idea what the enemy is up to.

Wednesday, August 20

A woeful day indeed, courtesy of Ruff 'n' Tumble Dog Walking

Services; chairperson and chief walker, the seemingly impossible-to-eradicate Molly.

I was patiently ignoring the Owner's attempts to make me 'come' as usual when an all-too-familiar voice called, 'You're doing that all wrong, you know.' And there she was, being towed across the park by a pack of eight dogs like an Inuit who'd forgotten to bring the sled. I was so stunned I just sat there with my mouth open until that little click behind my ear told me I'd been crept up on. He never misses a trick, the Owner.

He had a brief conversation with her, during which she told him all about this new plan to raise travelling money, but she couldn't stand still for long, being at the centre of a web of retractable leads whose occupants I was urging to run as fast as they could in the opposite direction at the top of my lungs.

It occurs to me that this could be an opportunity to revenge myself on her for all those little castration speeches she was so fond of.

Thursday, August 21

Another puppy has found a home. The particularly spotty little bitch whom Scottie had provisionally named 'Splotchy Morag' is now 'Allsort,' and a member of Liquorice's den. Liquorice and Allsort; it beggars belief.

Had some fun with Ruff 'n' Tumble Dog Walking Services by giving Molly one of my special unwelcome welcomes while she was particularly hard-pressed with her eight clients. As she tried to dislodge me a big black Lab got away and was immediately chased by the rest of her charges, 'charges' being exactly the right word on this occasion.

She was pulled across the park so fast that I'm surprised she didn't actually take off like a parascender. As she receded, the Owner called out jovially, 'Looks like you've got your hands full there, Moll.' Fortunately, her reply was lost in a sea of yaps and barks. I'm not an expert lip reader, but it looked like very unladylike language to me. Score one to Blake.

Friday, August 22

With no Ella to scoot with, our war on Razor at a standoff and the park all but empty, I was forced to play with the Owner today. He gets these urges sometimes, probably feeling guilty for the amount he neglects me. Usually I'm happy to ignore his stick-throwing and attempts to wrestle with me, but sheer boredom drove me to steal his new Frisbee and hide it today. I must say, watching him run 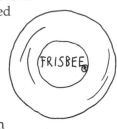 around trying to find it was more enjoyable than I thought it would be. After he'd finally retrieved it, he then threw it straight in the pond by accident. Much as I don't usually need any kind of excuse for a dip, today seemed like a good day to stay dry and look puzzled. At his urging to 'Go get it' I did test the water with a paw, but decided not to bother.

Eventually he had to strip off to his underwear and go get it himself. After which I decided that it might be a good time for a muddy swim after all. It's play like this that helps make the special bond between dog and owner.

Saturday, August 23

Another meeting with Molly today, and this time we were walking with Ella and Samantha. I don't think the females liked each other very much, as Molly insisted on cracking 'jokes' about when she and the Owner were an item, as if to remind all present that up until recently she had been sharing the den. It had the whiff of territorialism to me. Ella was equally unimpressed by Molly's comments about my behaviour.

Unfortunately, I was on the lead and wasn't able to avail myself of any mischief, but on the plus side five of the eight dogs that Molly was walking are un-neutered males and she was having serious difficulties keeping them under control with Ella present. A plan suggests itself.

Sunday, August 24

Another puppy down, this time to a first-time dog owner who happened to be walking past the box of cuties this afternoon. She's an older woman, a widow called Mrs Fortis who apparently wants a 'nice quiet companion' for her evenings at home. Oh boy, is she in for a shock, but if her idea of quiet companionship is constant yapping through *Antiques Roadshow* and cleaning puppy wee off the carpet, then she might be OK. Knowing Scottie's genes, it'll be huge holes all over her garden, having sex with her best tea cosy and demanding biscuits every two minutes.

This one is a perfect miniature version of Scottie, only with tiny little spots everywhere, and is now called Macintosh. Presumably the old lady likes her pets to be named after items of wet-weather clothing. Mind you, it's a slight improvement on Scottie's name for him – Acne.

Monday, August 25

Score two to Blake, and Ella. And this time I remain completely blameless, a Good Boy, even.

As I had guessed, Ella had taken an instant dislike to Molly and it didn't take much to draw her into my conspiracy. In fact, she was keen to take some sort of revenge on Samantha's behalf. Apparently, she'd been quite put out by Molly's constant references to the Owner as 'my ex.' Ella agreed that my plan was beautiful in its simplicity and when we saw Ruff 'n' Tumble Dog Walking Services heading towards us this morning – no doubt to make a nuisance of herself again – we sprang straight into action.

By the expedient of my launching a sexual attack at her owner's leg and making free with it (as an added bonus I also enjoyed this immensely), Ella's lead was dropped. Her owner needn't have protected herself, mine pulled me off almost immediately, but I guess it's instinct to push away a libidinous beast intent on having its way with your lower regions. I was swiftly brought back to heel, but too late, Ella was away, sprinting across the park to Molly and ignoring her owner's calls, just as I'd taught her.

As I noted a few days earlier, five of Molly's clients are un-neutered males, and they all acted accordingly as they sniffed Ella approaching, followed by a number of loose park dogs. (Including Scottie again. I have made a mental note to have a firm word with him.) As the poor CEO of Ruff 'n' Tumble Dog Walking Services fought to keep her dogs under control, Ella circled them again and again, and they all followed, entangling Molly in an ever-decreasing net of retractable lead. With this done, Ella shot off back toward her 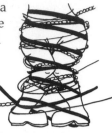 owner. As every dog sought to follow her (the two bitches and the eunuch had become caught up in the drama by now) Molly was pulled sharply off her feet and landed heavily, like a human cocoon.

Some of Molly's clients are big dogs and include a pair of huskies, but even so it's testament to the power of the bitch in season that they managed to drag their walker, screaming and struggling, across sixty yards of open field in their efforts to catch up with Ella. After a quick but rough-looking ride, Molly was deposited almost at Ella's owner's feet, among a baying pack of dogs. Among them was Scottie, who had decided that as his luck was obviously out with Ella he'd try it on with Molly's shoulder. Trussed like a Christmas turkey, she wasn't in any position to argue, save trying to bite at his legs.

Ella's owner looked down, smiled benignly in the midst of bedlam, and shouted, 'It's Polly, isn't it? Is everything all right, Polly?'

The Owner had turned away and his shoulders were shaking. For my part, I can see more clearly than ever why wolves mate for life. Ella is one in a million.

Tuesday, August 26

Samantha came over last night and put some clothes in a drawer in the bedroom. For the puppy's sake and for the love of Ella I just watched and let her get on with it without stealing so much as a thong. I should be given some sort of reward for my forbearance. As she unpacked I trailed around after her, catching whiffs of Ella and trying to keep my rampant lust under control. I failed, of course, and had to be beaten off the two humans' legs at least six times.

Wednesday, August 27

Uh oh. The first sign that we have been invaded. The sofa is now covered with throws and our homely old cushions that were crispy with old drool and flecked with tasty patches of spilled food have been replaced by new ones. Pretty soon it'll be frilly lampshades and constant cleaning. How can you call a den a home when everything stinks of chemicals?

Still, I have to say the new cushions are very comfy, and to do Samantha credit she was completely laid back about my reclining on them as soon as she'd finished.

The Owner looked at me suspiciously and asked, 'Should he be on there? He's going to make it all dirty again.'

Samantha just shrugged and said, 'It's all washable and I got dark colours on purpose. Just because I'm moving in, it shouldn't mean Blake has to suffer.'

A thoroughly commendable attitude, which is totally unexpected in a human. Of course, she wasn't so happy when I started humping the cushions, though calling me a pervert was a little harsh I thought. It's not as though I've got a soft-furnishing fetish, but they've made their views on leg-humping very clear and if Samantha is going to continue wafting Ella's scent around the den then they have to expect some consequences.

Thursday, August 28

Just as I predicted, Samantha spent the entire day cleaning the den. Where there were patches of fragrant old dirt behind the cooker, all is sparkling. The back of the sofa, once a haven for hiding the evidence of my chewing, and home to my impressive collection of shed hair, is now bereft of its homely lived-in charm and stinks of some vile powder she sprinkled all over the carpet.

It's true the Owner tried to stop her, but in his usual ineffective style. 'You don't need to do all this you know, Sam,' were his exact words. If he was serious about being an alpha one day he should have bitten off her mop-wielding hand.

'It's OK, it needs doing and I've got the week off. Besides, I'm moving into a bachelor's den. Even in my most wildly optimistic flights of fancy, I never imagined it would be anything other than a breeding ground for disease.'

'I think you'll find Blake and I are meticulous about our personal hygiene.'

'I can see that Blake takes personal grooming seriously by the way he spends most of the day licking his balls, but how do you explain this?'

Samantha held up the remains of Mr Femur, who I'd pushed under the sofa weeks ago and who appeared to have gone a bit nasty since then.

'Ah, that would be the thighbone of the last woman who attempted to clean behind the sofa. I always wondered what happened to her.'

Friday, August 29

We saw Molly in the park again today, but she was keeping her distance. Samantha took a break from shooing off all the dogs who were following us to wave at her across the meadow, but she appeared not to notice and scuttled off in the opposite direction. Hopefully, she's learned her lesson and won't be bothering us again. If she does, I have another little trick up my sleeve.

Saturday, August 30

I have come up with a plan for Razor's downfall. It's going to be a tricky one to pull off as it involves humans, well, one human to be exact – Constable's continent-sized owner. As she is the only creature in the park of whom Razor seems to be wary, we have decided that we must pit the two beasts against each other in a final showdown. Although neither of us condone organised dog-fighting, in this instance we're going to make an exception, and personally I shall enjoy the sight of the massive woman tearing Razor apart. The beauty of the plan is that involving a human in a dog territory dispute has never been done before; it's a move that Razor will never expect. Some might question its legality, but there's no denying that she is a part of our 'pack' and as such is within her rights to challenge any alpha male for supremacy, even if she's not aware that she's doing it.

It will be quite odd having a human female as the technical Pack Leader of the park, but as she's so far not shown much interest in marking territory or becoming involved in canine politics, her position will be almost entirely ceremonial, though if she were to bring down the occasional moose with her bare teeth it would really help cement her position.

Sunday, August 31

Met up with Scottie in the wasteland this evening, and we racked our brains for some foolproof way of bringing together Constable's owner and Razor. It will need to be foolproof, because inevitably Constable will have to be involved. As she fights like a lion to protect the idiot dog, he'll have to be used as bait in some way, but Razor is not stupid and won't touch the shaggy celebrity unless he knows he's safe from retaliation. I'm reminded of the battle tactics of Alexander the Great, who often put his infantry on the field while holding his cavalry hidden in reserve, to be unleashed upon his enemy when they were least expecting it. There are clear parallels between the destructive potential of the ancient Macedonian mounted forces and Constable's avalanche of an owner.

It's a conundrum, but we have time to solve it. Scottie and I agree that P.A.R.P. should concentrate on bringing every member of Razor's pack over before delivering the decisive knockout blow. It will complete his humiliation if he is alone at his downfall.

SEPTEMBER

Monday, September 1

The security around the plan will be as tight as possible, strictly a need-to-know basis. Unfortunately, Constable is the only dog who needs to know. As we'll be using him to lure Razor and pushing his owner into the ring it's only fair. He didn't hesitate to offer his services, even though it's certainly above and beyond the call of duty. It took him a while to get the hang of the idea though.

'So, you want my mistress to fight with Razor,' he pronounced after about half an hour's painful explaining.

'Yes, Constable. It will be a titanic battle.'

'Oh, on big ships?'

'No, Constable. With tooth and claw.'

'But the mistress hasn't got any claws. It's all the gardening she does. And her teeth sometimes come out when she chews. Like, it wouldn't be good if they fell out while she had Razor locked in her jaws.'

'No, Constable. But she'll probably do enough damage with her umbrella and boots once we've got her blood up, which – if you remember – is where you come in.'

'Right, so after the mistress has fought Razor, then it's my turn?'

'No, Constable. You let him see you alone and undefended. He won't be able to stop himself chasing you. You then bark as loudly as you can to attract your owner's attention. When she sees Razor about to maul you, her maternal instincts will kick in and she will rush forward in your defence.'

'But what if he kills me first? He doesn't like me at all, you know.'

'As we mentioned previously, a back-up team including me, Rudy and Liquorice will be hiding close by. If it looks as though he might hurt you, we'll all rush in and start biting chunks out of him.'

'And afterwards, my mistress will be like the queen of the park?'

'Yes, Constable.'

'Does that mean I'll be a prince?'

'If that's what you want, then everyone will call you Prince Constable.'

'Wow, OK then.'

'Tell me, Prince Constable, why is it that Razor detests you so much?'

Before we found out his mistress called him and he loped off to her side.

Tuesday, September 2

Scottie's owner hasn't had much luck finding homes for the last of the puppies. There are now four left, including the two that will be staying with Scottie and the one that is reserved for our den. I hope it doesn't take too long for the little mite to find someone to take her in. We see the others around the park a lot now, taking their first steps at the sides of their respective owners. Scottie is as proud as a dog with six bowls and even Dottie comes over for a sniff whenever she can, though her owner always calls her away if he sees her.

I'm pleased for Scottie and glad that the pups weren't mine, but the sight of them makes me wish that Ella and I were having some too. Her season is nearly over now and she's still being scrupulously kept away from any possibility of mating.

Wednesday, September 3

Oops, I've upset the next-door man again. The Owner was out all day and left me chained in the back yard, due to a slight misunderstanding over a book he'd just left lying on the coffee table as if it were a chew toy. Obviously, just because he was across town having lunch in a restaurant with Samantha, didn't stop me howling and barking to attract his attention. The howl of a coyote can carry for many miles in the wilderness, and I was stretching myself to full capacity in order to compensate for the noise pollution in this town.

Talking of noise pollution, I was halfway through a particularly emotive howl, when I heard the neighbour saying, 'And this is my pride and joy, the garden . . . That's just the dog next door, he's a lovely animal and usually as quiet as a mouse.' I could actually hear his clenched teeth.

'Anyway, why don't you have another look upstairs. Maureen, would you show Mr and Mrs Brown?'

Two seconds later his head had popped up over the fence. 'Shut up, shut up, shut up you filthy brute. If you don't ****ing shut up, I'll ****ing climb over this ****ing fence and rip your ****ing larynx out. And then I'll **** in the ****ing hole.'

Then there was the sound of a throat clearing behind him and another male voice said, 'Excuse me, I just came back to ask about the guttering.'

Thursday, September 4

The Owner didn't get back until late, but the neighbour was on our doorstep first thing this morning, shouting about 'losing a sale' and threatening me again. The Owner was quite chilly with him from the start; he's probably still upset about having to show submission in the Battle of the Chew Toy.

'Mr Turvey, I understand that you have cause to dislike Blake, but please remember that I have done everything in my power to make amends for the damage he's caused. I even offered to buy your wife a replacement, err, thingy.'

'And I've already told you, that would be highly inappropriate,' the neighbour shouted.

'One man's inappropriate is another man's gesture of reconciliation,' the Owner shrugged. 'The point is that Blake is a dog, although he's a spirited animal he doesn't understand that what he's doing is wrong, and he doesn't do it out of spite, so why don't you leave him alone?'

'I'll leave him alone when I've squeezed the last breath out of the disgusting beast.'

'Touch my dog, Mr Turvey, and I'll have the police on you so fast it will make your head spin.'

'You wouldn't dare.'

'Try me. And I'll also tell them that you attacked me in broad daylight with a thingy. I have plenty of witnesses, and they put people in the psychiatric wing for that kind of behaviour.'

The neighbour went purple and started spluttering, but my Owner slammed the door in his face. This evening he was treated to the Eyes of Complete Devotion, which are not seen in the den on a regular basis, I can tell you. Then I fell asleep at his feet. Every so often he deserves a bit of attention.

Friday, September 5

Denny the Flea became the newest member of P.A.R.P. today. We are now eight, or nine if you count our secret weapon. As he sat and scratched his ear, I asked him what had taken him so long.

'Would have come over ages ago,' he replied, 'but thought you could use a dog on the scene. Information and suchlike.'

This showed remarkable initiative for the old parasite magnet. 'Well, do you have anything?'

'Nah, I just got tired of Razor taking nips out of me every day. He's got something planned, but he's not telling anyone and he's getting madder than a cat with a lemon up its bum.' Denny paused for a moment. 'Thinking about it though, he might have a couple of spies running around.'

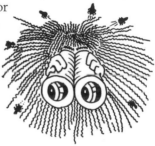

'What makes you think that? We've been patrolling the border regularly.'

'Yeah, but there's a couple of little dogs what get better treatment than the rest of us, and we don't see them often.'

This is bad news. We have been becoming lax over the last few weeks. It's time we stepped up the campaign before Razor has a chance to think up a nasty surprise for us.

Saturday, September 6

Well, Ella's season is well and truly over. Samantha's given her a bath to get rid of any lingering smell and she's allowed off the lead again. Nevertheless there was a tiny hint of it left and we were straight off to do what we'd both been longing to for the past couple of weeks. Afterwards we used the Scooting Place as Dog intended. It was good to have her back.

Now that Ella doesn't need to be kept away from me, they are moving in properly. There are loads of new and exciting things to chew spread all over the den, and once I'm off best behaviour I've already earmarked a few items that need my urgent attention. Ella's bed has been put next to mine in the kitchen.

Sunday, September 7

Like the Owner, Samantha works at home, too. After spending the day moving stuff around to try and make some more space with all her female clutter now squeezed into the office, Samantha stood back and said, 'It'll have to do for now, but I can't work sitting in your lap for ever. If this is going to be a long-term arrangement, then we're going to have to think about finding somewhere more spacious before too long.'

I knew it. Female humans are nothing but trouble. She's been here one day and already she wants to drag me away to Dog knows where, leaving Scottie and all my other friends behind and P.A.R.P. at the mercy of Razor.

I don't know why she doesn't use my kennel, I've hardly been out there at all recently and all that space is just going begging.

Monday, September 8

The owners have decided to go ahead with the adoption! We will be the adopted family of the last remaining male, a scrappy little fellow with one big spot over his left eye. He's going to be called Coleridge, which is a fine name of which I thoroughly approve. Scottie will be unhappy about the change though, as he had named the fluffball after his grandfather – Sporran. Of course, it'll make the den more crowded, but at least us dogs will now have the weight of numbers. In any truly democratic system, the den should now be run solely by and for the benefit of us dogs and the humans should be forced to service us.* As Lenin once said, 'A democracy is a state which recognises the subjecting of the minority to the majority.'

In preparation for the little fellow's arrival, the Owner's been reading again. Tonight he brought home a rag that had been rubbed all over Coleridge, to get me used to the smell around the den. I don't think my chewing it into tiny shreds went down too well.

* On reflection this is already pretty much how it works around here.

Tuesday, September 9

Coleridge came home with us today and made himself at home straight away by peeing on the entrance hall rug, leaving a little present under the coffee table and chewing the Owner's wallet. If I'd have done all that it would be six months without parole instead of a gentle 'naughty boy' and a bowl of extremely nice-smelling puppy food.

Ella and I were kept away at first, so that we got used to him running around, but the owners needn't have bothered; all we wanted to do was snuffle the little guy and watch him play. They must have been feeling expansive after becoming new owners again, because we both got some prime beef for dinner tonight.

Wednesday, September 10

It was a novel experience walking to the park as a family, but I was very proud of my new stepson, who shows a natural gift for disobedience already. I've always thought that upbringing is more important than genetic inheritance in the old nature/nurture argument.

It was a beautiful morning and the owners bought coffee and croissants. While they sat on the grass, Ella and I played with Coleridge, who isn't allowed off the retractable lead yet. Coleridge managed to steal three pastries, one right out of Samantha's hand while she was eating it, which is a brilliant tactic that had never even occurred to me. Perhaps I can get the food off the Owner's plate while he's actually sitting at the table. It will take practice, but it's worth patience to master a skill like that.

Thursday, September 11

This evening, the two humans started talking some more about moving, probably because all five of us were trying to find room on the same sofa, with Coleridge jumping over us trying to find a comfortable spot.

Samantha said that we badly needed more space, and a garden for the dogs, which showed that she was thinking of the right angles even if moving would mean leaving my precious den. The Owner frowned for a moment and countered that he liked the area and didn't want to leave. After a few moments of silence, he looked up, nodded at the wall and said, 'Of course, there's a very simple solution to the problem staring at us.'

Samantha smiled. 'Great idea, and with the added benefit of the look on their faces when you turn up on the doorstep. Let's go have a look at it and take Blake with us, too. Maybe he can parade around with some more evidence of their very active sex life.'

The Owner looked glum. 'Don't even joke about it. Perhaps it would be better if you went on your own.'

'Don't be such a coward, they'll have to find out eventually.'

Friday, September 12

Razor has struck, and showed his true colours today. No one would have believed that *any* dog, no matter how insane, could attack a defenceless puppy, but it seems that no crime is beneath him.

The stupid old woman, Mrs Fortis, hadn't bothered to learn the basics about dog care and just let Mackintosh wander free while she went to have a cup of tea. Full of the spirit of adventure, the pup ran straight through into the woods and into the jaws of Razor.

With his hostage clamped in that drooling vice, Razor immediately strolled triumphantly Westward. Rudy could do nothing but growl and bark a warning. I came running with Ella at my side and tried to reason with the pink-eyed pit bull, but as we watched, horrified, he just bit down carefully until flecks of blood started appearing on Mackintosh's coat. The poor puppy cried out, but it did him no good at all. I made to attack, but Razor snarled, baring his teeth, and increased the pressure. Thankfully Scottie wasn't there, as nothing would have stopped him going for Razor's throat.

Eventually, Razor spat Mackintosh to the floor, making sure he stayed within biting distance. Then he issued his demands: P.A.R.P. is to be disbanded and all members are to swear eternal submission. Anyone connected with the organisation must report to the woods at an arranged time for a private 're-education session'. I am first, Scottie second. If we do not comply quickly, the next puppy that Razor sees will die.

Saturday, September 13

Ella and I gave Scottie the news as gently as we could on the wasteland last night. As expected he took it badly. If the gate hadn't been closed I think he would have run all the way to Razor's den and chewed his way in through the door, or – more likely – broken his remaining teeth on it. Instead he vowed instant bloody revenge at the earliest opportunity. Luckily, the humans were deep in conversation, giving me time to talk some sense into my loyal lieutenant.

'Scottie, face the facts, even if you were in your prime Razor would tear you into a dozen pieces in five seconds. He's hoping you'll react like this, so he can sit happily over your body with his smug bastard of an owner saying you attacked first. We have to think, not fight.'

'Aye, and whut do you suggest then, ye grate puddin'? Wait until he's eaten all ma bairns and then get him when he's too full tae move?'

I have to admit that for the time being I was stumped. 'We may have to submit, for the puppies' sake.'

'Nae, Ah'll nivir surrender to that creature. Ah'd sooner eat the puppies mahsel'. Doomed, we're all doomed . . .'

Eventually, I managed to extract a promise that he wouldn't attack Razor before telling me. At least I'll be able to go with him if it comes to it.

Sunday, September 14

No sign of Scottie in the park this morning, but we put the word about that any P.A.R.P. member was to watch him carefully if he arrived during their watch and create a canine shield along the length of the woods if he made any move towards sneaking through. An emergency meeting by the dog toilet has been called for tomorrow. If I cannot think of anything by then, P.A.R.P. surrenders.

Monday, September 15

Scottie and I reconvened on the wasteland last night. He is calmer, but I could smell his rage all the same. Yesterday morning his owner went to visit Mrs Fortis, who was distraught over Mackintosh. The little fellow is doing fine, the wounds are all superficial.

'If ye talk tae me aboot surrender, ah shall bite yer cowardly balls off, ye dinnae deserve thum,' was the first thing he said.

'You're right,' I said. 'Not about my balls, but I agree if we give up now, it'll never end and Razor'll get the puppies eventually anyway.'

'Whut are ye thinking?'

'We've got about two or three months while the pups are still on the lead. Mrs Fortis probably won't let Mackintosh out of her sight ever again. We'll assign each one a bodyguard just in case and double the patrols again. If a crisp packet blows through those trees we'll know about it. It's not much of a plan, but it'll buy us some time.'

'Agreed on both counts.'

I just hope I manage to get my teeth into Razor before the war is over.

Tuesday, September 16

Two dogs who formerly had no allegiance or territory have asked to be admitted to P.A.R.P. Word of Mackintosh's plight has become a rallying call for every dog in the park. They are a poodle called Fabienne and an old Labrador/spaniel cross named Chutney. They will make useful lookouts.

Every member of P.A.R.P. has been safely escorted through enemy territory to the north gate and back. It's a lake of urine over there. A small human tried to sail a boat across it before his mother pulled him away, and a number of humans are going home with dripping shoes, spreading P.A.R.P.'s message of defiance far and wide across town.

Wednesday, September 17

Scottie and I were on puppy watch today. All the humans are still talking about the attack and though no one saw anything, they all strongly suspect Razor and are consoling Mrs Fortis. Even Molly brought a book on looking after puppies to the park. There are mutterings that 'someone should do something about that damn pit bull,' and Constable's owner is openly telling everyone that she'll tear Razor limb from limb if she sees him anywhere near Constable or Barkly. I can't speak for Razor, but if she had me in her sights I'd be slinking out of town under cover of darkness, probably wearing a false nose and moustache.

Samantha and the Owner are packing stuff again. Surely they can't be planning another holiday? The last thing P.A.R.P. needs right now is Ella and I doing another stretch in Stalag Woof.

Thursday, September 18

Now Dottie is seriously wounded. Barney was on patrol last night and says that she saw Razor and was across the park like a snarling bullet. She's no fighter, but still managed to draw blood before she was badly mauled. Once again, his owner is crowing that Razor cannot be held to blame if other dogs attack him. As far as we can tell the humans are just taking it as more evidence of Razor being responsible for Mackintosh's wounds.

Who could have guessed that she would do something like that? I hope that she'll pull through, poor bitch. I haven't had any time for her since her last season, but it looks as though I misjudged her. She is usually so haughty that I couldn't imagine her caring about the puppies, but I guess all mothers in the animal world will fight to save their offspring. It must be awful for her seeing them playing across the park every day and not being allowed to go and sniff them.

Friday, September 19

The Owner started loading the car up with cases last night. It was lucky that I warned P.A.R.P. that Ella and I might be doing stir again. This morning, after a quick run to the wasteland and back for our morning ablutions, we were all put in the car. At least, Ella jumped gracefully in, Coleridge was given a helping hand, and I was dragged barking and growling and held down while the door was slammed. It's a terrible time to be leaving the battlefield, especially to go back to that prison camp.

After an hour and still no sign of the guard towers and barbed wire I started to relax; so, too, did Coleridge's bowels. It was the first of many stops.

Four hours in a small car filled with two humans, three dogs and luggage is a very long time. Especially when the smallest of those dogs is sick twice,* incontinent and yaps constantly with excitement. Even with my head out the window it was actually a relief when the Owner set the Bee Gees to full volume.

We are staying in a small house close to a beach with rocks and pools. Best of all, the house has a proper garden, so we can run in and out all day carrying sticks or whatever else takes our fancy. Freshly dug vegetables for example, or a dead bird I found under a bush.

* I'm not complaining, this provided me with a couple of quite delicious snacks of puppy food that were already semi-digested, saving my stomach a lot of hard work. From the comments and looks I got I probably should have saved some for everyone else.

Saturday, September 20

All day on the beach today. This late in the season, it was almost empty and Coleridge was allowed off the lead for a while and Ella and I gave him his first swimming lesson in a rock pool. Afterwards he went and shook himself all over the Owner, who was lying on a towel. Later, he discovered crabs and has learned that they are More Trouble Than They Are Worth.

Due to her thick and lovely coat Ella gets quite hot in the sun, so we spent the rest of the day running in and out of the ocean. My Owner put sunglasses on me and Ella said I looked like Jackie Onassis. I got my revenge by stealing his Frisbee and giving it to Coleridge, who mangled it. He must get that from Scottie.

When the sun went down, the owners lit a barbecue and cooked enough food for all of us, then Ella and I wandered off to find a quiet spot and caught up with each other's backsides.

Sunday, September 21

First Ella, then I, climbed up on the humans' bed last night. Little Coleridge couldn't quite make it, and whined until the Owner reached down and gave him a helping hand. It was a scene of perfect family bliss until the humans realised that sharing their bed with three dogs – one of whom is intent on chewing their toes – isn't very sensible. Then Coleridge peed everywhere again. Then he had another dump, this time on the Owner's pillow. What a great little puppy he is.

I nearly burst with pride this morning when the humans stomped around the kitchen cursing and asking each other whose idea it was to get a puppy. I'm no anthropologist, but this kind of human behaviour is very familiar to me and I reassured Coleridge that it is just their way of showing us appreciation for the non-dull moments we provide. Then I pointed out a pair of new sandals to him that smelled suspiciously like hand-stitched Italian leather. Well, it's a family tradition.

After more cursing we walked to the beach with the Owner's sandal flapping off his foot most amusingly. A swim seemed to calm him down though and he started some playful wresting with Samantha, during which their clothes fell off. Me, Ella and Coleridge joined in the fight, but they seemed to lose all their enthusiasm when we did.

Monday, September 22

It was a long drive home last night, but Coleridge fell asleep and Samantha refused to listen to the Bee Gees again, so it seemed to pass a lot more quickly. Halfway home I realised I hadn't brought anything for Scottie. He would have liked one of those ice-cream wrappers that were just lying around a dustbin for anyone to pick up.

During our absence five more of Razor's pack defected to P.A.R.P. – it seems that their leader's attack on Mackintosh was more than they could stomach. Even Claude, who I thought was a lost cause, has seen the light in the darkness that is the Park Animals Resistance Party.

Razor's pack now numbers just four dogs, three of whom are apparently so terrified of him that they pee whenever he comes into the park. The other is an antisocial Jack Russell called Croxley whose owner treats him badly. There is hardly a dog in the park who is not a member of P.A.R.P. It is just as Scottie and I planned.

Tuesday, September 23

According to Claude, Razor is frothing with rage and swearing that he will pick P.A.R.P. off one by one. As a military strategy it has the subtlety and complexity of a dog biscuit. Nevertheless, we have doubled the guard on the puppies.

Apparently, he has also taken to barking uncontrollably at the slightest noise and attacking anything with the scent of P.A.R.P. Claude thinks he's becoming unhinged.

Wednesday, September 24

The extra muscle is making it much easier to guard the puppies and the more dogs we have the more sophisticated is our early-warning system. Accordingly, it has been decided that P.A.R.P. will no longer slink in the shadows. We now enter Phase Three, all-out psychological warfare. Any dog quicker than Razor and Croxley will from now on harass the enemy on their own territory, showering them with P.A.R.P. propaganda. Our urine will flow freely across all four corners of the park.

Thursday, September 25

The new phase commenced today. Myself, Claude, Liquorice and a greyhound/whippet cross (a 'grippet' or 'whiphound' as he likes to call himself) known as Floyd stormed through the woods in perfect formation and out into the meadow beyond. Razor's last stronghold. The four of us then began an elegant series of manoeuvres, weaving around the short-legged enemy and barking, 'Down with the puppy killer,' 'P.A.R.P. for peace' and 'Disposable Razor' while urging his last pack members to join us. The pit bull was almost foaming at the mouth, but we easily outdistanced him and his cronies on their stubby little legs.

Finally he half-barked, half-whined, 'You can't run forever, and you can't watch those puppies all the time.'

I am going to enjoy turning Constable's owner loose on him. I only wish I had one of those telephones with the camera inside.

Friday, September 26

I realised today that it has been a while since I chewed anything or went through the garbage. Well, not with real passion anyway. It's like I'm just going through the motions for the sake of appearances. For a second I panicked. Does this mean I'm becoming a Good Boy? A run through my mental checklist put my mind at rest though. I might muster a 'sit' now and then, but it's evens at best unless there's food involved. 'Down' is 3–1 against, and the odds on my obeying the command 'come' still wouldn't attract the most optimistic gambler. Plus, I'm still giving the postman his daily dose of fear with all the verve and vigour of old and can still be counted on to snatch any food that's left within reach. Obviously, the next-door neighbour's psychopathic hatred of me is a big stud on my collar. Yes, I've still got what it takes.

Feeling slightly better, I noticed there were three people on the TV who were watching a succession of humans howl. Frankly, even Denny could do better than most of them, but that didn't stop me joining in, and Ella soon started with a few verses of 'Doghouse Blues,' too. During the show, two cushions, a slipper, one of Coleridge's chew toys and the remote were thrown at us. Eventually we were banished to the kitchen. I prepared myself to sleep with a warm glow of satisfaction in a job badly done.

Saturday, September 27

Looking torn and sore, Dottie returned to the park today. Ella, Scottie and I trotted over to see how she was. Motherhood seems to have taken the edge off her haughtiness a little. Although she looked sad, she was even affectionate with Scottie, bumping him with her nose and calling him a 'cheeky old dog.'

For once her owner didn't shoo us away, just stood talking to Scottie's human while we told Dottie that Mackintosh

was fine, all the other puppies were thriving and that each one had two dogs and a human guarding it at all times.

We hadn't been listening to the humans, but suddenly Dottie's owner leaned over and picked the last puppy that needed a home out of the box. Holding it to his chest he twitched Dottie's lead gently and said, 'Come on, Dot, let's go.' As she turned obediently, she looked nothing like the cold and aloof pedigree Dalmatian of a few months ago.

Sunday, September 28

Although raids on Razor's territory continue on a daily basis, it is proving difficult to dislodge the last members of Razor's pack. Despite our security measures and P.A.R.P.'s parkwide supremacy, every dog in the park is quivering with nervous tension and are sure that Razor will try something soon. Although he's cracking up, he still won't come near a human and we haven't come close to bringing him near Constable's owner. Just in case we cannot engineer a meeting between them, Rudy, Claude and myself are all in training. One of us may have to take Razor on. Scottie insists on joining us and has also taken up yoga to 'increase mah flexibility when I tak' on that gormin' brute.' He's particularly keen on the 'Down Dog' position and can often be found doing 'Salutations to the Lamppost.'

The Owner and Samantha are going to look at the house next door tomorrow. The plan is to knock some of the walls down and make one big den with a garden for us dogs. He did insist that the appointment was made in her name though.

Monday, September 29

It was a complete surprise to the neighbour when the Owner turned up on his doorstep with his prospective buyer today. Ella and I were listening carefully while Coleridge quietly chewed the TV remote, and even through the wall I could tell he had gone purple again.

'You! How dare you come round here. You know perfectly well the only reason we're moving is because you and your dog have disgraced –'

'Now, Brian, calm down,' his wife interjected, though her voice was also tense with disapproval.

Then my Owner's voice. 'This is uncomfortable for all of us, but it's purely a business transaction so let's try and be civil. If we like the house as much as we think we may then we can offer full asking price in view of the part that Blake might have played in your decision to leave the neighbourhood.'

'That damn animal needs putting out of everyone's misery.'

'However, every time you make a comment like that one our offer will be reduced by a thousand. We have the money ready, so you could be out quickly, and we won't even ask you to fix the guttering.'

'I'd rather choke myself than have that ****ing dog running around my lovely garden.'

'That's two thousand. And if that's your final word then good luck getting a better price.'

'Brian, come here, would you,' his wife cut in sharply. There was a muffled conversation, then the neighbour spoke again, but more politely.

'I've just remembered, I have an urgent appointment, Maureen will be happy to show you round.' Then the door slammed.

Mrs Next Door must be a much more adept salesperson than her husband because our owners finally agreed on the full asking price before he returned.

We're going to have a garden, with a swimming pool and plants to dig up. It'll be like an adventure playground for Coleridge.

Tuesday, September 30

We met Dottie and her puppy while out walking today. For once her owner didn't shoo us away, but let us have a sniff of the pup. I instinctively went to have a sniff of Dottie's bum, just out of habit, but pulled away when both Ella and Dottie's owner growled simultaneously.

Dottie hadn't even noticed, she was so caught up with her new addition. 'We're calling her Spotty,' she told Ella proudly. 'It's a mix of Scottie and Dottie, just like she is. And because she has spots, of course.'

'I see,' said Ella. 'That's, umm, very clever. Such an unusual name, too. But I thought your owner didn't like mixed-breeds?'

'Well, after I attacked Razor, he could see how much I was missing my pups, and he adores me. Once he'd calmed down, I think he was quite taken with them. Spotty spends every night sitting in his lap now. It's all I can do to get a scratch behind the ears. It helps that Scottie is a pedigree West Highland terrier, of course,' Dottie smiled.

'Is he?'

'Yes, didn't he tell you?'

'Of course,' I lied. 'Remind me what his full name is again.'

'Laird Scotland McIvor of Strathpeffer.'

'Ah, yes, of course.' I grinned. 'A fine name for a fine pedigree dog.'

OCTOBER

Wednesday, October 1

We met Scottie in the wasteland this evening, but it doesn't seem kind to laugh about his preposterous name. Not now anyway. It's something to be saved up for a special occasion.

Thursday, October 2

I suppose Coleridge has the whole cute and fluffy thing working for him, but he seems to be getting a lot of attention from the Owner that should rightfully be mine. Quite often I've found that I've had to squeeze myself between them, moaning for even a scratch behind the ears, while Coleridge spends half the day on his back having his tummy tickled. When you find just the right spot on his ribcage, one of his back legs starts going like the clappers. It's quite funny the first time you see it, but gets boring after a while, though the humans are at it all the time. It doesn't take much to amuse their tiny primate minds.

Friday, October 3

A spot for the final battle between the forces of good and pit bull has been selected. It is a patch of clear land on the shore of the pond, close to the woodlands. We have been observing Constable's owner, and she makes a slow but routine circuit of the Western Park as regularly as a well-tuned digestive system, always along the same path that takes her close by. The path itself is shielded from view by a small hill, so Razor will have no idea of her proximity. In future times the area will probably become known as Razor's Folly, Pit Bull's End, or something like that.

Saturday, October 4

Scottie, Ella, Constable and I are considering the best way to lure Razor into our trap, and have decided to recreate the conditions as exactly as possible in order to spot any problems that might occur. All professional modern armies play war games to simulate real-time battle experience. We also need to test the reaction time of Constable's owner so that we can synchronise our efforts and give Razor the smallest possible window of opportunity to savage the sheepdog. Scottie will take the part of Razor, Ella will be me concealed in the undergrowth, and Constable will have to be himself, though I wish we could substitute some dog who might make a better job of it. Needs must when there's a pit bull cocking his leg on your lamppost.

Sunday, October 5

Having made sure that Razor was absent and his pack kept busy by a P.A.R.P. propaganda raid, we began our dummy run of Operation Cutthroat.*

Shrouded in utmost secrecy, Ella took cover under a convenient bush, Constable disappeared into the woods to practise baiting and Scottie followed him. From the small growls and snarls that escaped him, I guess he was trying to enter the mindset of a psychopath. When Constable's owner was approximately three minutes from the battle site, I gave the signal and then trotted off to meet Razor's nemesis. I was greeted with a pat, and noticed with satisfaction that Barney and Claude were following at a discreet distance, keeping an eye on Barkly. In the distance I could hear Constable barking, 'Come and get a bite of best-of-breed then, loser.'

As far as baiting goes it was lame, and I made a mental note to work on this with Constable later. The important thing was that the two of them were now crashing through the woods, and Constable was barking in terror and panic. I was surprised at how convincing he was, but then he is the veteran of a series of paint adverts and was once 'Dog Being Trained' in a children's TV show. I suppose he's been to some special acting classes where all the dogs have to wear legwarmers and ripped pullovers or something.

It did the trick. Constable's owner immediately stiffened and broke into a trot towards the sound, but then Scottie started barking and I heard her sigh with relief.

'It's all right Barkly, it sounds like Constable's playing with your peculiar dad.'

Over the hill I could hear, 'Och, that's not bad acting, mind. Did I really hurt ye?'

To which Constable replied in a less than pained voice, 'No, not at all, you were great actually. It's all about identifying with the character and staying with it. You're a natural.'

'Och, well, I dinnae ken aboot that.'

As we crested the small hill, the two of them trotted up, still congratulating themselves on their performances, and Ella squeezed slowly out from under the bush, complaining about twigs getting caught in her coat. It must have been the most pathetic battle-scene simulation ever.

* As in 'cutthroat razor.' Another fine operation name that sailed so far over every dog's head that it may have actually achieved orbit.

Monday, October 6

It wasn't safe to have another trial today as Razor was in the park and dribbling mad, sniffing about like a bloodhound and zigzagging crazily around the park, trying to close in on any member of P.A.R.P. As usual he found nothing but dogs walking obediently close to their owners, distant rustles in the trees and the longer-limbed dogs always on the other side of the park. Eventually, he savaged someone's kite, presumably just to keep his paw in. There was an interesting scene with his owner who eventually had to get his wallet out.

Tuesday, October 7

Constable and Scottie seemed to get the hang of it today, with some especially fine work from the sheepdog. Who would have thought that beneath his dimness was such a talented thespian? His barks of anguish were so convincing that I was afraid that Razor had actually caught him for real, and his owner moved with impressive speed. We'd still misjudged though; by the time she arrived at the scene, Scottie's jaws were tangled into the fur at Constable's throat and, though he hadn't got hold of any actual flesh, was swinging around like a circus act with Ella trying to talk him down. Once he'd been pried gently free, he explained that Constable had been giving him lessons in 'Method' acting and he got locked into character.

If it had been for real, Razor would have torn his throat out. Hopefully one or two more dry runs will resolve these teething problems, if we're all to survive the real thing.

Wednesday, October 8

I know he's just a puppy, but my adopted son needs to be taught some manners. Not only has he almost completely usurped me when the affection is being handed round, but he's started sleeping in my bed when he has a totally adequate cardboard box of his own. Today, he chewed up a book on puppy training and left it there. I got the blame while he sat looking sweet and innocent on his pee-drenched newspaper.

Plus he keeps helping himself to my food. If I go near his I get A Shaking. Not sure why he'd want it, he gets plenty of that delicious-smelling puppy stuff while I'm currently on Super Budget brand, which has all the nutrition of the Yellow Pages and tastes suspiciously of rat.

Thursday, October 9

In time-honoured style, I finally wended my way back to the Owner this morning, taking time to sniff the daisies as I went (you never know who might have peed on them or if a cat has passed recently – it's all part of being alert), and found him deep in conversation with Ruff 'n' Tumble Dog Walking Services. After all I've done to neutralise her on his behalf. His gratitude should be overwhelming, but I don't think I've been whelmed at all, not even enough to be underwhelmed.

To cap it all she was giving him advice about making me come, with a little smile on her face that looked like she knew he'd come crawling back eventually. Huh, he doesn't stand a cat's chance in a pit of starving Rottweilers. If only he'd stop these ridiculous attempts to bend me to his will; it's so undignified.

Unfortunately, she seems to have learned her lesson and had only four dogs on retractable leads, none of whom looked particularly husky-like, so I couldn't even make good my plan to have her dragged into the pond. Closer inspection, however, revealed that one of them was my old friend Snowy from obedience classes. When he saw me approaching he tried to climb up Molly's leg and then peed on her open-toed sandal, which was something. The excitement of seeing me again must have been too much.

Friday, October 10

Thanks to Molly I had to endure a lengthy training session in the park. With Ella scampering off to help with the war effort, it was a frustrating and completely meaningless way to spend the morning. Obviously, 'come' was on the menu again. This time with the retractable lead. I'm sure Molly could have told him that success doesn't involve him hauling me across the park like he was landing a marlin, but from the praise I got when I was flopping at his feet and trying to get as far away from him as possible, you'd have thought I was some top circus performer.

Saturday, October 11

Ella and I are mostly to be found peering out from under the kitchen table at the moment. It's about the only place that isn't piled with boxes. Coleridge is having a great time chewing through them all and dragging the contents around the kitchen.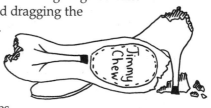
Until now I have resisted everything, but today my nose found a new one that smelled delicious and proved to be full of old shoes.
One pair had the label 'Jimmy Choo' in it, so presumably it was some kind of shoe-shaped choo toy. Being a generous, if increasingly stern, father I pushed it toward Coleridge and then went and hid with Ella at the opposite end of the kitchen.

From the reaction, I think it's safe to assume that Coleridge will not be receiving any tummy tickles tonight. I haven't seen such an explosive display of human emotion since the Owner came down naked to get a glass of water in the night and leaned over the electrified bin.

Sunday, October 12

I am In Disgrace again. Some men came to the house to look at the wall, measure the wall, rub their chins at the wall, knock on the wall and sigh at the wall. As befits a mature dog I limited myself to a thorough security check at the door, followed by the traditional ear-licking, face-barking Blake welcome and challenge to a fight. After I'd been shouted at a bit I retired to my old spot on the sofa to watch the proceedings. Coleridge, however, took the full ankle-nipping, trouser-biting, 'aaaaargh gerofff' option, which is often favoured by younger small dogs, and was shut in the kitchen for his youthful dedication to ridding the den of intruders.

One of the men went to get something out of their van and left the front door open. It being too good an opportunity to miss, I trotted out onto the street, then ran as fast as I could, careful to watch the road and ignore the shouts behind me.

It's a big world out there, and amazingly full of cats. Why is it that we dogs are shut up against our will all day long, chained, tethered or pining behind closed doors, while cats are free to wander hither and thither, like leaves blown on the breeze? I'm sure there's a poignant political point to be made from this, but I have to admit I was momentarily more concerned with getting my teeth around a large, ripe moggie. That ginger tom next door wasn't available (probably hiding in a tree), but his continual escaping had given me a sharp hunger for cat.

Most ran away when they saw me coming, but with the pursuit shaken off I could afford to take my time. Eventually, I found just what I was looking for, an old and fat smoky grey creature with its back to me. Going low and stretching my tail out behind me I stalked it, with just the tiniest of growls when I came close enough to pounce.

I was banking on a good chase ending with me sinking my teeth into it, but it just turned round and looked at me quite unconcerned, with slitty green eyes. Devil's eyes. I was taken aback. Between me and you, diary, I've never actually caught a cat before and I wasn't so sure what to do. Rip it apart, obviously, but I've never ripped anything apart either – not anything alive anyway – and when it comes right down to it, where do you start?

It was obviously either too stupid to realise the danger it was in, or too scared to move. Either way there was nothing to stop me munching it right up. I thought I'd get going with a sniff, just to get warmed up to the idea, the saliva flowing sort of thing, so I lowered my nose. Just as I was taking in it's unnatural clean odour, the damn thing put up a paw, hissed at me and scratched me all the way down my muzzle and nose with claws like electric needles.

I did what any sensible dog would have done and ran for it. All the way back to the den.

Monday, October 13

A humiliating day, and as always the root of my pain is Molly. After my small excursion yesterday, the Owner says that he's lost patience with my failing to obey the command 'come'. At the park I was forced to walk between him and Samantha for hours, each time one of them said 'Blake, come.' All the while Ella sat and laughed at my being in 'remedial' class. She was joined by Scottie, then Constable wandered over and finally Barney, Chu Chu and Fabienne, too. An audience of dogs, all barking encouragement and commenting on my performance. Although the occasional small piece of sausage helped take the edge off my embarrassment, it was pretty awful.

If that wasn't bad enough, Molly told the Owner that he has to make himself an exciting prospect to come back to. It would be funny if it wasn't so very sad. In his twisted mind an 'exciting prospect' is half an hour of bloody fetch and playing chase. Eventually I had to head-butt him in the crutch and pretend it was an accident.

Molly will suffer for this.

Tuesday, October 14

I was woken up last night by sharp little teeth dragging at my ear again. I suppose all new parents go through this, but I'm getting fed up with it now. It's been every night for over a month and growling just seems to make him worse, like I've challenged him *canine à canine*. He's got some of his dad's spirit, I'll give him that, but does he have to have it in the middle of the night?

Wakened by my growling, Ella opened one eye and said, 'Ahh, he just wants to play with you, it's sweet. Ignore him if you don't want to.' She was snoring again within seconds.

It's not so easy to ignore your ear being slowly shredded. In fact, I'd go as far as to say it's annoying, but Ella was right. Coleridge did eventually get bored. Instead, he cocked a little leg and peed in it.

'That's nice,' yawned Ella, 'he's claiming you. He must really respect you.'

It's the Owner's fault for being too soft with him. When I was his age it was the Rolled-up Newspaper morning, noon and night. Youngsters these days just don't know how lucky they are.

Wednesday, October 15

A close shave with Razor today. He was hidden in the woods and his little pack chased Claude and I straight to him. It was so subtle that we didn't realise we were being herded until it was too late, and there was no hint of his scent. Luckily, he sprang his ambush a couple of seconds too early and we were able to swerve away from him. Even so I could see the pink veins in his eyes and felt his breath as he snapped at me.

It looks as though he's adopting P.A.R.P.'s guerrilla tactics. A most disturbing turn of events. He could hide anywhere.

Thursday, October 16

P.A.R.P.'s alert level has been raised to orange. No dog is to venture into the woods unaccompanied, and our best and fastest sniffers have been assigned to sweep ahead for signs of ambush. Raids into Eastern territory have been reduced. They don't seem to be having much effect anyway. Ella has suggested that where a show of force has failed we might succeed in parting Razor from the remainder of his pack with a softer approach. As the least threatening looking members of P.A.R.P., Chu Chu and Fabienne have been appointed liaison officers. If the members of Razor's pack that are staying out of fear can be separated, the two miniature dogs will be smuggled through the trees to offer them protection.

Meanwhile, we continue to practise the final showdown. Scottie and I are racking our brains for a fail-safe way of making sure that Razor follows Constable. Increasingly, it looks as though everything will rest on the final battle.

Friday, October 17

Another brush with Razor. This time he was waiting by the dog toilet for me. There were too many humans around for him to strike though. As I watched him for the slightest muscle flicker that would indicate that he was preparing to attack, I could see Barney and Liquorice from the corner of my eye, tense and snarling.

'Blake,' said Razor. 'You smell like a coward and you act like one too. Why all this rustling around in bushes, stealing my pack and running away? Is it because you are afraid to face me? Is it because I nearly ate you? Did you know you taste like a coward, too?'

I could feel my hackles rising. So, he wanted to goad me into a fight in front of all these humans. I forced myself to be calm. 'Razor!' I said in mock surprise. 'You can talk! And here I was thinking you had the mental capacity of a rubber mouse.'

'Words and insults. You think like a human, coward. You are a disgrace to dogs.'

'You dare to call me a coward, when you prey on innocent puppies,' I snarled back.

'He was on my territory, it is my right to do whatever I want on my territory.'

'P.A.R.P.'s territory. Your days as Pack Leader are few and getting less.'

'Then you will fight me? Good. Why not here? Why not now?'

'Do you think I'm as stupid as you are?'

'I think you are a coward.'

I should have just walked away, but I just couldn't leave it there. Not with P.A.R.P. dogs looking on. Banking on him being not quite mad enough to fight I decided to let rip.

'Well, let's celebrate the famous Razor's wit and clever tactics, shall we? Oh, poor little Blake, overcome by the intellectual prowess of the pit bull, resorts to violence. Listen, Razor – sidebar: totally ridiculous name by the way – you obviously want me to attack you in front of all these humans, so that they can all say, "but the ruggedly handsome and beautifully toned mixed-breed attacked first," thus saving you from the execution by lethal injection that you so richly deserve, but newsflash Toothbrush, sorry, uh, Razor. Headlines are "Blake in More Clever Than the Braindead Bathroom Accessory Shock". Do you get what that means? In simple language easily understandable to lamebrain pit bulls, it means that you are going to lose. No more Razor. Bye bye. I could come over there and pee on your head and there isn't anything you could do about it except tell me what a Bad Dog I am.'

And for a second I actually considered doing it. Nevertheless, I didn't want to push him too far, not here and not now. Choking back my rage, I turned my back on him and walked away slowly.

Saturday, October 18

Liquorice and Barney have broadcast my showdown with Razor around P.A.R.P. and every dog wanted to congratulate me today. It felt like a hollow victory though – we won't win by sitting and barking at Razor and he was right, I am afraid to fight him again.

Sunday, October 19

More 'come' training. This time Molly has advised the Owner to attach me to the end of two washing lines tied together, which is apparently supposed to give me the illusion of freedom while making it impossible to ignore him when he wants to recall me. By dint of some artful dodging I managed to bring down three joggers and a rollerblader with it, but also nearly garrotted myself while chasing a squirrel. When humans weren't screaming curses at the Owner they seemed to think it was funny to shout things like,

'You'll never get that kite off the ground,' and 'Yeehah, rope that steer, dogboy.' Finally he untied me after I lashed a pigeon-feeding old lady to a park bench. I loped off to find Ella, leaving the idiot human trying to placate her while Coleridge went berserk at the pigeons and Samantha tried to untangle the washing line from the old lady's shopping trolley.

Monday, October 20

Razor sent Croxley over to challenge me to a duel in the deep woods, where no human is likely to disturb us. On close inspection the little Jack Russell is a nasty piece of work, the sort of dog that sits in his owner's favourite chair and snarls if anyone tries to move him. He came trotting into P.A.R.P. territory flanked by Rudy, looking around at the playing dogs with a sneer of contempt.

'Zis vun vants to talk with you, Blake. Be careful, he is now Razor's zecond in command.'

'I think we'll be all right thanks, Rudy. Hello, Croxley, have you come to join P.A.R.P.?'

'Don't be absurd, I wouldn't join your pathetic gang of outcasts if you paid me. I bring a message from Razor.'

'I thought that might be the case. Still upset that I got a bit annoyed with him is he? Tell him I'm very sorry and I'll sniff and make up if he will.'

'Razor says that if the coward Blake wants to settle this he will be in the woods tomorrow.'

My eyebrows twitched. I was expecting something like this.

'He doesn't expect you to come, but he thought your pack should know what a coward you are.'

'Is that right? Well, you can go back to your funny little friend and tell him that I'll meet him there.'

After Croxley had left, looking extremely pleased with himself, Rudy turned to me and said, '*Gott in Himmel*, you cannot do zis.'

I woofed back, 'Rudy, if Razor wants to go and sit in the woods on his own for an hour just think of the fun we can have on his territory.'

Tuesday, October 21

Gathering every P.A.R.P. dog in the park we set off on a raid to the East with Ella keeping a careful watch on Razor as he sat waiting in the woods. There was pee everywhere. All over his owner again, across his meadow stronghold and around the north and east gates. In fact, P.A.R.P. obliterated his scent completely. It'll take him weeks to re-mark it and until then he'll be constantly reminded of us.

Wednesday, October 22

It was Coleridge's turn to get some training today, and I stuck around to help as I was on puppy watch anyway. Watching treat after treat disappear down his throat I couldn't help but get involved, though weaving through the Owner's ankles barking orders at Coleridge and trying to gain access to the bag of sausage parts in his pocket was not deemed helpful. What a surprise.

Actually, the little fellow seems to be learning fast. Although this means he is advanced for his age, it looks as though he's inherited some of his mother's unfortunate eagerness to please. I shall have to start teaching him about the iniquitous system that humans impose to keep dogs in servitude. There is a fine line between accepting treats as a fair redistribution of wealth and becoming a running dog for an unelected dictator with pretensions to being an alpha male.

Our surveillance teams report that once again Razor is barking with rage. I was tempted to launch a raid to goad him further, but with the plan not yet ready, decided to let insane dogs tear around the Eastern Park, peeing indiscriminately.

Thursday, October 23

An early start today, and as the only member of Razor's pack in the park was Suki the spaniel, Ella and Fabienne were dispatched with promises of protection and the better life that P.A.R.P. can offer. Even from across the park I could see Suki shaking like Mr Wobbly with fear, but Fabienne was eloquent and Ella offered a personal guarantee of safety. Finally, the three of them trotted off to the north gate and Suki added her mark and pawprint. Then she ran to her owner as if the hounds of Hell were behind her and sat trembling in her lap.

Friday, October 24

An excellent obedience-training session this morning. I worked really hard and managed not to be there for the entire thing. Coleridge had a really good run with the Owner as they dashed hither and thither across the park trying to catch me. Exercise is so important for a growing pup who is growing fat on your dinner.

On the way back to the den we walked past next-door's ginger tom. For the sake of appearances I gave the impression that I was straining at the lead to get to it, but my nose still hurts from my last feline run-in. For the future, I'm considering adopting a policy of disdain. Distant disdain. After all, the antipathy between cats and dogs is probably an outmoded stereotype.

Saturday, October 25

Another chance to go through our battle plan presented itself this morning. As I crested the hill to watch for Constable's owner I could hear Scottie behind me shouting, 'OK, dogs, places, places. Noo does iviryone ken their lines? Ella, what's yer motivation, love?'

'Umm, to protect Constable from Razor?'

'That's right, darlin', an' ye'll be marvellous.'

Senility can take many forms, though I think Scottie's is the plain old 'barking mad' variety. Still, it got the job done. From the other side of the hill it sounded like a vicious battle was in progress and Constable was getting the worst of it. His owner ran to the top of the hill on cue, with another impressive burst of speed for a human of her size, just as the two dogs burst out of the woods.

As the human laughed and walked away, Scottie leaped about, barking, 'Och, it's such a privilege tae work wi' real talent.'

I think he should swap his tartan doggie coat for one with a few more buckles.

Sunday, October 26

Coleridge's behaviour is starting to worry me. He's only a few months old, but is already starting to sit on command like a Good Boy, and he trots along next to the Owner with barely a pull on the lead. I've told him again and again about the joys of attempting to pull the human arm out of its socket, but he's just not paying attention. For a pup who showed such early promise, it's not at all encouraging. As if this weren't bad enough, at walk time he sits quietly and waits for his lead to be put on. I thought jumping up and down barking manically was instinctive. I don't like to brag, but I've destroyed several pieces of expensive furniture in my excitement at going for a walk before now, not to mention the Owner's nerves.

Giving fatherly advice is like peeing into a drain. Coleridge just jumps up, bites my ear and hangs there like a large, growling, pendant earring.

Chained in the back yard again. It's only a matter of time before the Owner buys one of those medieval cage things and leaves me to dry out in the wind with ravens pecking at my eyes. This time my crime was trying for a little affection while he was sitting at the computer. I am the alpha around here, and Coleridge is getting far more than me. It's not my fault he doesn't keep all the wires underneath the desk tidy. You would have thought he might show some sympathy for a dog caught up and panicking, but he was more concerned about the computer banging about on the office floor than he was for a fellow mammal being strangled by office equipment.

The day was not wasted though. Oh no. For this afternoon, at approximately 3.47 p.m., the post to which my chain is attached finally gave in to the inevitable and parted beneath my mandibles of power. With the gate closed my only option was the fence again, but luckily he hasn't bothered to clear away the crate and the water butt. I was on the shed roof and leaping onto the lawn next door within seconds, alighting with the grace of a ballet dancer to find the place empty and the gate open. Freedom beckoned. But first, I couldn't resist peering through the kitchen door. Like our den it was covered with boxes, and one of them was causing one or two cells in my incredibly powerful nose to twitch. The unmistakable aroma of an old friend.

Unfortunately, the smell was coming from a box that was much more tightly secured than the rest of them and I only managed to get the tape off the bottom before footsteps coming down the stairs forced me to reconsider my position. Not wanting to be trapped in the kitchen with Brian the testicle thief, I beat a retreat and headed off down the path at the side of the house, consoling myself that there's a garbage pile at the back of a pizza place a few roads down that I've been longing to investigate. Damn my luck today though, I was just slinking quietly past our front gate when the Owner emerged shouting, 'Blake! Blake!'

With a length of chain and the remains of the post impeding me it wasn't even worth running. I lay down by the gate and tried to look as though I was just making my way back. Now I'm hitched to a much sturdier fence post, and with the neighbours moving out soon, it looks like Mr Wobbly might slip away forever, without even the chance of a tearful farewell.

Tuesday, October 28

It's getting increasingly dangerous in the park. Razor has finally realised that the war will not be won by brute force and has switched his tactics. Instead of trying to run down P.A.R.P. members, he has adopted a policy of intimidation as well as some of our own strategies. He and Croxley are concealing their scent, slipping through our lines and lying in wait for the weaker dogs. They then follow them and their owners around snarling quiet threats. Our guards are powerless to intervene unless he attacks first. P.A.R.P.'s sniffer dogs have also twice been ambushed by the pit bull and his Jack Russell lieutenant. It's only their longer legs that have saved them. Combined, the sight of our forces fleeing and the constant fear of reprisal is having a devastating demoralising effect on the more nervous members of P.A.R.P.

Wednesday, October 29

Spirits are definitely plummeting, as if I didn't have enough on my plate with the Owner constantly hassling me over the 'come' issue. It's taking all my skill and tactical know-how to avoid him long enough to catch up on the latest reports these days. Scooting with Ella is a forgotten dream. Meanwhile, there are whispers that P.A.R.P.'s protection may not be complete. Croxley has taken to shadowing Chu Chu and Fabienne, so all further attempts to persuade the remnants of Razor's pack to defect have been suspended. The Jack Russell only responds to force, and our heavy troops are ready to strike at him as soon as an opportunity presents itself. If we can neutralise Croxley, Razor will be effectively isolated. This may be all we can achieve in the run-up to the final battle. The remainder of his pack will have to be liberated after the war.

Thursday, October 30

The situation is deteriorating quickly; Razor is targeting the more nervous ex-members of his pack and promising extreme punishment if they do not return. One or two dogs are so scared that they have openly questioned whether it is not worth trying to live in peace with Razor. P.A.R.P. is a democracy, and their free speech is assured, but such defeatism must be quelled before it spreads.

Scottie and I have called a general meeting for any dog in the park tomorrow morning, that's if I can shake off the human limpet for long enough.

Friday, October 31

Eight dogs made it to the meeting this morning, and by maintaining a semblance of good behaviour all the way to the park I was allowed out of the Owner's sights for a few minutes. I took my place by the poop disposal bin, after acquainting myself with its contents, and began my address. It was powerful stuff, and it should be – I stole most of it from what I remembered of a Winston Churchill speech that was on the radio once, and the rest from the Beastie Boys.

'We shall go on to the end. We shall fight in the meadows, we shall fight by the pond and around the coffee stand, we shall fight in the air, and we shall fight on the overgrown patch of brambles behind the swimming pool. We shall fight for our right to party. We shall never surrender, and even if we are subjugated, then Scottie will fight on alone, until finally we are liberated by the old.'

I thought it had gone pretty well. Political hounds like myself have to have some oratory skill, and indeed, there was a stunned pause at the end of the speech. Then Scottie ruined the atmosphere of determined resolve.

'The air? An' hoo are we guan tae fight thum in the air? Huv ye a hang-glider noo? Or is it the jet-pack ye're planning oan? I cannae wait tae see the dogfights.'

I must have been a bit carried away, but rallied immediately. 'It's a metaphor, Scottie, obviously. When I say fight them in the air, it's like P.A.R.P. will be everywhere.'

'Och, I see, an' me takin' on Razor an' the whole pack. Is that a mettyfor, too?'

'That was a rhetorical device implying that we should hold out for our freedom until help comes from an unexpected quarter.'

'Och, a rhetorical deevice was it noo? An' there wus me wi' the impression it wus just the worst speech ivir made.'

I sighed. It looked as if old Winston wasn't hitting the mark in the modern era, so obviously it was time for plain talking. 'Look, this new behaviour of Razor's is a final attempt to frighten us all into submission, the tactics of a tyrant who knows he is beaten. He will not attack if you remain close to your humans. He's not completely stupid and won't risk a one-way trip to the vets.'

Barney interrupted. 'But when are we going to get rid of him? I'm tired of running and hiding.'

I was on firmer ground here. 'This question of vanquishing Razor once and for all has not been neglected. Constable, Ella, Scottie and I have been drawing up Top Secret battle plans. When the time comes I assure you that P.A.R.P. will triumph.'

Scottie chimed in again. 'That's right, it's going to be a wonderful show –'

'Thank you, Scottie. We cannot divulge the details right now, but it is an audacious strategy that has been finely honed to absolute precision.'

Just then a bark from one of our sentries warned us that the enemy was approaching. As P.A.R.P. dissipated, I could hear low grumbles. Not every dog was convinced.

NOVEMBER

Saturday, November 1

Scottie is down and may be dead. No dog knows. We were wrong to think that Razor would stop at merely stalking. It was all leading up to something much, much more sinister. Of course, we knew he was somewhere in the Western Park this morning, but he'd concealed his scent again, this time with the urine that P.A.R.P. had conveniently left for him by the north gate. In fact, he was hidden in a thicket of bushes that line a path along which Scottie was trotting behind his owner, who was busy trying to separate Edina and Jock. With nothing but the familiar smells of P.A.R.P. on the breeze, Scottie took a few seconds for a bit of genital licking. Razor darted out of the bushes, grabbed him and dragged the poor Westie beneath the leafy canopy. Chu Chu was  watching, horrified, and said that it was all over in seconds. Scottie barked a panicked warning, and his owner immediately turned and started poking furiously through the bushes. By the time he found his dog, it was too late. Razor had gone and Scottie looked like he'd been in a fight with a blender, bleeding from too many holes and shaking uncontrollably. As his owner picked him up, swearing and shouting revenge, Ella and I arrived panting. From his owner's arms the old boy, stained with the blood of battle, held out a paw to me.

'Awld friend, mah time hus come. Ah kin feel mahsel' slippin' away.'

Ella and I followed him as his owner hurried to the gate, dragging the two puppies behind him.

'Blake,' Scottie whined over his shoulder. 'Dinnae let the Mad Dog win. Fer the puppies' sake, Blake.'

'I won't, Scottie, I won't,' I barked back. A hush had dropped across the park. We could just hear Scottie moaning, 'Aye, Mother, ah see ye. Ah'm comin', Mother. I'm comin'.'

Razor will pay for this.

Sunday, November 2

There is a time for caution and a time for instant and unlimited retribution. During a shocked meeting with Constable this morning it was agreed that the plan would be launched immediately. There weren't many dogs in the park, but we managed to round up Rudy and Liquorice and brief them. They will conceal themselves where they will be able to reach Constable if anything goes wrong.

Both dogs warned me that Scottie's attack has affected some P.A.R.P. members badly. There is fresh talk of opening diplomatic channels in order to negotiate peace. I growled that there would be no peace in the park while I was still on four legs and off the retractable lead. It would be an insult to the Westie's memory if the pit bull was allowed to escape justice for his crimes.

No Scottie or puppies in the wasteland this evening. If he's still alive he will need to relieve himself, so where can he be?

Monday, November 3

An early run this morning. Razor was not in the park though we stayed as long as we could before the wretched humans caught us. Constable's owner was complaining that Constable has never disobeyed an order before. She thinks I'm a bad influence. The lack of human insight into the complications of canine relations and politic astounds me. Obviously, I am a bad influence though, and proud of it.

Tuesday, November 4

Again Razor has escaped our reprisal. Today, he was in the park, but Constable was missing. Dogs are following me about at a discreet distance waiting for something to happen, but without Constable's owner on hand there's nothing I can do but keep an eye on the pit bull and worry about Scottie. Still no clue as to whether my friend and advisor is alive or dead.

Wednesday, November 5

The weather was fine, and the park full. Perfect conditions for Razor to meet his comeuppance. Rudy and Liquorice ran over as soon as they saw Ella and me, and together we found Constable. With Scottie's wounds still fresh in our minds there were few words, but we wished each other good luck and took our positions. Rudy and Liquorice disappeared into the undergrowth, Ella vanished into the trees to watch for Razor, Constable sat quietly at the edge of the woodland and I ran to the edge of the path, looking out for Constable's owner.

After a few minutes, we heard Ella's signal bark through the trees. The target was identified and in position. Down the path, Constable's owner was slowly walking towards me. Closer and closer. As she passed the third lamppost on the left, I gave the order for Constable to leave. We were in a Go situation.

After two minutes the colossal female had reached the second lamppost. Barkly stopped to pee on it. Precious seconds ticked by. In the distance I could hear Constable barking, 'Hey, Razor, came bottom at the show last week again I heard. I expect you're too ugly to meet breed standards. With a face like that, the judges probably couldn't tell which end was which.' In the rush to put the plan into action we had no option but to trust that Constable's odd taunting would lure Razor. Fortunately, it seemed to have worked.

He must have been running already, because the barking got closer. As did his owner. She had reached the first lamppost and was only yards away now. Through the trees, Constable had found his theme. 'I won best of breed again. I saw your name on the result board. They spelled it L-O-S-E-R.'

There was a bark close behind him of purest rage, and as they got closer I could hear twigs snapping as Constable fled towards the safety of his owner. I barked to summon any P.A.R.P. member close by the scene of Razor's defeat.

By now Constable's owner should be running to him, but something was wrong. She was taking no notice at all. Instead she looked down at Barkly and said, 'Sounds like Constable is playing with your daddy again.'

Oh Dog, she hadn't heard that Scottie had been attacked and we'd made her practise this too many times. It was just like that story about the wolf who cried 'Boy'.

'Abort, abort,' I barked, streaking back towards Constable just in time to see him come crashing through the trees with Razor at his hind paws.

The world slipped into slow motion, as it often does at times of great stress. The same thing happened when the Owner found me with the hand-stitched Italian leather shoes. I barked again and dashed down the hill towards the two dogs. Razor looked up, saw me, and instantly forgot about Constable. I was running straight into a yawning cavern of teeth, packed into jaws that could grind bone like dog biscuits. The pain and fear of the last time I fought with Razor rushed back, and for a moment I almost stumbled. But then the image of Scottie, tattered and struggling to breathe, came back to me. I put my head down and willed my paws to carry me faster. My mouth curled into a snarl, I charged at the puppy-mauling, friend-killing monster. In the space of maybe one or two seconds all the dog fell away from me, leaving pure wolf, hungry for blood.

As I opened my own jaws ready to lock onto Razor's flesh, Rudy and Liquorice charged his flanks. His momentum ruined, the pit bull fell and rolled. At the same time, Ella's lithe, powerful shoulders pushed at me, forcing me to turn my attack into an escape. As we fled I could hear Razor laughing, 'The Westie tasted horrible. Old dogs are so bitter.'

Thursday, November 6

The plan has failed and due to my stupidity half of P.A.R.P. was there to watch it fail. The fragile unity is breaking apart around me. About half the dogs in the park today are supporting a fresh attack. The other half say they want me to head a peace envoy. What they really want is for me to offer myself as a sacrifice to appease Razor.

If I hadn't promised Scottie I would be tempted to make an attempt to negotiate with the pit bull. He's not so stupid that he won't have recognised a trap, and Constable's owner must now be mothballed. Our only hope of beating Razor is now decommissioned.

In the circumstances, I have made it known that I will fight on until the last, but that any member of P.A.R.P. who wishes to leave may do so unimpeded.

Friday, November 7

Thank Dog Scottie's owner was in the wasteland this evening. I couldn't get much sense from the pups, but he is still alive. However, Edina and Jock tell me that he is so badly hurt that he has made his final will and testament. Edina is to have his collection of chew toys, while Jock has been left his beloved food and water bowls with the words, 'As I telt ye son, one day all this wud be yours.'

With our only plan in tatters, I could really use the old dog's advice right now.

Saturday, November 8

With Scottie down and a P.A.R.P. ambush foiled, Razor is capitalising on his success. New scent markings are appearing all over the Western Park. Reminders that the territory officially belongs to him. Croxley has been jumping out at smaller dogs, pretending to play, but warning them that Razor is coming to get them. No more news of Scottie, and the dogs who remain steadfast have no suggestions for a new plan that might defeat the mad pit bull. Surely, this is the park's darkest hour.

Sunday, November 9

The spaniel, Suki, who Chu Chu and Ella liberated, has gone back to Razor, begging to be 're-educated.' Apparently Croxley found her unguarded yesterday and gave her a vicious bite as a taste of what Razor had in store. Ella blames herself, but as we weren't in the park at the time there was little she could have done.

No other P.A.R.P. members have gone back yet, but a little spaniel/Labrador cross called Barnaby found me today to ask if I was planning another attack. He implied that around six of the smaller dogs are planning to go back if they are not reassured that P.A.R.P.'s failure would be rectified.

I guess it must be hardest for the small dogs. They've been tagging along with their owners for months, unable to do anything but wait fearfully and trust that one day they will be able to run around the park and play unmolested.

Monday, November 10

Ella and I talked late into the night trying to identify a new secret weapon. But who?

Scottie's owner is too infirm, even if he were available to us; Liquorice's wanders around with headphones on; Ella's is so small that we couldn't be sure of her winning. Claude's looks like he would make mincemeat of Razor, but walks about the park so aimlessly that it would be impossible to predict his location. For one reason or another every dog owner is out of the running.

We even considered attacking as a pack, but it is in contravention of all treaties and international codes. The end result would be that Razor's claim to the territory would be strengthened.

It seems inevitable that I will have to step into the breach. Ella forbids it, but there doesn't seem to be an alternative, and I would not ask another dog to go in my stead. As a founder member of P.A.R.P. and *de facto* Pack Leader it is my responsibility to protect the park dogs.

Tuesday, November 11

Training in the park today, with Ella running by my side telling me that there has to be another way. In fact, she spent the entire day trying to talk me out of fighting Razor, with rising urgency.

Eventually, while we were lying at the humans' feet, she looked up and said, 'What about him?'

'Who, Coleridge?' I replied, glancing at the pup who was draped across the Owner's lap with his back leg pumping.

'No, your owner, idiot.'

'What about him?'

'Why not get him to fight Razor?'

'You have to be kidding me.'

'Well, why not?'

'Just look at him. He's got the muscle tone of a well-chewed bone and the killer instinct of a damp towel.'

'Are you sure about that?'

'I've known him a lot longer than you have and I assure you that there's more chance of Razor being overpowered by a day-old kitten. His own duvet's been known to beat him in a fight.'

'But he looks pretty fit when he's running and doing all those exercises.'

'Appearances can be deceiving. Unless you think Razor might succumb to a Rolled-up Newspaper?'

'You just don't want him to become alpha male through right of conquest, then you'll have to obey him.'

'Don't be absurd, I just don't want his tin-opening opposable thumb chewed off.'

And I hoped that would be an end to it. He's not much of a human, but he's all I've got. Razor would probably make mincemeat of him and it's a risk I'm not prepared to take. We've become used to each other and I'd hate to have to spend the rest of my life pining on a cold gravestone.

Wednesday, November 12

Last night, when Ella and Coleridge were asleep, the Owner came down to the kitchen for a glass of water. He was naked, and the dim hallway light gleamed off pectorals and biceps that I don't remember seeing before. He was slimmer than ever, taut in what I assume are the right places on a human, and for a moment looked like a sleek fighting machine. I started to think that maybe Ella was right after all, my Owner could be the saviour the park was looking for.

Then he skidded in Coleridge's pee, tripped on Ella, and fell flailing into a pile of boxes. Grabbing blindly he pulled the oven door open, straight onto his head, and crashed back to the floor swearing.

Then again, Ella might be completely and utterly wrong.

Thursday, November 13

Razor tried his new trick again and this time brought down one of his ex-pack members, Barney. Fortunately, Barney's owner came looking for his dog immediately and Razor didn't get to finish the job, but Barney will be limping for a while to come. Meanwhile Croxley is still on the loose, spreading his poison  around the park. The bigger dogs chase him off time and again, but he always pops up somewhere different, intimidating the smaller breeds and sniffing around the puppies.

P.A.R.P. is still terrified, but just about holding. If I don't have a plan together quickly though, it's finished.

Friday, November 14

Our reconnaissance team report back that although Suki hasn't been physically assaulted, her owner can barely pull her into the park she's so frightened and almost has to carry her around. Nevertheless, when Razor or Croxley barks she runs to them and immediately lies on her back with her belly exposed. Poor thing.

I have to do something, but it would be stupid just to get myself torn up again unless I absolutely have to. I need to think clearly. How did Caesar continually beat armies twice the size of his own forces? How did the Spartans drive off the mighty Persians at Marathon?

Without Scottie I am forced to seek the judgement of other dogs. Constable's advice was no use at all.

'I heard this horrible story about a human that poisoned a dog next door by mixing petrol in its food. It was very sick and the dog's owner bent down to see what was wrong with a cigarette in his mouth. Maybe we can do that to Razor.'

'That is horrible. What happened to the dog?'

'Well, apparently, it went *woof*.'

'I see.'

'Does Razor's owner smoke cigarettes?'

'No, I don't think so.'

Saturday, November 15

Some of the P.A.R.P. dogs have suggested that we make
another attempt on Razor using Constable's owner, but I
have vetoed it, unwillingly. Last time we were lucky. If we try
it again, Constable might not make it through. The sheepdog
was willing to take the risk (I have to hand it to him, what he's
missing in the brain department he makes up with a courageous
soul), but it's too dangerous.

Instead, I told them that I would be going into battle alone.

This is the plan. As before, P.A.R.P.'s troops will keep Razor's
small pack occupied, though I have ordered them to be as gentle
as possible with Suki. They may do what they like with Croxley.
We will extensively mark an area by the pond as a P.A.R.P.
stronghold. Razor will bring his pack to claim back the territory
and as he does so, P.A.R.P. will surround him with its full
strength. We are still fifteen dogs, and hopefully the threat of our
massed forces will strike some sort of fear into his vicious heart.

As the P.A.R.P infantry engages the Razor pack, I will fall like
a hammer blow upon him from the woods. And this time it will
be a fight to the death.

Essentially, it's the same plan as last time, but whatever
strategy I have considered, it will all come down to me versus
Razor. Beyond trying for the most advantageous ground, there
are no tactics that can help in the white heat of single combat.

Sunday, November 16

Ella is furious and pushing her plan to use my Owner harder
than ever. She's not convinced by the argument that putting my
life in the hands of that bumbling incompetent is tantamount to
jumping in a sack and throwing myself into the pond.

In some respects she does make sense. It's me that Razor
wants to chew on more than any other dog in the park so it
would be a cinch to lure him into a trap, no matter how wary he
is. Plus, I'm pretty sure the Owner would do the best he could,
after all he did wade in when I was fighting Claude and I haven't
forgotten the care and attention he gave me after my last bout
with Razor. But when I see him on all fours pretending to bite

Coleridge's tummy or singing 'Copacabana' while he's making breakfast it's difficult to maintain any enthusiasm for the idea.

Monday, November 17

Scottie's back! Thank Dog. He's still not up to a long walk in the park, but his owner is now bringing him to the wasteland in the evening. I was overwhelmed with joy, jumping around him like a puppy.

'Aye, ah thought ah was a gonner there,' he told me when I'd calmed down enough to say how glad I was to see him.
'When ah woke up there wus voices calling tae me and a light at the end of a tunnel.'

'You mean you had an out-of-body experience. Wow. Did you see Dog Heaven?'

'Noo, after a couple o' minutes ah realised ah jest hud this flippin' funnel oan mah heid.'

I didn't want to worry him with the war of the park while he was still convalescing, but he insisted, so I told him about Barney, Suki, P.A.R.P. threatening to disintegrate, my desperate plan and even Ella's idea of using my Owner.

'Ye're a brave heart, right enough, but if ye should go heid tae heid wi' Razor agin, ye're a fool, as well. A foool, I tell ye.'

'But there's no other way.'

'Huv I taught ye nuthin', ye prize parsnip? There's always another way. Let me think on it, an' we'll talk some more on the morrow.'

Tuesday, November 18

Scottie's had 24 hours to think and I'm not sure I like his conclusions. We met in the wasteland and he looked grave and dour, not that dour isn't his usual expression.

'Och, it's a pickle that we're in an' that's fer nuthin'. But if ye want mah opinion it's no a bad idea o' Ella's tae use yer owner, he's a big lad. No as tasty as yon Constable's, but a canny second choice.'

'We are talking about the same human?' I replied. 'Runs like a duck, cuts his fingers opening tins?'

'Aye, but he'll do his best by ye, sure enough. While ye wus at the vet's las' time he came doon the park an' hud a terrible shout at Razor's baldie human.'

'He did?' This was news to me. Razor's owner is a pit bull walking upright.

'Aye. Ah thought he wus guannae stick the heid on hum he wus that angry.'

'Why didn't you tell me?'

'Och, ye ken ah'm gettin' jest a little bit forgetful in mah old age. Did ah tell ye I goat a brand new bowl? Seems in mah delirium ah bequeathed the last one tae Jock, an' the little bugger will nae let us eat oot o' it noo.'

Scottie went misty-eyed. 'It's silver, wi' little bones embossed oot o' the metal . . .'

Wednesday, November 19

This is the new plan.

1. Scottie will defect to Razor's pack, telling him that he submits after his defeat. He will then feed Razor all the information P.A.R.P. wants him to know, including my regularly visiting the Scooting Place at certain times of the day, unaccompanied except by Ella.
2. I will taunt the Owner with my failure to 'come', making him chase me to the Scooting Place on Scottie's signal.
3. I will engage with Razor, and pray to all that is Howly that the Owner doesn't trip over his own feet, get distracted by Coleridge, decide to have a coffee, lose interest and go to feed the pigeons, or otherwise fail to turn up.

It's bold, audacious and simple, but at the same time success hangs on the dependability of a human being who cannot be relied upon to tie his shoelaces properly. Just thinking about all the things that could go wrong makes my bowels loosen. I guess that the worst that could happen will be me and Razor fighting it out as originally planned, but between me and you, diary, though I was being all noble about it, that scares the shit out of me too.

Thursday, November 20

With the park pretty full today, a hasty general meeting was called and I explained the new plan to the dogs of P.A.R.P. If Scottie is to defect, the rest of the party need to know that it is on a highly dangerous Top Secret mission demanding courage and cool nonchalance in the face of mortal danger. What better dog for the job than an elderly and slightly mad West Highland terrier.

After I had reassured them that Scottie's apparent going over to the other side was not a desertion of his friends and fellow soldiers, a good idea came from an unexpected quarter: Constable.

'Like, why don't we all defect? Except me, Razor hates me.'

Some of the dogs looked quizzically at him, and I was fairly bemused, too. You could see the effort of thinking playing out across his overgrown face as he struggled to explain himself.

'If Razor, like, thinks he's almost won, won't he be even more likely to come after Blake and finish it, thus not considering that he may be leaving himself open to human intervention?'

Constable lay down, panting.

'Yeah, that's right, that's good. Well done, Constable, you're a great dog, good dog, yeah. Brilliant,' chipped in Liquorice.

'And it would also mean we could look out for Scottie,' said Barney.

'Plus, we'd be on hand to help you out if anything goes wrong,' suggested Claude.

There was a murmur of agreement, with Chu Chu telling anyone who would listen that she would take Razor's genitalia home in a paper bag if he hurt me again. Even the dogs who advocated a peace mission nodded agreement. I guess if this plan fails, they've got nothing to lose by having returned early.

It was unanimously decided that when Scottie returns to the park the whole of P.A.R.P. would defect with him. Except for

Constable. After the taunting he gave Razor, we decided that it would be best for him to stick to his owner.

Friday, November 21

Yesterday's meeting reminded me of something and as Constable and I trailed around after Barkly on puppy duty today I asked him, 'What was all that taunting about with Razor anyway?'

'Well, his owner keeps entering him in dog shows. Razor hates it and he never wins anything anyway. He's even been entered in the fancy-dress parade, which is like the most desperate way to win anything. It's worse that I win a cup or two every time he goes and he has to sit there watching while I sit on the winners podium with people clapping and giving me prizes. It's all rubbish really, I'd rather be jumping around in the pond, but it makes mistress happy.'

I'd never seen this side of Constable before. 'So you don't like celebrity?' I asked him.

'No.' He paused for a second. 'I'm not keen on leeks, carrots or fennel either.'

'Hmm. Just out of interest, what costume does Razor wear in the fancy-dress parade?'

'Marilyn Monroe. He's got a blonde wig and sparkly dress and everything. It doesn't really suit him though.'

Just when you thought you'd heard everything.

Saturday, November 22

Despite P.A.R.P.'s support, I still have grave misgivings about the plan. And 'grave' is exactly the right word. If anything goes wrong I'll probably die. Scottie, Ella and the rest of P.A.R.P. are convinced that it cannot fail, but just in case I have decided to put my affairs in order. Before I go I would like to complete my life's work:

1. A last act of revenge on Molly, after which I think we should be quits for her testicle-severing advice.
2. One final showdown with the postman, just so he won't

forget me too quickly. If I get it right, I could leave him with mental scars that will fester and lead to a healthy phobia in time.

3. Give next-door's ginger tom one last treeing, though taking care to keep out of actual scratching distance.
4. Dispense some fatherly advice to Coleridge to keep him off the slippery path of obedience.
5. Give the Owner some affection. After all it won't be his fault if I die, he can't help being a complete idiot, and he has sort of been good to me. Not always in the matter of food, but since the demise of the Rolled-up Newspaper things have been a lot more harmonious. As it may be my last chance I am even considering bringing him something he likes, but as he doesn't smoke a pipe or wear slippers and always gets to the newspaper before I have a chance to shred it, I'm not sure exactly what.
6. One last scoot 'n' sniff with Ella, my mate for life.

Sunday, November 23

I began the countdown to Doomsday, when Scottie is well enough to return to the park, by testing the Owner over the command 'come.' Today, I was more concerned than usual about his reaction, but right on cue he began chasing me around the park waving his arms. It seemed like a good idea to give him a longer run than usual – I need to keep him in tip-top condition – and was gratified to see him covering the ground like a startled gazelle. However, my optimism was slightly dampened when he threatened me with the retractable lead if I continue to be 'too bloody stupid to learn the simplest commands.' It might be best to keep him happy for a little while. There's no chance of luring Razor to his fate if I'm towing a human on a piece of string around the park.

Monday, November 24

Well, no dog can say I didn't do my best to make the Owner feel wanted. Having thought long and hard about what he likes best, I remembered how much he loves a piece of steak. Obviously, taking a piece to him would be an extremely appropriate way of expressing what little devotion I have. Seeing that the fridge lock had been left off, it was the work of a moment to paw the door open, grab the big slab of meat within and – after the tiniest of licks and nibbles to make sure that it was of superior quality – walk nobly to the sofa for a grand presentation. Curiously, he didn't seem at all grateful. Probably because Coleridge made a spectacle of himself by pulling at a corner while I tried to drop it in the Owner's lap.

Not to be disheartened by the cursing and clutching of the brow, I tried again later by climbing into his lap and giving his ear a licking it won't forget in a hurry. A response a little more heartfelt than 'Ugh, gerroff, Blake,' and pushing me to the floor would have been nice, but at least that's one duty discharged.

Steak for dinner tonight. Although he hid it under an exterior of grumpy churlishness, I could tell that he was deeply moved by my behaviour. He'll miss these little affectionate moments when I'm gone.

Tuesday, November 25

That's another final request fulfilled. The postman will be having nightmares about my mandibles of death for years to come thanks to Ella. With my Owner safely upstairs in the office, she sat by the door and whined as if urgently needing to relieve herself. Having little experience of my postie-bothering history, her human obediently opened the door on cue, allowing me to accost the letterbox-rattler as he turned down our path. I was also determined to give Coleridge a practical lesson in how to treat tradesmen, postmen, religious types and anyone else impertinent enough to beat a path to our den. I must say he didn't disappoint, though he's already shown some natural ability in that area.

Today, he was there before me, and after some preliminary jumping about, yapping and ankle-snapping, attached himself to the postman's bag with an expression that said it would only be prised out of his cold dead jaws, and probably not even then, an excellent move well suited to the smaller dog.

With dear old postie already under siege, it was a pleasure to turn up the heat a little. With practised ease I had my feet on his shoulders and was woofing into his face using an eardrum-rattling D flat from the very bottom of my considerable range. For good measure I snapped my powerful jaws about an inch from his nose. Ella joined in with some restrained growling from the front step. Ladylike, but adding an extra layer of menace; it was a nice touch on her part, I thought.

We only got a few seconds of course before the owners spoiled the fun, but we made them count. By the time I was yanked off and Coleridge's jaws were pulled open, the postman was almost crying. I don't think my Owner's speech made it any better.

'I've been reading about this. They react like this because you're invading their den. What we need to do is get them used to you so that they can see you're a friend.'

By this time the postman was on the other side of the fence and retreating rapidly. Nevertheless, the Owner called out hopefully, 'I don't suppose you've got time to come in for a coffee and to get to know them?'

Apparently, 'You must be out of your ****ing mind' means 'no,' though I have to say it showed an unexpected acuteness of perception. I gave him a final fierce bark, partly in agreement, partly to see him off.

Wednesday, November 26

I took Coleridge aside today and attempted to impart some pearls of wisdom, as behoves an older, wiser dog. I'd prepared a few words for him to think back on in years to come and as he looked up at me with his head cocked to one side in awe I let the legendary Blake eloquence flow. I touched briefly on cats (claws, the sharpness of), begging (it's all in the eyebrows) and bitches (though with his father's genes he's probably ahead of the game already), before moving on to my main theme: obedience.

I pointed out that history is littered with examples of dogs who have shown remarkable loyalty to their humans. Greyfriars Bobby is one who makes me feel particularly ill. These dogs are no better than quislings. Filthy traitors to their own species, giving humans expectations of faithfulness that no dog could or should live up to. There's nothing wrong with showing a tiny amount of affection now and again, especially as it usually pays dividends in the way of treats and strokes, but in general no human command should be obeyed without the promise of a fair day's pay. Obedience is a valuable commodity in a modern world driven by market forces, and to just give it away is inviting oppression. Of course, the history books are quiet about the other great dogs, the dogs who have fought for our freedom, so I told Coleridge about some of the hounds who have inspired us all with their acts of heroism: Sheep Worrying Nedley, Never-Seen-Him-Again Satch who had sixteen owners, none of whom could keep him more than a month, and – of course – the great Defecating Bob.

In fact, I was just warming to the question of 'Biting the Hand That Feeds You' (which by the way is perfectly admissible if it's holding a small sausage and you can make it appear an accident) when I noticed Coleridge was snoring at my feet.

Ah, well, perhaps youth has its own wisdom. I lay down next to him, he shuffled into the warmth of my belly and we both dozed off.

Thursday, November 27

Scottie is back in the park. His stitches are out and although he's still sore, the vet has given him a clean bill of health. To avoid suspicion, he will have to go and submit to Razor immediately. We have settled on tomorrow.

After discussion in the wasteland this evening it was decided that he will initially take Rudy, Claude and Liquorice with him. They will appear to be P.A.R.P.'s first returning penitents, but in reality will form a bodyguard for Scottie. Once safe passage is assured, the rest of P.A.R.P. will follow the day after or as soon as they are available. The only exceptions will be myself, Ella and Constable. Scottie will tell Razor that we are too stupid to realise that the war is lost, then he will supply information that will lead to our defeat with the readiness of the complete convert.

Friday, November 28

It is done, and Scottie told me all about it last night, being careful to keep his distance from me so no hint of my scent is upon him tomorrow.

At approximately 10 a.m. this morning, Scottie, Rudy, Liquorice and Claude entered the enemy's territory with every appearance of submission, and lay down peacefully as Razor approached. He was panting with glee.

'You're either brunch or you're here to submit,' he said.

'Aye, ye beat me fair an' square.'

'And the other three?'

'Our pack kens when it's beaten. This is jest the advance perty. If ye promise tae be a Good Boy and not eat thum all, the rest will be here on the morrow.'

'Blake?'

Scottie told me that as he said my name, Razor cocked his leg and peed furiously.

'Nae, that one's all yours. Constable tells me he'll be takin' his chances on his own too. But iviry other dog in the park will be in yer pack and it willnae be long before ye have yer chance tae teach Blake and Constable the error o' their ways.'

'And supposing I don't promise to be a Good Boy?'

'Well then, it makes nae difference tae me, I ken the rules o' combat, but I'm thinkin' it might be a while til ye can say ye're Top Dog agin. This way, ye'll ha' won by tomorrow.'

Razor thought about this for a few moments. 'As Pack Leader I might have to dispense a few nips here and there to maintain discipline.'

Scottie told me he had trouble not throwing himself on Razor, but calmly responded, 'An' that's yer prerogative noo.'

'Well then, I won't kill any dog who comes back to where they rightfully belong, unless they step out of line or are caught with that traitor Blake, who I beat and who owes me his life.'

As Scottie and the other dogs took the position of submission, Razor gloatingly added, 'A debt which I shall be calling in very soon.'

Saturday, November 29

As the rest of P.A.R.P. straggled over to swear allegiance to Razor, Ella and I took what could be our last opportunity and ran to the Scooting Place. As we romped in the pond, rubbed our bums down a bank and spent half an hour in blissful sniffing and playful chasing, it occurred to me how long it has been since we've been able to just enjoy each other. The privations of war are terrible, but this tiny slice of paradise reminded us what we were fighting for and I swore to her that even if the Owner failed me I would fight to the last woof in my body to vanquish Razor. As I snuffled her white fluffy bum, death didn't seem to matter too much.

Across the park, dog after dog swore loyalty to Razor for as long as he is Pack Leader. Little does he know that he only has a matter of days.

When our owners called, Ella and I streamed straight back to them.

Sunday, November 30

It is unnaturally quiet in the park. The ex-P.A.R.P. dogs were avoiding me and huddled together in wary-looking groups. Watching them from afar made me realise how much I missed the comradeship of our struggle. Razor wasn't there, but I am on a knife edge. Ella and I stuck close to the owners and Coleridge for company, though we stopped to pass the time of day with Constable, who is keeping so close to his mistress that he has tripped her up half a dozen times already this morning.

This evening Scottie reported that while Razor has not savaged any dog, he has been liberal with his 'instructive nips,' which are getting less instructive and more brutal hour by hour. He also confirmed he has told Razor that I can often be found in the clearing near the pond, and passed the word around ex-P.A.R.P. members to keep a close eye on it. Convention or no convention, they have unanimously agreed to come to my aid if necessary.

DECEMBER

Monday, December 1

As Ella and I quietly watched the meadow for any sign of Razor today, it occurred to me that I didn't get the chance to even the score with Molly. A pity, as I had a great move worked out. I was going to give her my normal welcome while Ella crouched behind her. When stumbling backwards under my considerable weight, she would trip on Ella and end up flat on her back with me keeping her pinned to the ground.

Some would think that this is a lightweight plan, not up to my usual standard of subtlety and quiet malice. However, when applied correctly – say in the dog toilet just after her clients had relieved their bowels – then I have every confidence that it would have been one of my very best yet.

Simple, but effective and based on a close observation of human behaviour. It takes a keen eye to notice that humans have an aversion to rolling around in dog mess. Ah well, 'What's gone, and what's past help, should be past grief,' as the Bard once said. As I sit here at the edge of the woods awaiting my doom, there's no time for puppyish play. If I live though, I shall enjoy rolling her around in the poop.

Tuesday, December 2

The owners wanted an early run, so once again our timing was all out, despite my hiding behind the sofa and dragging on the lead to slow him down. Coleridge tried to help by peeing on the entrance hall rug. All to no avail. It was still dark when we arrived and the only animals there apart from us were owls. With the park empty, the Owner let Coleridge off the lead for the first time as the sun came up, and he and Samantha, Ella and I spent half an hour chasing the little tyke around the meadow, after which Ella and I introduced him to the pleasures of an early-morning dip.

He may be small but the shagginess of his coat makes for excellent shaking, and the humans went home covered in mud.

Wednesday, December 3

We had been in the park for ten minutes this morning when Ella and I watched Razor arrive, chastise some of his pack with the usual round of vicious nips and make his way towards our Scooting Place. An expectant hush fell across the park and P.A.R.P. members started edging closer toward the clearing. I sent Ella back. It was now all down to me and my Owner. With my bum in my mouth I watched from concealment as the inept human started looking around for me. A few minutes later he was shouting, 'Blake! Blake! Aaargh, that bloody dog,' in those dulcet tones of his. I resisted the temptation to answer. If I went now and never left his side again, the final battle could be avoided. Then I remembered the casual way that Razor bit a puppy and savaged the dogs of P.A.R.P. – my dogs. My determination hardened like an old bone. I waited.

Five minutes later, the Owner had started rushing around, calling my name and cursing. It was the cursing I was waiting for. His temper was my cue to act.

Jumping out of the bushes I ran around him in a large circle, taunting him, but not getting close enough to be caught. He reacted perfectly, chasing me and cursing louder, while yelling 'come' at the top of his voice.

I took a deep breath, turned and sprinted for the Scooting Place, with him following. And there, as I crashed through the trees, was Razor waiting for me and snarling a challenge. The Owner was about fifty yards behind me and closing fast. I needed him to see Razor attack me first. Would he, knowing my human was so close? I was banking on his mad fury, but it seemed my luck had run out.

'Smells like a trap, but you won't last long without your pathetic P.A.R.P. to shield you. And your pal is going to die for trying to put one over on me.' He turned to walk away.

The Owner had reached the edge of the clearing. There was only one chance left and I took it.

'Suit yourself, *Marilyn*. Maybe you could batter me to death with your handbag next time, eh?'

For a second I didn't know if it was going to work, and then he rounded, his eyes staring the bloodshot gaze of a truly Mad Dog, and started running straight at me. With my eyes closed and my teeth clenched in anticipation of pain I sat and waited: *I must not be seen to be aggressive.*

And then he hit me, like a car, and his teeth fastened on my undefended throat. So fast, so powerful. The breath was being choked out of me and my flesh was parting beneath those terrible teeth. I couldn't help it, I rolled and began to thrash about, seeking any way to be rid of this savage who was killing me more quickly than I could have imagined.

From across the clearing, there came a long, drawn-out 'Nooo' and the sound of running feet across the grass. I was already close to passing out, but on the edge of the darkness I could hear the Owner – Dog bless him – spitting out curses as he charged Razor.

Suddenly the pressure on my throat was lessened. There was no dragging this brute off me by his hind legs, and as I opened my eyes I saw that the Owner had his hands around Razor's jaws and was slowly forcing them apart. An inch more and I broke free, panting and rolling away. With a muscular twist, Razor transferred his jaws to my Owner's arm. He was biting a human. Uh, and indeed, oh.

His face transformed by a truly frightening human snarl, my Owner wrenched Razor's teeth out of his arm, tearing his own flesh. The insanely twisting dog was now held by his collar and a back leg. More humans were arriving: Samantha and Molly. Ella was sprinting towards me and Croxley had also appeared, closely followed by the dogs of P.A.R.P. who were baying in a circle around the clearing. The Jack Russell followed his Pack Leader's example and jumped at my Owner, burying his teeth in an ankle. With him hanging from one leg and Razor held at arm's length before him, the Owner strode to the pond, swung the pit bull round in a circle, and hurled him into the middle shouting, 'That should cool you down, you little bastard.' At that moment, Razor's owner joined the bedlam in the clearing, just in time to see the pit bull hitting the water with a huge splash.

'Oi, what are you doing to my dog?' As he closed on my Owner he noticed the blood pouring down his arm. 'You must've provoked him, Razor wouldn't hurt a –'

He got no further. With his good arm, the Owner caught him a punch that knocked him to his back.

'No, Razor's just a big old cuddly wuddly, you moron.'

The Owner didn't seem to notice that Croxley was still gnawing furiously at his ankle, but by this time, Molly had handed the leads she was holding to Samantha and walked quietly across the clearing. Looking serene, she drew her leg back and kicked Croxley hard enough to send him into the pond with Razor.

'Sometimes,' she said, 'you have to take a firm line with them. Biting is not permitted.' Looking at the two paddling dogs in the pond, she barked, 'Bad dogs! Naughty boys!', once more confirming my deeply held belief that humans are crazy.

Thursday, December 4

What has happened to Razor? Have there been any reprisals? Are the P.A.R.P. dogs OK? My Owner won the fight and by all the codes and conventions, now has the right to all of Razor's territory, but I wouldn't put it past the pit bull to commit some revenge atrocity or even try and bend the rules, after all the Owner's not likely to go out of his way to defend his new territory. That's if Razor hasn't already been destroyed. Every dog knows that ripping big holes in a human is a capital crime.

The not knowing is driving me crazy, but Ella, Coleridge and I are strictly on the wasteland so that the Owner can keep me 'close by.' No sign of Scottie either. It's so unfair, I've only got a few stitches, some bruising and another funnel. He's got his arm in a sling and everything and still managed to go out for most of the day. Not that I'd dream of complaining. The Owner knows best, I'm sure. Oh, who am I kidding? He's still an idiot, but Dog, I'm proud of him.

Friday, December 5

Even though I can hardly think straight for worrying about P.A.R.P., I am on my best behaviour. Who would have thought the Owner would prove such a fearsome gladiator? I'm still amazed at the way he pulled Razor's jaws apart to free me with no regard for his personal safety. They must have taken stupendous strength. Plus the final throw into the pond was an awesome display of muscle combined with total humiliation for his opponent. A brilliant move.

Ella reminds me that he's now the alpha male, by right of conquest, as if I needed telling. I'd resigned myself that this was the price to be paid for delivery, but now it's actually happened, I find that obedience to such a heroic and valiant warrior is not difficult at all. In fact, it's quite a relief not to have to constantly think up new ways in which to assert my authority. Obviously, it's meant some adjustments in my behaviour and I've already started showing him a bit more respect. I'm not sure he's getting the message though. I sat quietly today while he put the retractable lead on, and trotted obediently by his heel, just like Molly taught me, but all he did was pat me on the head and say, 'Not feeling yourself today, Blake? Still a bit woozy I expect. Never mind, you'll be running me ragged around the park in no time.' All right, he's a bit slow on the uptake, but such generosity of spirit shows real promise in an alpha.

Talking of Molly, I've readjusted my opinion of her, too. What a trooper. Not only did she show a hitherto unseen, but very attractive, side to her personality by giving the Jack Russell a good kicking, but she couldn't have been more of a dog person afterwards. The owners went off to the hospital to get the Owner's arm looked at while she dropped her clients off at the obedience school and took me to the vet. In the waiting room it was all strokes and murmuring consolation and afterwards she stopped at the butcher's for a new bone. Mr Clavicle alone would have made me reconsider the whole dog-toilet plan, but now I'm wondering where I can get hold of a pipe and slippers to take her.

Saturday, December 6

At last, the Owner seemed satisfied that I wasn't going to slip into a coma at any second and took us for a longer walk in the park today. Mostly, I think, because Coleridge has been getting fractious about being cooped up. I remonstrated with him, but he insists on running about like an attention-seeking missile.

Ella and I stared in wonder when we got through the gates. No longer are dogs hiding in bushes or staying close to their owners. The smell of the place is completely different. It smells of freedom. Dogs were chasing each other about, or having mock battles over their new territory, sniffing in bins and generally living the dog's life to the full. Even the humans seemed to have realised something was different. For the first time we saw Barkley running off the lead, chasing Constable. It was like watching a mouse trying to bring down a moose. Across the meadow Scottie was trying to give Edina and Jock wrestling lessons while Dottie looked on with Spotty sitting proudly next to her.

The hero of the hour didn't escape attention long, and within two shakes of a poodle's tail almost all the old P.A.R.P. dogs were running around us. My part in the plan and nearly broken neck had been forgotten I noticed; they all came for a sniff of the Owner. Some of them jumped up and licked him, and one even started humping his leg before I growled him off. Alpha or not, that's *my* leg.

As the crowd dispersed from around the bewildered human, I noticed Constable standing before us with his head bowed.

'Welcome, Prince Blake, Princess Ella, to our humble park.' Then he started sobbing, 'It should have been me,' and ran away.

The last dog to get to us was Scottie. He ignored the human and just said, 'Ye did all right there. An' ye're not too hurt noo, are ye?'

'No, just a few cuts and bruises.'

'Good, 'cos the big collar dinnae suit ye at all. There's been a bit of bothir over who's havin' whut territory, but I kep' yon clearing in the woods free fer ye, so ye'd better go mark it.'

The sun was shining and it seemed like too good a day to stand around chatting. The Owner bent over and unclipped us all and Ella and I walked across the park to the Scooting Place with Coleridge scampering around us.

'By the by,' said Scottie as we departed, 'Iviryone kens what ye do with ye're buttoms in there.'

So much for the returning hero, veteran of the Great Park War and nemesis of the evil Razor. I thought they'd have written a song about me for sure. Or at least some poetry. I mentioned this to Scottie over my shoulder.

'Ah'll see whut ah can doo, but dinnae hold yer breath, laddie.'

Sunday, December 7

P.A.R.P. has been officially disbanded. Razor hasn't been seen since his dunking, but the consensus is that he's a spent force. Even the last terrified members of his pack have been heard making nervous jokes about cross-dressing. Across the park the party atmosphere continues, as does the Owner's amazement at my new attitude. He just has to purse his lips these days and I'm at his side like a rocket, chivvying Coleridge along, sitting without being told and offering my collar for the lead to be clipped on. My 'heel' is second to none. If I got any closer I could ride home on his shoe. I've even been turning the word 'master' over now and again. Trying it on for size, you could say. It trips off the tongue nicely, I've noticed, and quite suits him really.

Monday, December 8

The next-door neighbours have finally left. All day Ella and I watched with our paws on the window as box after box was loaded into a waiting van, until finally a cluster of people from other houses up and down the street gathered to wish them well in their new home. My master and Ella's mistress went out and we followed them hanging over the wall as goodbyes were said, and the last box was brought out.

I recognised it immediately and instantly went for the gate to investigate, but at a word from my master, returned to his side and sat quietly. Unfortunately, Coleridge hasn't got my exquisitely honed manners. He ran through everyone's legs, and true to form jumped up and buried his teeth in the bottom of the box.

I guess I must have weakened it quite considerably because the bottom dropped out almost immediately. As the next-door neighbour's wife clutched her husband's arm and said, 'Oh no,

Brian, not that one,' it deposited a great heap on the pavement in front of the thronged well-wishers.

At the bottom of the pile was a large DVD collection. Some of the titles suggested that despite my experience of them they are committed animal lovers. As you might expect there were several movies about pussies, but more surprisingly they also had a documentary about doggy style, which I guess must be all the latest Milan fashions of the kind of coat that Scottie wears. And I thought they didn't like dogs! It just goes to show that you should never judge humans. The one about someone's ass looked interesting, too. The plight of many donkeys around the world is often overlooked by animal lovers, so it was nice to see someone had made a film about kissing them.

As well as the movies there were items of underwear made out of fur-lined leather, which looked very sturdy and much more warm and sensible than thin cotton and the silky things our humans wear. I noted the metal studs with approval. They're all the rage on collars too and are much more respectable than ribbons and lacy bits. I could see where they might help protect against dog bites and suchlike also.

The *pièce de résistance* though was sitting on top of the pile. Not the original version, but something that looked even better, if that's possible. Beneath the transparent purple rubber there were what looked like treats and widgets stuck out at angles. It was bigger than Mr Wobbly, too.

All the humans had gone very quiet for some reason, and there was a small gasp as Coleridge darted forward and grabbed Mr Wobbly II in his mouth. He must have pressed something because it started whirring and buzzing, exactly like the first one. He looked overjoyed and ran back into the house. Lucky little tyke.

This time the master didn't bother chasing. He stuck his hands in his pockets, smiled cheerfully, looked the next-door man in the eye and just said, 'I'll post that on to you, shall I? Can we have the keys now?'

Strangely, the neighbours staggered to their car clutching their chests and drove away in complete silence, though some people at the back of the crowd seemed to be snorting and turning an odd colour. They left their pile of belongings, too. As I have had occasion to observe previously, humans are crazy.

Tuesday, December 9

Last night the humans smashed down the back-yard fence with a sledgehammer. We now have our very own garden to play in while the humans start redecorating next door and workmen make holes in the walls. Obviously, the first thing that Ella and I did was jump in the pond while Coleridge obeyed his terrier instincts by beginning a respectable hole in the lawn. Not as impressive as his dad's network of tunnels by the pond in the park, but not bad for a beginner.

After a few minutes of wallowing we realised it was a bit cold at this time of year so went inside for a good shake and a lie down in front of the fire. Unfortunately, it soon became apparent that duckweed on the furniture and muddy footprints are not permissible and in fact Likely to Cause a Breach of the Peace. I tried for the Eyebrows of Penitence and Adoration (usually a powerful combination), but we were still dragged straight outside again.

Wednesday, December 10

Having a garden is the best. No more standing with my paws on the windowsill watching the world go by; adieu spending days sleeping because there's nothing else to do; farewell to getting under the master's feet all day. Instead my days are now spent romping around with Ella and Coleridge, rolling in the grass and snuffling at every corner of our new territory. There's also a constant stream of interesting-smelling people coming in and out of the new den, delivering things, banging holes in the wall, painting and generally making life interesting. Moving their tools and equipment to the bottom of the garden when they're not looking is the latest craze in our den and Coleridge is particularly good at burying screwdrivers.

Nevertheless, I can envisage a time when the garden might become too small for a dog of my capabilities, and

I've noticed that the fence on one side is rotten at the base. It won't be long before I can roam the back yards of the whole street at will.

Thursday, December 11

Spending the whole day out in the fresh air with room to run around certainly makes a difference, I slept like a cat on a velvet cushion last night. Plus we still get walks in the park, though by the time I've had a run around the garden for an hour while the humans have their breakfast, I'm much less excited at the prospect. The days when the Owner would get his arm half pulled off are definitely over.

Friday, December 12

For the first time since Razor's downfall, Croxley was spotted in the park. He's been keeping himself to himself and hiding under bushes apparently, but Barney and Liquorice hounded him out and herded him over to where Scottie and I were running around in pursuit of the puppies.

As we walked over to him for a sniff, it was obvious that he hadn't seen the error of his ways. Standing stiff-legged and growling, it didn't seem to have sunk in that the pack he once ran with was a spent force.

'Hello, Croxley,' I growled softly.

'Hello, Coward,' he replied. 'What do you want with me?'

'Only to say that if you fancy it, P.A.R.P.'s former members have agreed that you can have a small patch of territory of your own, and your past crimes, *such as biting my master*, will be forgiven. It's only a small patch and not prime land, but if you can prove you can behave then who knows what the future might hold.'

It was a generous offer, considering.

'I don't want your scrappy territory, Coward. When Razor returns, he'll take back all that is his and your stupid master won't step in a second time if he knows what's good for him.'

'In that case I don't want to keep you from lurking under bushes. You can be on your way.'

As the Jack Russell turned to leave, I growled at him. 'Just one more thing, Croxley.'

He turned.

'If you touch a single hair on any dog in this park, you'll find out just how much of a coward I am. And when I've finished with you, you'll have to deal with every other dog in this park. There will be no more territory fights and no more Pack Leaders. Understood?'

Croxley snarled but, I noticed, ran away as fast as his legs would carry him, peeing as he went.

Saturday, December 13

Yesterday's interview with Croxley did bring up a serious point, and one that has been all but overlooked by all the celebrating dogs in the park. What are we going to do about Razor when he returns? I asked Scottie what he thought.

'Och, dinnae worry aboot it, it'll be fine. Ye'll see soon enough.'

'Why, what do you know?'

'I clear forgoat tae tell ye aboot the day aftir the fight. Ah'm losing mah faculties an' noo mistake.'

'What happened?'

'Wull, yer owner came doon the park, an' hud a quiet word wi' Razor's. There wus a lot o' gesticulatin' wi' that bandaged arm an' a list o' demands tae stop yer owner goin' straight tae the police.'

'Demands?'

'Aye, I reckon ye're gaunne see a wee change in Razor's attitude.'

'Tell me everything, right now, you horrible ball of fluff.'

'And ruin yon surprise, I dinnae ken aboot that.'

Sunday, December 14

I didn't have to wait long to find out what Scottie was being so secretive about. Razor made his first appearance today. At first, I couldn't believe it was the same dog walking towards us, picking his way daintily through the grass.

About three feet away, he sat down awkwardly. It was a bit

difficult for him to speak with the huge muzzle strapped to his head, as well as the funnel, but he tried anyway.

'Ee chussst wainted tthh thhay tthhorry foor bffiting you.' Then he giggled with just a hint of his old madness. 'Eee'm a goood boy nowwff.'

With that short speech he wandered off. I couldn't help noticing that the vet had removed some very important parts of him. He smelled different, too.

'Aye, that'll be the hormoans he's takkin'.'

It was a pitiful sight, but one I wasn't sorry to see.

'An' did ye notice, he wus battin' his eyes at ye?' Scottie asked. 'Ah ken he might huv fallen for ye.'

Monday, December 15

Ella, Coleridge and I were following the humans around the park this morning when Constable and Liquorice came bounding up with Scottie.

'You've gotta see this. It's brilliant, mate, brilliant,' Liquorice barked out breathlessly.

We followed them through the woods, where they slowed down and led us stealthily to a clump of bushes in what was once Razor's stronghold. Beyond, I could see Croxley jumping around after Razor and barking at him. Although we were quite a long way away, it was just possible to make out what they were saying.

'But Razor, you've got to fight back. They can take your balls, but they can never take your mindless violence.'

'Thdon't fbee tthuch a fbig thilly Thcroxthley. Wouldth thyou thlick my thtitcheth ffor me againth. The're chuttht a fbit itchy.'

Obediently, Croxley moved up to Razor's backside and licked the place where Razor's testicles had once been. From the look of it he had been providing this service all morning and wasn't very happy about it. Razor sighed, 'Ahhhh yetth. That'th fbetter.'

'Come on, Razor, pull yourself together. Blake is laughing at you. All the dogs will be laughing at you if they see you like this.'

'Oooo Fblake! Thdo you thknow, I hadth neffer thnoticed fbefore what a fbig thdog he ith. He'th thquite thcary.'

'Master, what are you talking about? You came within an inch of killing him a few weeks ago.'

'Yeth, fbut that wath fbefore I thtarted to embrathe my inner fbitch.'

Croxley stared at his old Pack Leader in horror.

'Thtalking off Fblake. He'th thvery handsthome, ithn't he? Thdo you think he fliketh me now?' Razor did a little spin on the spot. In reply, Croxley turned tail and fled.

If I hadn't heard it with my own super-efficient ears, I'd never have believed it.

'Ye see,' said Scottie. 'Ah telt ye he fancied ye. Better watch that one Ella.'

'That's true,' replied Ella. 'We all know how much Blake likes pedigrees.'

I chased her all the way back to our owners.

Tuesday, December 16

News of the change in Razor has spread across the park like wildfire, and dogs are queuing up to see him for themselves. It seems like it was the last thing that was needed for a real peace to finally descend.

Wednesday, December 17

All the humans who were working on the house have finally left, and I must say it's great to have a bigger den to hang out in, especially as the postman hadn't realised that it's now one big house and is still delivering to both letterboxes. I suppose he's used to having a little moggie winding around his legs when he goes next door, and he actually screamed when he heard my impassioned barking and the door started rattling on its hinges today.

There's new furniture as well, and now Coleridge has mastered the art of peeing outdoors he's claimed a whole sofa to himself. Ella and I prefer to curl up on one end of the old one. It's got history, that sofa, and smells like it.

The humans spent the evening putting a tree up in the lounge and covering it with twinkly lights and chocolates. Very peculiar behaviour. Unfortunately, we were banished to the kitchen for the night so there was no chance for a sample.

Thursday, December 18

All sorts of fine cooking smells have started coming from the kitchen, which is novel. It doesn't seem long ago that the master would throw a lasagne in the microwave (and still manage to burn it), now there's all sorts of tantalising odours making my mouth water. Unfortunately, Samantha banned us and we've been huddled in the shed all day. After the master put some old blankets and chew toys in, it's become quite the dog palace.

Friday, December 19

Though the atmosphere is much different in the park now and all the dogs are by and large happy with their territories, there have been a couple of minor border disputes. For some reason I always seem to be the dog that has to sort them out. Today, Rudy and Liquorice brought Suki and Fabienne over. To our surprise, with the threat of Razor gone, Suki has turned out to be quite feisty over perceived encroachment on her territory and Fabienne was whimpering in distress.

I resolved the situation by clearly marking the boundary between the two territories and made the spaniel and the poodle apologise in best dog fashion. I left them breathing in each other's anal secretions.

Saturday, December 20

Another day, another spat between dogs to sort out. In the wasteland this evening I asked Scottie why they were all coming to me when they had a problem.

'Och, ten thoosand years o' history cannae be undone in one day.'

'What's that supposed to mean?'

'Well, whithir ye goat the title or no, the dugs all look at ye as the Pack Leader.'

'You're kidding me, that's not what P.A.R.P. was all about.'

'Aye, but all the same ye're still the new Pack Leader. I cannae see yer master runnin' around widdlin' oot border markin's or tellin' the big dugs tae lay oaf the wee dugs. Plus ye fought Razor twice and it wus yer strategy whut finally vanquished the Mad Dug.'

'Yes, but –'

'Noo buts aboot it now. If ye want mah opinion, it could be a worse dug, ye've come oan no badly in the last year, so ye huv.'

'But –'

'Och, shut up, wud ye. It's no often I'll say somethin' gude aboot ye, ye great haggis.'

'No, but –'

'It doesnae mean ye can start humpin' Dottie agin noo, ye ken?'

Sunday, December 21

I asked Ella about my being Pack Leader last night and she confirmed what Scottie had told me. Apparently, though no one is calling me by the name, every dog regards me as the authority in the park who should be obeyed for the good of the pack.

'But I don't want to be Pack Leader any more, all I want to do is play with you and my friends and have the occasional medicinal scoot.'

She sniffed me gently. 'And that's what makes you a good Pack Leader.'

'In that case I order you to go and fetch Mr Clavicle for me.'

'Don't push your luck. You may be Top Dog after all, but I've still got the best backside in the park and if you want your nose anywhere near it you'd better watch your manners.'

Monday, December 22

The year is drawing to an end, and I remembered that there was one piece of unfinished business that I still had to deal with. Walking in the wasteland with Scottie this evening, I asked him where his name came from.

He looked at me as if I had suddenly turned into Constable. 'Weeell, ah'm a West Highland Scots Terrier, ye ken. A Scoattish dog, in fact. An' mah owner? Well, he's Scoattish, too. De ye get the connection, ye dumb mongrel?'

'Ah, I see, so your real name is "Scotland"?'

He tensed. "Whut did ye say?'

'Oh nothing, I was just thinking about humans that give their dogs ridiculous names like Constable's. "Baron Constable Fluffykins of Stupidsville" or something isn't it?'

'Aye, whut of it?'

'Well, I was just thinking. However silly Constable's name is, it's not quite as breathtakingly awful as Laird Scotland McIvor of Strathpeffer.'

As I've had occasion to mention before, dear diary, I'm a big dog in prime fettle. Even so, I had real problems beating off the crazed attack of Laird Scotland McIvor of Strathpeffer.

Tuesday, December 23

Molly came over tonight. Since the fight the two humans have been quite friendly with her and for once she even seemed to enjoy my effusive welcome. It seems she's finally going away to save animals in far-off places, and this was a farewell dinner.

After the humans had finished a couple of bottles of wine, the conversation turned to us dogs. The master sighed and said, 'Sometimes I don't know why we bother. They're such a tie and they wreck everything. The vet's bills from this year alone have been more than the GDP of some small countries and I don't like to think about the state of my lungs after inhaling some off the gasses that come out of Blake's backside.'

'Well, Ella was always perfectly behaved until she met Blake. He's been a bad influence on her.'

'Sorry, he is a very bad dog, I know, but I can't help loving him. He helps keep me active, he's great company when he's not pulling the house apart and he does this adorable thing with his eyebrows. He's quite useful too. I always know when the postman's coming, and the way he reacts about leaves blowing against the window, I reckon we're pretty safe against burglars.'

'I've been watching him in the park recently,' said Molly, 'He seems much more obedient suddenly.'

'Yes, it's odd. Ever since that fight he's spent every evening climbing all over me, which is annoying, but he does seem to be getting the hang of basic commands now.'

In the corner of the kitchen my eyebrows flickered. Annoying? *Moi*?

Molly laughed. 'I think you've finally convinced him you're the alpha male in the pack.'

'If I have I hope he tells Coleridge. That puppy's going to the dark side already, and I thought he was going to be much better. Still, if nothing else, Blake's a great dustbin. Not an ounce of food ever goes to waste.' With that he threw me a piece of pork with traces of a rather nice Madeira, parsley and caper sauce still attached. I went from half asleep to snatching it out of the air within half a second.

'You shouldn't do that you know . . .' Molly started. Then she stopped. 'Sorry, I know I sound like a dog-training manual most of the time.'

At the table the humans continued with their blah, blah, blah. Just because he's alpha male it doesn't mean he's interesting. I got up and smooched Ella. With Coleridge in between us we started to doze off.

Wednesday, December 24

Tonight Ella said to me, 'Have you noticed my mistress smells different?'

'Yes, what's with that?'

'She's going to have a puppy, she just doesn't know it yet.'

Thursday, December 25

The owners left the kitchen door open a crack last night and when all was dark and silent throughout the house, Coleridge crept into the lounge. I opened one eye, but decided I didn't want to know.

The disaster scene this morning was unprecedented. Not even in my worst moments have I ever caused so much havoc. The occasional shoe or newspaper is one thing, but this was spectacular, my boy is an artist, a destructive genius.

For a start the tree was on its side, its chocolates long chewed out of their sparkly wrappers and now filling Coleridge with a sugary rush. Presumably that's where he got the energy to chew the paper off all the boxes that were under the tree, tear them open and strew their contents around the room. When the humans came down, with Ella and I looking between their legs, he was bouncing off the walls with a small plastic human with wings in his mouth. When he saw the master he ran over to him and was immediately sick all over his bare feet.

For a second I thought we were going to see the return of the Rolled-up Newspaper. Then with a deep breath, Samantha said, 'Coleridge seems to be full of vim this morning. Look, he's made a little bit of a mess. Why don't you take the dogs for a walk and let him run it off? I'll clear it up and get dinner started.'

Friday, December 26

What a dinner last night! It almost made up for being fed indescribable meat product, horse parts and gravel all year. I was too full to move after. The humans might want to reconsider feeding us sprouts in future though. As they settled down in front of the fire, Coleridge, Ella and I collapsed asleep in front of it like a dog bomb had gone off and farted in unison throughout the evening. Every so often the sound of the owners gagging for breath woke us up. For all his complaining, I noticed the master slipped out one or two of his own in and blamed it on us.

Saturday, December 27

After two days of sitting around the house and garden with occasional short trips to the wasteland the lazy humans finally took us back to the park today. The first dog we saw was Razor. We gave him a small patch of his own – a piece of territory around the north gate. It's so soaked with the scent of P.A.R.P. it'll probably never quite wear off, but he seems happy with it and for the most part just sits there smiling at something that no other dog can see. He calls himself Marilyn now.

Sunday, December 28

Well, it's been an interesting year, and I slipped up on most of my resolutions. I'm still scooting, though Ella and I have decided to try and cut down together next year, and I never did perfect the ultimate cat-torturing device. I also completely failed to save my master from romantic attachment, though there have been some compensations there by way of sharing my bed with Ella every night, Coleridge joining us and, of course, having a garden.

On the other paw, I certainly got it on with Ella (and Dottie) and there's been a definite improvement in canine–human relations, though I'm proud to say that I'm still keeping him on his toes as far as 'fetch' is concerned. There's a fine line between being a loyal lieutenant and being a slave to the master's every whim. A line I intend to keep very much on the right side of.

Instead of expanding my territory as far as the bandstand, I'm now the honorary Pack Leader of the entire park. This probably means they'll put up statues of me in the future, but that's all part of being a dog of fortune, the chosen one of fate. I have decided to use the power wisely, which basically means doing whatever Ella and Scottie tell me to.

Monday, December 29

The humans found out today that they were going to be parents. There was much vomiting, then shouting and hugging of dogs, though I'm not expecting the latter will last. If my experience is anything to go by the master is not going to enjoy being woken up by a small human peeing in his ear or trying to bite it off.

Tuesday, December 30

Tonight in the wasteland Scottie announced that he had written a poem about my heroic exploits.

'Aye an' it's a belter. An epic o' legendary proportions. A roosin' battle hymn fer the republic. They'll be recitin' it tae yer grandchildren, and great-grandchildren and great-great-grandchildren . . .'

'Let's just hear it, Scottie,' Ella sighed.

'Och, alreet then. It goes:

> 'There wus a mongrel called Blake,
> Whose friend wus a bit o' a rake,
> He trusted the Scotty
> Not tae boink Dottie,
> Whut a bloody stupid mistake.'

He ran off into the darkness, laughing like a maniac, with Ella and me hot in pursuit.

Wednesday, December 31

Blake's New Year's Resolutions:

1. Be a Good Boy. The threat of that trip to the vet seems to have passed completely and the master feeds me well, looks after me and has even started grooming me regularly when Samantha reminds him to do it. This breaks down into sub-resolutions as follows:

(i) ~~Fetch paper, slippers, pipe, whatever.~~
Yeah, right, the alpha hasn't been born I'd do that for.
(ii) My 'welcome home' routine has come on remarkably in the last year, but a dog on such form can't rest on his laurels. With a little more practice I could be Olympic standard. This year I'm going for the triple ear lick, barking hump manoeuvre. They say it can't be done, but a dog of my talent might just prove them wrong.
(iii) Quit chewing completely. For some reason I just don't feel the urge any more and besides, Coleridge is chewing enough for all of us.
(iv) Fetch is a lost cause, but I'm becoming increasingly

addicted to lying with my head in his lap. He seems to like it too so long as I can keep the drooling to a minimum. Samantha thinks he's incontinent.

2. Keep the Republic of Acorn Park free of tyrants, and make sure the underdog is doing all right.
3. ~~Develop a mature and enlighted attitude to cats.~~ Just keep away from cats. Period.
4. Cut down on the scooting.
5. With another human on the way, I need to redouble my efforts to guard the den. Next year no one will pass on the street or walk down the path without the master knowing about it.
6. Impregnate Ella. I love Coleridge as a son, but with genes like these it would be a crime not to pass them on.